DEAD LITTLE DARLINGS

USA *TODAY* BESTSELLING AUTHOR

RITA HERRON

Beachside Reads
Norcross, GA 30092

Cover Design: Jeffery Olsen
Cover Photo: 123RF.com
Print Design: Dayna Linton, Day Agency
eBook Interior Design: Dayna Linton, Day Agency

ISBN: 978-1-949178-08-1 (Paperback)
ISBN: 978-1-949178-06-7 (eBook)

First Edition: 2019

10 9 8 7 6 5 4 3 2 1

Printed in the USA

In memory of my mother who taught me to never give up.

DEAD
LITTLE
DARLINGS

◆ ◆ ◆

With Bonus Material:
The Prequel to
DEAD LITTLE DARLINGS

LITTLE
WHITE
LIES

LITTLE WHITE LIES

CHAPTER ONE

New Year's Day—1995

NEW YEAR'S EVE WAS always a bear when you were a cop. Last night proved no differently. Detective William Flagler rolled over and groaned at the sound of his phone.

Dammit, he was tired as hell. He hadn't gotten home till after seven A.M. He was getting too blasted old to pull all-nighters.

Although crime on Seahawk Island usually consisted of underage drinkers, DUIs, an occasional accident, domestic call, or someone setting a bonfire on the beach, everyone had been on alert last night. New Year's Eve always brought the partiers and the crazies.

A break-in at an apartment near the beach turned out to be a bunch of students looking for a place to ring in the New Year. Then some poor guy threw himself off the bridge at the pier because his girlfriend had dumped him. The Coast Guard reported they found the man alive.

Then he'd busted up a bar fight that had broken out over rivalry football teams. At four a.m. when he thought he was done, a couple called frantic that their sixteen-year-old son hadn't come home. Will found the kid passed out drunk in the park and drove him home. His parents had been relieved he was all right but threatened to ground him for life. They'd also thanked Will profusely for not arresting him. No need to saddle the boy with a record when he was just being young and stupid.

Will had been young and stupid himself once, too. Another officer, his boss and Chief of Police now, had cut him some slack. Will was paying it forward.

His phone buzzed again, and he snatched it up. "Flagler."

"We got a call. Three teenage girls missing." Chief Rodney Mantino said.

"How long?"

"Not even twenty-four hours, but the parents are freaked out. Sure something bad happened."

Will's gut tightened as an image of his own fourteen-year-old kid, Piper, flashed behind his eyes. If his daughter was missing, he'd be calling out the damned National Guard.

He threw his feet over the edge of the bed, grateful that he was alone, although not a day passed that he didn't miss having a wife.

Betsy had missed him, too. So much that she'd replaced him with a pool guy named Eddie. Now Eddie got to spend his nights in her bed.

No way on God's green earth would he let Eddie replace him as Piper's father though.

Last night he'd tried to devise a plan to win his family back. But Betsy had demanded he leave his job.

Could he?

"Flagler?" Mantino's gruff voice jerked him from his thoughts.

"I'm on my way." Will headed to the bathroom.

"I'd meet you there, but I think I caught a stomach bug last night."

More like too much brown whiskey. But hey, his boss was close to retirement and who was Will to judge?

"No problem. I'll keep you updated once I talk to the parents. Hopefully the kids just snuck out and they'll turn up by the time I get there."

"That's what I was thinking." A pause. "Sending you the name and address now."

A voice echoed in the background, a female's voice. So Mantino wasn't alone. Hell, good for him. At least somebody should get laid on New Year's Eve. It sure as hell hadn't been him.

He hung up, jumped in the shower for a solid three minutes, then dried off and dressed.

He checked the information his boss sent. Howard and Phyllis Darling. Three daughters: Candace, Deborah and Polly. Parents hadn't seen the girls since the night before when they left the girls home alone and went to a party.

It was possible they'd snuck out to meet friends, gotten wasted and hadn't yet found their way home.

Still, three teenage girls alone at night could spell trouble.

A number of scenarios raced through Will's mind, none of

which led to happy endings.

He strapped on his weapon, snagged his keys and new police issued cell phone, then headed outside to his black SUV. He'd pick up coffee on the way.

CHAPTER TWO

WILL CHECKED HIS WATCH as he parked at the Darling house. Two P.M.

If the Darlings had discovered their daughters were missing this morning, why had they waited so long to report it?

Suspicions immediately reared their ugly head. But he had to refrain from jumping to conclusions until he talked to the family. There could be a logical explanation.

He didn't know what that would be, but he would see what they said.

The small brick ranch was situated on a side street and had been built in the 1950's. Weeds choked the front lawn and flowerbeds, and the back was patchy and had been left natural. Wood shavings and rocks covered the brittle grass.

Badge in hand, he surveyed the drive and carport as he approached the steps to the front door. An ancient blue Chevy pick-up was parked beneath the covering along with assorted tools, an old lawnmower, spare tire, and three bikes that must belong to the daughters.

He raised his fist and knocked. Seconds later, footsteps sounded, and a weathered looking man who looked mid-forties answered, a lit cigarette in hand. Gray streaked his wiry brown hair, and his eyes looked bloodshot.

He flashed his badge. "Detective Flagler. Mr. Darling?"

The man nodded but didn't quite make eye contact. "Howard."

"You reported your daughters as missing," Will said.

"Yeah, that's right." Darling's voice cracked slightly.

The older man looked upset, confused. As if he hadn't slept? Or maybe he'd imbibed too much the night before?

"May I come in?" Will asked.

Darling made a low sound in his throat, then stepped aside and motioned him in. "My wife . . . she's having a hard time . . ."

"I understand," Will said. "Can she speak with us?"

Darling scraped an arthritic hand through his hair. Fresh scrapes streaked the man's knuckles, stirring more questions in Will's mind. A sob echoed somewhere close by, and Darling's jaw tightened.

"Phyllis is in the den."

Will followed the man to a small living room cluttered with threadbare furniture, newspapers, and laundry. Mrs. Darling sat hunched on a faded plaid couch, a tissue knotted in her hands. Her chin length brown hair was as disheveled as the tattered blue shirt and jeans she wore. She looked up at him as if lost in a nightmare.

He introduced himself and claimed a seat in a chair facing

her. Mr. Darling sat down beside her and rubbed a hand across her shoulders to soothe her.

"Have you heard from your daughters?" he asked.

Darling and his wife both shook their heads, and she swiped at more tears.

"Have any of the girls disappeared or run off before?" Will asked.

"Our girls are good girls," Mrs. Darling said in a broken voice. "They never snuck out or anything like that."

Or if they had, she didn't want to admit it. Parents often lied when first interviewed, afraid of being perceived as bad parents. "Let's get something straight," he said. "I'm not here to pass judgment. I have a teenager of my own, and I'm well aware that as parents we don't always know what our kids are up to or thinking. They're adept at hiding things from us that they don't want us to see." He paused. "My daughter says it's just little white lies. But little white lies often lead to bigger secrets."

Mrs. Darling shot up from the sofa and glared at him. "Our girls are not like that. They don't hide stuff from us. We're a happy family."

Her defensive reaction said the opposite. There was trouble at home with the Darlings. He automatically conducted a visual sweep of Phyllis Darling's face, arms, and hands for bruises or signs of abuse.

Mr. Darling coached his wife back onto the sofa. "Phyllis, calm down. He's here to help. We have to cooperate."

Her face crumpled, and she collapsed in her seat again. But this time she reached for the glass on the table. Vodka.

Will preferred whiskey himself. But it was a little early in the day.

Under the circumstances though, he guessed he couldn't blame her for having a drink. Although he wanted her clear headed.

"I assume you checked with the girls' friends and their families before you called the police," Will said.

Mr. Darling worked his mouth from side to side. "The girls don't have friends. At least none that come over here. They got each other."

Will arched a brow. No friends? Seriously. Teenagers were social animals.

"We thought they might have gone to their grandma's," Mrs. Darling interjected. "But we called her, and she hasn't seen them or talked to them."

He leaned forward with his hands clasped. "All right. Let's start from the beginning," Will said. "Tell me about your daughters. What are their names and ages?"

Mr. Darling stood and removed a photograph from the side table, then pushed it toward Will. "Deborah is the oldest, sixteen. Candace is the middle one, fourteen." He paused and swallowed hard as he looked down at the third girl. "And that's little Polly. She just turned twelve."

"They're pretty girls," Will said in an effort to create some camaraderie.

Mr. Darling nodded, and Mrs. Darling sniffled and lifted her vodka with a hand that trembled.

"I promise you I'll do everything I can to find your daughters and bring them home safely," Will said. "We already alerted authorities to look for them. If I can get a picture of the girls before I go, we'll pass that along to law enforcement agencies."

Emotions twisted the mother's face while Mr. Darling squeezed his eyes shut for a minute. Then the mother rose, walked over to the desk in the corner and returned with three school photographs.

Will's heart gave a pang as he studied their faces. Candace had long wavy blond hair and looked confident in her pose with her head tilted slightly upward. Deborah, the middle daughter, had auburn hair, and freckles dotted the bridge of her nose. Polly was a mixture of the two of them. Small framed, she hadn't quite hit puberty as the other girls had.

"Why don't you walk me through what happened last night and this morning," Will said.

The father released a weary sigh. "Last night Phyllis and I went to a party at the American Legion in Brunswick. Our group had been collecting blankets for the homeless and the veterans."

"And the girls stayed home alone?" Will asked.

Mr. Darling's face tightened. "That's right. Candace offered to babysit so we left her in charge."

"Does she babysit a lot?"

Darling narrowed his eyes as if he didn't understand the reasoning behind the question. "Not really," he finally answered. "But if we ask her to, she would."

Will wondered if Candace had a plan in mind when she'd offered that night. "Do you think the girls might have invited friends over for a little party of their own?"

Mrs. Darling looked alarmed at the question. "I told you our girls weren't like that. They were good girls."

So, she kept saying.

"They didn't have anyone over," Mr. Darling said. "Like I said, they didn't entertain friends at the house."

"Did you notice anything different when you arrived home?" Will asked. "Anything out of place?"

Darling shook his head no, grim faced.

"You keep alcohol here." Not a question but a statement. "Could they have snuck into it, gotten drunk and decided to go somewhere and hide until they sobered up, so you wouldn't know."

"Why do you want to keep insisting that our girls did something bad," Mrs. Darling shouted. "Someone must have taken them and you're suggesting they're off partying somewhere!"

Will strived for a calm tone. "Ma'am, I'm not trying to offend you. As a detective, I have to consider all angles," Will said in an effort to calm her. "As I mentioned, I have a teenager myself."

"Well, if these are the kinds of things she's doing, maybe you should go home and be a better father to her."

Will clenched his jaw. Her verbal blow hit home.

"Now, Phyllis," Mr. Darling murmured in a placating voice. "He's just trying to help."

"If he wants to help, then he should go out and look for our girls." The woman lurched up and staggered down the hall, ranting that she didn't like his accusations.

Mr. Darling dropped his head into his hands. "Sorry about that. She's just upset and scared."

Will nodded, although he couldn't shake what she'd said.

His wife had accused him of putting his job before her. Of putting it before their family.

Of missing out on Piper's life because he'd rather chase criminals than be a father.

CHAPTER THREE

WILL DIDN'T HAVE TIME to think about his own family right now. Three girls were missing, and it was his job to find them.

He cleared his throat. "So, you and your wife went to the party and you got home at what time?"

"Not till about three this morning," Mr. Darling said.

"That seems late for an American Legion function," Will said.

"Yeah, but it was New Year's Eve, and they had a dance, and everyone was having fun . . . and Phyllis didn't want to leave till the end . . ." He let the sentence trail off.

"What happened when you got home?"

The older man looked down into his hands as if they held answers. Or maybe he was remembering something, that he'd used his fists against his wife or daughters?

"Phyllis had a little too much to drink and went straight to bed." He rubbed at his leg. "By then my arthritis was acting up, and I was dog tired, so I went, too."

"You didn't check on the girls?" Will asked.

Darling shook his head. "Door was closed. We figured they were asleep and didn't want to wake 'em." His expression turned contrite. "I guess we should have. But they were old enough, I didn't even think about it."

Will decided to let it slide. Either he or his wife always checked on Piper before turning in. Was Betsy's boyfriend looking in on her now?

A sour taste filled his mouth at the thought. "So, you went to bed and woke up at what time?"

"Wife slept in till about ten. I took a pain pill for my leg and overslept, too."

"Were the girls usually up early?" Will asked.

"Nah. On the weekends, we have to make 'em get up and do chores."

"Did you hear any noise this morning? Their voices or the TV?"

He scratched his head. "Not that I recall."

Will glanced at the loaf of bread on the counter. "How about the kitchen? Were there signs that they'd made breakfast or eaten anything?"

He mumbled no.

"Didn't you think that was odd?"

His gaze shot to Will's. "I thought they were still in bed. Went to wake them up. That's when I found their beds empty."

"What did you do then?"

"Checked the house then outside and looked for their bikes. Thought they might have gone for a ride."

"But the bikes were still under the carport?"

"Yeah. I ran in and got Phyllis up. She figured they'd gone to her mama's house, so she called her."

"But the girls hadn't gone there?"

He shook his head, his face full of misery. "I figured they'd just snuck off to the park down the way. So, I got in the car and rode down there, and looked all over, but they weren't there either."

Panic tinged his voice. Will felt his own rising as he listened. If it was Piper, he'd be out of his mind with worry.

"I decided maybe they'd snuck some cash and walked to the store to buy snacks, so I drove to the quick market, but clerk hadn't seen 'em. Kept telling myself maybe they'd come home so I drove back here, but Phyllis was hysterical. Said she hadn't heard a word. She'd looked in their room and the girls' backpacks were gone."

Will offered the man a sympathetic look, although if something bad had happened to the girls, the parents would be prime suspects. Howard Darling was a big man. He imagined if Darling was angry, he could be formidable.

He stood. "May I look around in the girls' room?"

Darling pushed to his feet with a groan and rubbed at his bad leg. "Down the hall."

The sound of Mrs. Darling's crying echoed through the hallway as he followed the man into a small room. Three single beds lined the walls, one covered in a yellow spread with butterflies, one purple with blue and pink stripes, and the other bright orange.

"Was anything missing other than the girls' backpacks?" Will asked.

"Not that I know of," Darling replied.

"How about clothes? Make up or toiletries?" If they'd taken those, maybe the girls had run away.

"I don't think so," Darling said. "But my wife would know better. I stayed out of my girls' personal things."

Will acknowledged his comment and wondered if he could believe the man. Something about the time lapse and the parents insisting their daughters didn't have friends didn't feel right.

He gave a pointed look at the man's fists. "Mr. Darling, how did your hands get bruised?"

Alarm flashed in the man's eyes as he glanced down at his knuckles. "Working on my pick-up."

Will gave a non-committal response. The question had definitely triggered a panicked response.

"I'm gonna check on Phyllis." Mr. Darling fled toward the back room as if desperate to escape Will's interrogation.

Will mentally catalogued every nuance of the couple's behavior to scrutinize later if needed. Time to search the daughters' room now.

He walked over and examined the bulletin boards above the girls' beds.

Butterflies cut from art paper were tacked on the board above the bedding with the butterfly theme. There were also several pictures of dogs clipped from magazines. She'd drawn a circle around a small poodle and written—this is the one I want. Polly.

His heart tugged. Piper had begged for a dog last year for Christmas, but Betsy refused, saying she didn't have time for an animal with Will gone all the time.

Maybe this year . . .

Above the purple covered bed hung a board with a movie ticket stub. Flier about a school dance. School paper clipping about the 4-H club. A shot of the park that had been taken with a Polaroid camera. A school math paper, grade A+. The middle daughter Deborah's.

The third bulletin board held magazine pictures of a boy rock band, along with photographs from a fashion magazine. Candace's.

He checked the desk drawers for a note indicating where the girls might have gone or signs they'd been communicating with friends their parents knew nothing about.

No diary. No secret box of love notes. No pages with boys' names scribbled on them as if one of them had a crush.

If there was anything indicating their plans, they hadn't left evidence of it behind. And if they'd taken their backpacks with them as the Darlings claimed, they'd walked out of the house on their own volition.

Damn. He'd have to ask Mr. Darling for permission to search phone records. Maybe one of the daughters had made plans over the phone last night.

Twelve, fourteen and sixteen–vulnerable ages for girls.

And the perfect ages for predators to target.

Chapter Four

Will checked the windows. Locked. No signs of forced entry.

"You done in here?" Howard Darling asked from the doorway.

"For now." Will followed the man back to his den. The house was quiet, almost an eerie quiet. No TV. No radio. Just the creak of the old wood floor as he walked across it, and the wind whistling through the eaves of the house. "Your wife okay?"

"She's a wreck," Mr. Darling admitted. "I told her I'd handle things, for her to get some rest."

People handled trauma in different ways. If his kid was missing, there was no way Will could take a nap. But the girls' mother had been drinking. "How is your marriage, Mr. Darling?"

Mr. Darling's face turned red, and he clenched his fists. His eyes darted toward Will. "My marriage is fine, and none of your business."

Will let the silence stand for a minute. "Again, I didn't mean to offend you, but understanding the family dynamics might offer insight as to whether your daughters ran away or if they were lured away by someone else."

Emotions darkened Darling's face.

"Did you and your daughters get along?" Will continued.

"When they were little, I used to play catch with 'em and take 'em fishing." Darling said. "But they're teenagers now and didn't want to hang out with me anymore. They closed up in their room and listened to music and kept to themselves."

"Typical for teenagers," Will admitted. He used to kick the soccer ball around with Piper, and they'd make elaborate sandcastles on the beach. When had they stopped doing those things?

"Sometimes girls clash with their mothers," Will said. "Did your wife and daughters get along?"

Darling glanced at the hallway leading to the bedroom. What was he hiding? "They did fine. Phyllis is a good mother."

And the girls were good girls, according to her. Except Will sensed everything wasn't as good as they kept insisting.

Talking to the neighbors and the girls' teachers would offer more insight into the family. Typically, if a parent was abusive, he focused the abuse/anger on one child..

Will didn't see signs of a struggle in the house. No blood or indication that Darling had killed his daughters here.

"Mr. Darling," Will said. "Has anyone been out to the house to do repairs recently? Maybe a painter or gardener or even a cable or power company employee?"

The man scrunched his face as if thinking, then shook his head. "I work construction, so I take care of repairs around here."

"Are you currently working a job?"

Darling knotted his hands in front of him. "Afraid not. Hard during the winter."

Will gave an understanding nod. If Mr. Darling had done something to his daughters, a construction site would have been the perfect place to bury their bodies. Of course, he could have dumped a body or bodies at an old work site.

"How about your wife? Does she work outside the home?"

"She cleans houses," he said.

Will fought surprise. The woman certainly didn't use her skills in her own home. Dust coated the end tables by the sofa, the bookshelf was cluttered, and something sticky was on the floor in the hall.

"What does her job or mine have to do with finding our girls?" Darling grumbled.

"Maybe nothing," Will said. "But it's important I know everything possible about your family and daughters, so I can explore all angles." He paused. "One more question. Did either one of your daughters have a boyfriend? Or maybe a guy they were interested in at school?"

Darling's face turned ruddy. "No, they weren't into boys. They had too much studying to do."

Either he had buried his hand in the sand or he was in denial. Or he knew something he didn't want to divulge.

"Can you think of any place the girls might go? Did they

like the library or the park? Was there a favorite place you took them as kids?"

"We used to crab out at the marsh," Darling said. "But I checked there already."

"I'll have people check again." Will removed his card and laid it on the table. "I want to talk to the grandmother, and your neighbors and the teachers at school. Maybe they can help."

Darling rubbed a hand over his eyes, took the card and studied it. He looked miserable as if he was about to break down.

"I need the grandmother's name and contact information," Will said. "And a list of all your past work sites."

Darling's brows climbed his forehead. "What for?"

"Just to check in case the girls decided to go there."

Darling's mouth tightened, but he snagged a scrap of paper from the table and scribbled a name and address on it. With a grunt, he listed two different work sites near Pooler.

Will thanked him. "Call me if you think of anything else or if you hear from your daughters. I'm going to take a look around outside."

Darling opened his mouth as if to argue, then snapped it closed and nodded. Will let himself out. If the girls had run away, they might come back on their own.

But if they'd been lured from the house and kidnapped, the first twenty-four to forty-eight hours were key to finding them.

Several hours had already passed. The clock was ticking.

Chapter Five

WILL PHONED THE CHIEF as soon as he walked the Darling's property and asked him to have someone check out Darling's past work sites for the girls' bodies.

He'd hoped to find a note dropped from a backpack in the back yard, a phone number of a friend, an address where the girls planned to meet someone.

But nothing.

"What's the verdict?" Chief Mantino asked. "Did those girls show up?"

"Not yet, and the parents haven't heard anything. Mother is a wreck. Not sure about the father. He seems upset, but that could be guilt talking."

"You think he did something to his daughters?"

"Too early to say, although I sensed he was hiding something. I'm sending pics over for you to pass onto authorities and the National Center for Missing and Exploited Children."

"Of course. I checked, and you may be right. There was a call about a domestic disturbance at that house a few months ago. No charges were filed, but I'm reviewing the report now. Officer who answered the call said the couple had definitely been fighting. The Darlings couldn't get rid of him fast enough."

So, his suspicions about Howard Darling might be spot on. "We need to organize a search team to comb the marsh, parks, the Village, and the beaches."

"I'll get on it," Chief Mantino said.

"I'll talk to the grandmother and neighbors and try to get in contact with teachers at the school to see if they can fill me in on the family. The father and mother claim the girls didn't have friends over to their house, but –"

"Teenagers lie to their parents," the chief said.

He thought of Piper and prayed she never pulled a stunt like sneaking out. "Exactly."

Although the holiday was going to make it more complicated to track down teachers, but he'd find someone at the school who would talk.

"I'll have Roberta call you with contact information for the school," Chief Mantino said. "Meanwhile I'll work on organizing that search party."

Will scanned the ground, the carport and outside the girls' bedroom window. No signs they'd snuck out through the window or sign of a break-in. "Alert port authorities, train and bus stations, too," Will said.

"On it. Keep me posted."

Will hung up, then surveyed the neighborhood. The houses

were set about a half-acre apart. The closest one to the Darlings was a gray ranch with overgrown bushes dividing the property. On the other side, a dilapidated white ranch looked vacant.

He backed onto the street, then drove to the neighbor's and parked. Christmas lights still dangled from the awning of the house, a plastic wreath on the door. He hadn't noticed any signs of holiday decorations at the Darlings. Then again, some folks took theirs down as soon as Christmas was over. And others didn't bother to decorate.

He was guilty of that. Why decorate a tree just for himself? It would only be a reminder that he was alone for the holiday, that his family was broken. Like Humpty Dumpty, he didn't know how to put it back together again.

He'd have to figure it out later. The case took precedence.

He knocked on the door, his badge in hand as it opened. A middle-aged woman with curly brown hair peered at him over wire rimmed glasses. She introduced herself as Mrs. Beverly Clemson.

Will quickly explained about the missing girls.

Alarm crossed her face, and she averted her gaze. "I haven't seen them, if that's what you're asking."

"Mr. and Mrs. Darling claim they attended a party last night and were gone all evening. They didn't arrive home till three a.m. The girls were home alone."

She pursed her lips in a frown.

"Did you see or hear anyone over there last night? Perhaps the girls had friends over or a boyfriend showed up?"

She shook her head. "I'm sorry, I go to bed early. About

ten o'clock. Everything seemed quiet. It's not always like that though."

Will narrowed his eyes. "What do you mean?"

"They get into it over there sometimes," she said. "Especially when Phyllis takes to drinking."

"Did you ever report this to the police?" Will asked.

She shivered, fear flickering across her face. "Once, but the cops didn't do anything. The next day though Mr. Darling came over and threatened me."

Will tensed. "Tell me exactly what happened? Did he get physical?"

"Well, no," she said, her voice warbling. "But he told me to stay out of his family's business or I'd be sorry."

That certainly sounded like a threat.

"Do you live here alone?" Will asked.

She nodded. "My husband passed two years ago. Colon cancer." A sadness passed over her face. "He was a good man."

"I'm sorry for your loss, Ma'am." Will paused while she collected herself. "Mrs. Clemson, was Mr. Darling abusive to his wife or daughters?"

She clenched the door edge with a white-knuckled grip. "I . . . can't say for sure."

"But you suspected he was?"

Wariness darkened her eyes as if she was still afraid of the man. Then she gave a small nod. "I stayed away from them though because of what he said." Tears filled her eyes. "But if something happened to those children because I didn't call the law again, I'll never forgive myself."

God. He patted her hand. "This is not your fault. At this point, we don't know what happened. The girls could have snuck out to meet friends and be hiding out somewhere." Maybe too afraid to come home and face their father's wrath.

He pushed his card into her hand. "Call me if you think of anything else." He cut his gaze toward the Darlings. "Or if he bothers you."

She clamped her teeth over her lower lip, then closed the door. The sound of locks being moved in place echoed behind him as he walked back to his SUV.

If the neighbor was afraid of Mr. Darling, his daughters might have been as well.

He drove to the grandmother's next. She lived in a retirement community about two miles from the Darlings. The apartments were built of tabby and looked old, although the property looked well maintained. A groundskeeper was picking up limbs that had snapped off in a storm.

The grandmother introduced herself as Effie Litman and offered him coffee and teacakes as she led him into a small living room that overflowed with her collection of ceramic cats.

Will accepted the coffee, touched by the elderly woman's attempt at social graces, but shook his head at the teacakes.

"I know you came about the girls," she said, her chin quivering. "I'm terrified that something happened to them."

"I understand." He joined her at the small kitchen table and noted the dishcloths and tablecloth were also embroidered with cats. "Mr. and Mrs. Darling thought the girls might have come to see you. Do they drop by often?"

She blinked back tears and stirred sugar into her coffee. "No, I wish they'd come more. I get so lonely here."

His heart squeezed. "How about your daughter? Does she come regularly?"

Effie shook her head. "She has to work, you know."

"She cleans houses?" he said.

She nodded and ran a feeble looking hand over her graying hair, hair she wore in a bun. "I wish she stayed home more. Girls need their mothers."

"Were the girls and Mrs. Darling close?"

She worried her bottom lip with her teeth, her hand shaking as she dropped it into her lap. "I think they had issues," she said. "But my daughter loved her children. She was hysterical when she called me this morning."

He reached out and patted her hand. "I understand this is difficult, but anything you can tell me about the family might help. Do you think the girls would run away from home?"

She lifted her head, silence stretching between them. When she looked back at him, confusion clouded her eyes. "What were we talking about?"

Will sighed. "Your missing granddaughters."

She shot up, knocking the table with her sudden movement. Coffee slashed onto the table and the cup rattled. "What do you mean? My granddaughters are missing?"

Will frowned.

"Your daughter called this morning. The girls—"

She swung her hand toward the door. "I don't know who you are or how you got in here, but you need to leave before I call the police."

"Effie, I am a detective," Will said, troubled by her agitation. "I need you to tell me about your daughter and her husband."

She went still, then grabbed a dishcloth and began wiping the coffee spill. "I think they're having a baby," she said, a softness returning to her eyes. "I hope it's a girl."

Will swallowed hard as the truth dawned on him. Effie was obviously suffering from dementia.

He laid his business card on the table. "Thank you for the coffee, Effie. If you think of something else you want to share with me about your daughter and her husband, please call me."

Frustration filled him as he walked back to his car. If Effie knew something helpful, it might be lost in her memories.

But she had been coherent when he'd first arrived and said the girls hadn't been to see her. That matched the wife's story.

Still, the parents had to know more than they were saying.

Chapter Six

WILL HAD WORK TO do, but three missing girls were enough to make any parent panic. If he was wrong about Mr. Darling, and there was a predator lurking the streets preying on teenaged girls, the town should be alerted.

Fear swept through him. He needed to hear his daughter's voice.

He called Betsy's number as he settled in his car. Thankfully Piper answered, not his ex.

"Dad?"

"Hey, kiddo," Will said, grateful she was home and safe. "Listen, a case came up. Three teenaged girls have gone missing. You may know them. Polly, Candace and Deborah Darling."

Silence for a minute. "Yeah, they go to my school," she said flatly.

"Their parents haven't seen them since last night. How well do you know them?"

"Not well, Dad. Polly is sweet, but she's two years younger and shy as all get out. She barely looks at you when you try to talk to her."

"And the older girls?"

Her breath hissed out. "I don't hang out with them," Piper said. "Deborah is okay, I guess, but she follows her sister around like a puppy. They're always trying to flirt with the jocks, but the boys don't go for them."

"Why not?" Will asked.

"Dad," Piper said in an exasperated voice.

"So, your old man is clueless, fill me in."

"I don't know. You do remember high school, don't you? The jocks and the cheerleaders."

"Clicks," he said.

"Exactly."

What about Piper? Was she popular? Making friends? She played forward on the soccer team. What else was she into?

God. Was *she* starting to like boys?

There was so much he didn't know about his own kid . . .

"Dad, I gotta go."

"Wait." He didn't what to hang up yet. "Did you ever hear gossip about the girls being abused?"

A heartbeat passed. "No. You think they were?"

"I have to explore all angles. Find out if they had reason to run away or if something else happened."

"You mean, like they were kidnapped?" Piper asked, her voice rising an octave.

Betsy would be pissed that he shared information with their

daughter. But if there was a predator, he wanted Piper to be alert.

"That's what I'm trying to figure out." He hesitated, an image of her sweet face haunting him. "Sweetheart, promise me you'll be careful. That you won't go anywhere alone."

Another heartbeat of silence. "So that's the reason you called. To tell me not to go out alone."

"Well, yeah. I'm your dad. I worry about you."

She heaved a sigh that spoke volumes. "I thought you were coming to pick me up and we were going to get pizza."

Shit. He hated to let Piper down again.

"I'm sorry, Piper, we'll have to postpone. With missing person's cases, the first twenty-four hours is crucial. We have to get search teams looking, alert authorities."

"Fine, Dad, I should have known you wouldn't show."

"Honey, it's not like—"

"I know, I get it," she mumbled sarcastically. "Your job is more important."

He opened his mouth to apologize, but the line went dead.

Dammit, his sweet daughter had hung up on him.

Chapter Seven

Dammit to hell. Will wanted to drive straight to his ex's house and see his daughter, take her to get pizza, show her that *she* was the most important thing in his life.

But . . . every second that ticked by meant the Darling girls could be suffering if they'd been abducted. They could be getting farther and farther away on their own—or a predator could be transporting them to another town or state, even to another country.

He'd make it up to Piper later. She'd understand. She'd have to.

He drove to the precinct to drop off the photos of the girls to be passed along to the authorities. An hour later, the pictures had gone out and the local news had aired a segment about their disappearance.

"We checked those job sites for Mr. Darling. So far, nothing."

He supposed that was a good sign.

"We've set up a tip line," Chief Mantino added. "Hopefully someone has seen or heard something that will be helpful."

"And if the girls are hiding out with friends, maybe the news clip will scare them into coming home. Or at least into calling to let their parents know they're all right."

"We could ask the mother to make a plea on TV," the chief said.

Will quirked a brow. "Think we'd better hold off on that. She was not in a good way. Too much booze to ease the pain."

Chief Mantino's brows raised in interest. "Think that's a habit?"

"Maybe. Husband said she'd had too much the night before and went to bed as soon as they got home." Will scratched his head. "Of course, he could be lying."

"Maybe she's drinking because she's scared of him," the chief suggested.

"Can't rule out anything at this point." Will tapped his foot. "Except I don't expect this to be about a ransom. Family didn't appear to have money. Mr. Darling works construction and at the moment, is out of work. Wife cleans houses for a living."

"You're probably right about the ransom." Chief Mantino handed Will a sticky note with a phone number and address on it. "We located the school counselor, Evelyn Morris. Talk to her."

"On my way." Will checked the address. Evelyn lived on the island not far from the Village. It took him less than ten minutes to reach her house.

Her place was a small bungalow about two miles from the Village. A great location if you liked the beach. Judging from the bright blue paint and seashells lining the front porch ledge, she was a beachcomber.

She was late thirties with her blond hair in a ponytail. A breeze had picked up, rustling the palm trees and bringing the scent of salt air. She tugged her sweater tighter around her and ushered him inside.

He identified himself, then settled in her den facing her. The house smelled of cinnamon and pumpkin and pine, inviting and homey, as if Christmas still lingered inside.

"I saw the news a few minutes ago," she said, worry flashing in her eyes. "I can't believe there's been an abduction right here on Seahawk Island."

Her choice of words caught his attention. "What do you mean? Do you know something about what happened to the Darling sisters?"

She drummed her fingernails on her leg. "No, I didn't mean that. I just meant that if someone kidnapped them, it's scary. Everyone at school and in town will be in a panic."

"We don't know that they were kidnapped, but if you have reason to think so, please share it," Will said.

She fiddled with the pillow on the sofa. "No, I guess it's just gossip. I was at the diner when the news aired, and people started fearing the worst."

"I see," Will said. "For now, we're considering all possibilities."

"You mean that the girls may have run away," Evelyn said quietly.

Will nodded. "Did you ever see bruises on the girls or hear talk about abuse at home? Maybe one of the girls came to you."

She shook her head. "I did see bruises a few times, and asked, but Deborah and Candace both clammed up. Made up different stories. One time it was a bike wreck. Another they'd been playing tag football."

Typical of abuse victims to cover for their abuser.

"I talked to the parents, but need more information on the sisters," Will continued. "Mrs. Darling insisted that her daughters were good girls. Both parents also commented that the girls didn't entertain friends at their house. And that they didn't like boys."

Surprise flickered on the woman's face.

"I take it that's not exactly true. Which part?"

She pulled at a loose thread on the pillow edge. A nervous gesture.

"Please, Mrs. Morris, anything you can tell me would be helpful. If the girls are in trouble, every second counts."

She gave him a wary look. "They didn't have a lot of friends," she admitted. "But there were two girls who hung around with them. Aretha Franton and Mellie Thacker."

Names were helpful. "I'll need their contact information in case they know where the girls are."

"I can get it from school," she said. "Although Mellie and her mother moved away three weeks before Christmas. Mrs. Thacker told the school that her mother was sick, and she had to take care of her."

"All right. Then I'll need Aretha's number." He twisted his mouth. "Is there anything else?"

She studied her fingernails for a minute. "I'm the school counselor. The things my students share with me are supposed to be confidential."

Will cleared his throat. "I respect your job, but these young ladies might be in danger, Mrs. Morris. So again, *anything* you tell me might help us find them."

She inhaled. "Another girl in school came to me and said Deborah and Candace were teasing her. Bullying her."

Will had been forming a mental image of the girls, but that wasn't what he expected. Although sometimes abused kids turned into abusers themselves. "What was the girl's name?"

"I shouldn't say."

Will reached out and patted her hand. "I won't tell her that we talked. I'll just explain that we're questioning as many students as we can."

The woman nodded slowly. "Her name is Libby Barrett. She's a freshman. A quiet, shy girl with big glasses. She likes to read and volunteers on the yearbook staff."

"Thank you." He started to stand, but she caught his hand.

Regret darkened her eyes. "Detective, I hope you find them. Like I said, I can't be certain that the girls were abused, but something was going on in that house. Something that wasn't right."

Chapter Eight

An hour later, Will parked at Libby Barrett's house. According to the analyst at the precinct, she lived with her mother, a single parent who taught at the elementary school on the island.

He knocked and identified himself. The short, chubby woman led him to a den where she was obviously putting away holiday decorations. Dry needles from her Christmas tree dotted the floor, the tree bare of ornaments, making it look sad and empty. "Such terrible news about those girls," she muttered. "I hope you find them all right."

"We're searching everywhere," he said. "I wondered if I might speak with your daughter Libby."

She raised a brow. "Why would you want to talk to her?"

"Routine. We're interviewing as many students as possible hoping someone overheard something."

The woman nodded in understanding, walked to the hall

and called her daughter to come down. Footsteps clattered a minute later, and a thin red-haired girl with freckles and big square glasses appeared, hugging a copy of *Wuthering Heights* to her chest.

Wariness flickered across her face when she spotted him.

"Honey, this is Detective Flagler," Mrs. Barrett said. "He needs to talk to you about the Darling girls."

Libby pushed her glasses up on her nose and crossed the room to stand by her mother.

"I don't know anything about them," Libby said.

"You weren't friends?" Will asked, studying her reaction.

Her glasses slipped down her nose as she shook her head no.

"I've been talking with as many students as possible," he said, bending the truth. "A couple of them commented that Deborah and Candace bullied you."

Mrs. Barrett gasped. "Honey, is that true? Why didn't you tell me?"

Libby's face reddened with anger. "Because it was no big deal," Libby said. "They just teased me about my glasses and freckles, that's all."

"Oh, sweetheart," Mrs. Barrett said sympathetically. "I'm sorry. Teenagers can be so cruel sometimes."

"Were they mean to you?" Will asked bluntly.

Libby glanced at her mother then at him, some emotion akin to panic streaking her face. "Like I said, it was just some teasing, nothing I haven't heard before or can't handle."

Will offered her a smile. "Can you think of any place the girls might go if they ran away?"

Libby shook her head. "I avoid them," she admitted.

"Kids talk though," Will said. "Would they have gone to a boy's house?"

Libby shrugged. "I don't know. You should ask Aretha Franton or Mellie Thacker. They were tight with them."

Will thanked her, then left his card, hoping she might decide to open up later.

He drove from the Barrett's to Aretha Franton's house. The woman who met him at the door looked irritated when he explained the reason for his visit.

"I heard the news," she said tersely. "I'm sorry about those girls, but my daughter can't help you."

Will narrowed his eyes, noting that she hadn't invited him inside. "I had the impression they were friends."

"You had the wrong impression," she said stiffly.

He spotted a slender dark-haired girl with big brown eyes behind the woman. Fear strained the girl's face, and her eyes looked red rimmed as if she'd been crying.

"Please, Mrs. Franton," Will said. "Let me speak with your daughter for a moment. Mr. and Mrs. Darling are frantic that something bad happened to their children."

Mrs. Franton pursed her lips. "Maybe they should have been better parents then."

Her tone reeked of anger. "What exactly do you mean?" Will asked.

She gripped the doorjamb, still blocking his entry. "Nothing. I . . . am sorry their girls are missing. They probably just ran away."

"We're looking into that angle," Will said. "That's another reason I wanted to speak to Aretha. I thought the girls might have told her if they'd planned to leave home, and where they were going."

"My daughter doesn't know anything," Mrs. Franton said.

"Please, Mrs. Franton. Aretha might know if there's someone the sisters might call. Maybe they went to meet some guys or snuck out to a party last night?" Will said. "They could be in trouble and need help."

"I told you Aretha doesn't know anything. She hasn't spoken to those girls in weeks."

Without another word, she slammed the door in Will's face.

CHAPTER NINE

WILL SPENT THE REST of the day questioning people in the Village while the Coast Guard searched from the sky, and other officers and locals combed the beaches, the marsh, parks, anywhere they could think of that a teenager might go. They even checked the high school inside and out, but the girls weren't there.

Chief Mantino had their analyst pull the Darlings' phone records, but they found nothing suspicious. The tip line sent them racing to an abandoned ship at the marina, but it was a false lead. No Darlings, just a homeless man who'd sought shelter while he slept off his nightly binge. Police on I-16 heading toward Macon discovered a stolen car, but the prints inside belonged to a guy who'd held up a gas station the night before.

No stowaways reported. No bus tickets for three teenaged girls. And no one at the local airport spotted the sisters.

He ducked into the diner for a quick meal and ordered

a burger from a waitress named Susan who'd waited on him before. She was always friendly although not flirtatious, but today she looked antsy and spilled a tray of drinks and brought a couple the wrong order.

Her little girl Marilyn was sitting in the corner with a notepad and pencil. He heard the six-year-old liked to draw and scribble down things she overhead people say. Marilyn once told him she wanted to be a TV reporter when she grew up.

She kept hovering in the back and looking towards the door as if something were wrong. Susan delivered his burger and sweet tea and dropped the bill on the table.

"Everything okay?" he asked her.

She glanced back at her daughter, then bit her lip. "Yeah, guess the news about those missing girls has all of us freaked out. I can't imagine if something happened to Marilyn. She's all I've got."

"I understand," he said sincerely. "I had to call my daughter earlier just to hear her voice." He laid his napkin in his lap. "Did the sisters ever come in here?"

She shook her head. "Don't think I ever saw 'em here. Sorry, wish I could help."

A tall man with dark hair called her over, and Will realized it was Daryl Eaton, the lighthouse keeper. He supposed the women thought him handsome. From what he'd seen, the man kept to himself. He seemed friendlier to Susan than Will had ever seen him be to anyone else.

His phone buzzed, and he snatched it and answered, his pulse jumping. Maybe the girls had been found.

"Detective Flagler."

"Will, it's Betsy. What time are you bringing Piper home?"

He froze, his chest clenching. "What do you mean? I've been working and had to cancel. You heard about—"

"She's not with you?" Panic tinged his ex's voice, stirring his own.

"No, why? Isn't she with you?"

"No. I left her home earlier while I met some friends for dinner, and I just got back. She left a note saying she might spend the night with you."

Will shot up from his seat. "Listen to me, Betsy. She's not with me, but I'll find her. Have you called her friends?"

"I'm going to do that now."

"Is there any sign of a break-in at the house?"

A gasp escaped Betsy. "No, I don't think so."

"Was the door locked?"

"Yes," Betsy said.

"Is her bike still there?"

Footsteps sounded, and he realized she was running to the garage. "It's still here. God, Will, where is she?"

He wished to hell he knew. "Where would she go if she snuck out?"

"I don't know," she cried. "She was supposed to be with you!"

They'd planned to get pizza, but he'd let her down. Dammit to hell. If something had happened to her, he'd never forgive himself.

"I'll go look for her." He tossed cash on the table to pay for his uneaten food and hurried toward the door.

Outside, the wind picked up. A storm was brewing, dark thunderclouds rumbling and threatening heavy rain.

Fear seized him. His baby was out in this. Alone.

Sweat broke out on his forehead, fear choking him. Three teenagers close to Piper's age had disappeared the night before. And he had no idea what happened to them.

Dead God, was someone preying on young girls in the area? Did some crazy madman have his daughter?

CHAPTER TEN

THE NEXT TWO HOURS were a nightmare. Will thought he was going to lose his mind with worry.

Betsy called everyone she could think of. The officers in the Village were looking for Piper now, too.

Betsy wanted to join the search, but he asked her to stay home in case Piper returned or called.

He rode by the high school and checked the soccer fields, then the cove where he used to take Piper crabbing, but she wasn't there. Next, he went to the ice cream parlor, movie theater, then the putt-putt course.

Nothing.

She was fourteen. Where the hell did fourteen-year-old girls like to go?

The mall.

It was at least three miles from their house, but Piper was a runner and soccer player. Three miles was nothing to her.

Except it was dark now, and a storm was brewing. Lightning zigzagged across the sky.

The mall closed in an hour.

He was driving his own vehicle but set the siren on top of the car and flipped it on. Heart racing, he bypassed slower traffic, taking a turn on two wheels as he spun into the mall parking lot.

He threw his SUV into park, jumped out and ran toward the entrance, scanning the lot for his daughter and for trouble. If a predator was stalking teenaged girls, this would be prime hunting ground.

Earlier, one of his officers had canvassed the stores and owners for the Darling girls. It was possible though that they'd come here, and a predator kidnapped them from the parking lot before they went inside the mall. An officer was reviewing security footage covering both the inside and outside of the building, but so far, no report of the Darlings being sighted.

He burst through the front door, scanning left and right. He was surprised stores were open today, but sale signs hung in various windows. He tried to remember what stores Piper liked, but truthfully, he hadn't taken her shopping in ages.

He passed a teen clothing shop and glanced inside, but the store was practically empty. He flashed a photo of Piper at the store clerk, and she shook her head. He did the same with every store he passed. Finally, he spotted the food court.

He veered toward it, fear gripping him with every step. A group of teenaged boys were hanging out by a sports themed store. Families were finishing dinner and herding their kids to clean up, so they could head home.

He surveyed the area, perspiration trickling down his neck.

He was just about to give up when he spotted her.

Piper sitting alone in a booth in the pizza place.

They were supposed to get pizza. She'd come alone.

Because he'd let her down. Again.

Chapter Eleven

RELIEF MUSHROOMED INSIDE WILL. It was so strong it nearly brought him to his knees.

A second later, anger hit him just as hard.

She'd scared the hell out of him and Betsy. She knew better than to go out alone at night.

He gritted his teeth, desperate to hang onto his temper as he strode toward her.

When he'd almost reached her, she glanced up and spotted him. Wariness flashed on her small face, maybe even a sliver of fear. But sadness tinged her eyes, too, and a deep loneliness that made him ache inside.

He stopped in front of the table. He didn't know whether to hug her or yell at her.

He didn't say a word. He hooked his thumb toward the exit, and she stood and walked with him to the door. In the car, he remained silent and so did she.

But tension simmered between them, fueling the air.

As soon as he parked, she reached for the door handle. "Are you gonna tell Mom?" she asked.

He muttered a sarcastic sound. "She knows you were gone. She called me frantic."

Piper's shaky breath rushed out.

He climbed from the car and the two of them walked to the front stoop together. Betsy opened the door, dragged Piper inside and burst into tears as she hugged her. Will blinked back his own emotions.

It had been one damn hard day.

"I'm fine, Mom," Piper said, easing from her mother's arms. "I'm sorry I scared you."

"I was worried sick," Betsy cried.

Didn't she think he cared? For god's sake, he'd been out of his mind.

"We were worried sick," he corrected her, his tone harsher than he'd intended. "What were you thinking, Piper?"

"It was just a white lie," Piper said. "You and Mom tell them all the time. You say you're coming and then you don't."

"It was more than a little white lie," Will growled. "It was stupid as hell, Piper. You realize I've been out hunting for three missing girls today, three girls around your age?" His voice rose with pent up anger and frustration. "You could have been kidnapped or raped or even killed tonight!"

Piper burst into tears, the terror in her eyes sucker punching him.

"Stop it, Will," Betsy snapped. "You're frightening her."

"She should be scared," Will said. "Girls her age are perfect targets for perverts and murderers—"

"Don't pretend like you care," Piper screamed. "You're just

mad because you had to leave your job to come and look for me!"

Will was about to explode. "That's not true," he said in a quiet but lethal tone. "You have no idea the thoughts that ran through my head, young lady."

"Just go back to your job, that's all you care about, not Mom and me!"

He started to reach for her, but she bolted up the stairs. A door slamming indicated she'd locked herself in her room. The house vibrated with tension.

Betsy crossed her arms, her expression pained. "You should go now, Will. Thank you for bringing her home."

Dammit, he wanted to pull her and Piper both in his arms and assure them that they were important, that he loved them.

"Go," Betsy said. "I'll talk to her."

Their gazes locked, the memory of the day Piper was born taunting him. They'd been so happy.

That day he'd vowed to be a good dad just like he'd vowed to be a good husband.

But he'd failed at both.

He swallowed hard to keep from begging her for another chance. She'd made it clear when they'd separated that as long as he was on the force, there was no chance for them.

So, he turned and left.

Piper's words echoed in his ears. Her cries. The pain in her eyes.

Then her statement—*It was only a little white lie.*

What little white lies had the Darling girls told their parents?

Chapter Twelve

Three weeks later

THE CASE HAD VIRTUALLY gone cold.

Will spoke on the nightly news one more time. "I promise you the police won't give up until this case is solved. But we need your help." Photos of the Darling girls appeared on screen. "If you have any information regarding the disappearance or whereabouts of these three young ladies, please call our tip line."

Since there was nothing new to report, the questions were minimal. He couldn't tell locals that their children were safe. He couldn't tell them anything.

At least Piper was okay. She was still angry at him. He tried to make up to her for their missed pizza date, but she'd declined offers to have dinner with him. Betsy kept telling him to be patient, but every day that passed, he felt as if Piper was slipping farther and farther away.

At least she was alive. That gave him solace. He'd visited the Darlings again and again, and their despair kept mounting.

He was almost to the door to leave when one of the news staff approached him. "You have a call, Detective Flagler."

They'd chased so many false leads that he knew better than to get his hopes up. But false or not, they had to follow each one.

He stepped over to the desk area and took the phone. "Detective Flagler."

"Those girls had to be punished."

Will's blood went cold. "Who is this?"

"They got what they deserved."

The phone clicked silent. Will cursed and called Chief Mantino to see if they could trace the call.

"Did it sound like a man or a woman?" the chief asked.

"The voice was muffled," Will said. "Hard to tell."

"Let me know if you hear from the caller again. I'll see what I can do about the trace."

Will rolled his shoulders as he left the TV station. He hadn't slept a decent night since he'd been assigned the case. He probably wouldn't until he had answers.

Every day that passed lessened the chances that the Darling sisters would be found alive.

Weary and discouraged, he walked outside. Another storm threatened. The dark clouds kept coming, the winter wind picking up and beating him as he crossed the parking lot.

He climbed in his car, tempted to drive to Betsy's and beg Piper to see him again. When she was little, he could pick her up a candy bar or a stuffed animal, and all would be right with them again.

Nothing was right now. He didn't know if it ever would be.

That phone call disturbed him. What had the caller meant, that the girls deserved to be punished? Punished for what?

They got what they deserved. The caller implied he or she knew where the girls were and what had happened to them.

He drove from the precinct through the Village, the glow from the lighthouse twirling across the stormy sky, a guide for the ships at sea to find their way home.

He turned onto a side street, drove toward the beach and the place where he used to take Piper crabbing. How he longed for those sweet days again.

Just as he rounded the corner and drove across the causeway, a car crept up on his tail. He checked his rearview mirror, irritated at the vehicle's blinding headlights. The car inched closer, then suddenly slammed into his rear.

He braked and gripped the steering wheel to keep from losing control, grappling to stay on the road. But the car sped up and rammed into his rear again.

His vehicle went into a spin, skidded toward the edge of the bridge, snapped through the metal edge and careened over the ledge. He fought control again, but there was nothing he could

He flew through the air then, his SUV nosedived into the marsh. Glass shattered. Metal crunched. The impact jarred his body. He heard a bone snap. His head hit the windshield and dash. His chest slammed into the steering wheel.

The car sank deeper into the marsh, cold water seeping into

the car through the crack in the window.

God help him. He didn't want to die without making things right with his daughter.

Then the world went black.

CHAPTER THIRTEEN

Two weeks later

THEY WERE GOING TO pull the plug on him if he didn't wake up soon. They didn't think he could hear, but he'd heard every damn word they'd said. The doctors. Nurses. Betsy. Mantino.

Piper.

He didn't want to die and leave them. He had to drag himself out of this stupor.

Every time he'd tried before, his body felt so weighted and exhausted that he couldn't lift a finger, much less claw his way back to life.

Crying woke him this time. Piper. And Betsy.

"Shh, honey, I know it's hard," Betsy was saying.

"But I yelled at him the last time I saw him," Piper wailed. "And I wouldn't talk to him when he called. He thinks I hate him."

"No, honey, your father knows you loved him."

He did know that.

Memories returned. He'd been working the Darling case. Betsy called thinking Piper was with him. She snuck out to get pizza because he'd broken their dinner date. He nearly lost his mind looking for her.

Then he yelled at her.

If she'd been kidnapped or raped or murdered, it would have been his fault.

A warm hand touched his cheek. "Will, wake up and talk to us," Betsy whispered.

"Please, daddy."

Piper sounded so young. So terrified. Like she had when she was five and she had nightmares. He would slip into her room to soothe her, and everything would be alright.

He had to make it right now.

He blinked. Tried to move a finger. Blinked again and slowly opened his eyes. Just a sliver. The light hurt. His body ached. His head throbbed.

That soft hand again. Then another, Piper picking his hand up and cradling it in hers. Her palm felt so warm. So tender. It took away some of the ice coldness in his body. "Daddy?"

Her haunted whisper wrenched his gut. He summoned every ounce of strength he possessed and forced his eyes open. His fingers curled around hers.

"He's waking up!" Piper squealed.

"I'll get the doctor." Mantino's voice.

"Will?" Betsy whispered.

He blinked her into focus. Saw her tear-stained eyes searching his face. Heard Piper sniffle.

Then his daughter pressed a kiss to his hand. "Daddy, I'm sorry I yelled at you," Piper said in a raspy voice. "If you'll just be all right, I won't ever do it again."

A tiny smile tugged at the corner of his mouth. He shifted his head slightly and squeezed his daughter's hand. Then he reached for Betsy's.

He tried to speak, but his throat was so dry, he had to swallow twice to make his voice work. "Love...you...both so much."

"I love you, too, Daddy," Piper whispered.

Betsy pressed a kiss to his cheek. "Me, too, Will."

Hope mushroomed inside his aching chest. A second later, the doctor and nurse appeared. The doctor introduced himself, then shined a light in his eyes, and the nurse checked his vitals.

"You're going to be okay," the doctor said. "But you broke your leg and some ribs and have been in a coma for three weeks, so you're going to need some rehab time."

He didn't care. He was alive.

"We'll discuss a plan after you rest a couple more days here."

The doctor and nurse left, and Mantino moved up to the bed. "You scared the hell out of us," the chief said. "Thought we'd lost you."

He'd thought so, too.

"Do you remember what happened?"

Will struggled to recall details. "A car crash."

Mantino nodded. "You lost control?"

Again, a blank hole swallowed his memory. "I . . . don't remember."

A grave expression carved his boss's face. "The head injury. Doc said you might not recall the accident at all." Mantino leaned forward. "Your car nosedived into the marsh. It was pretty banged up, but we're going to make sure there was no foul play."

Mantino thought someone caused his accident?

The chief patted his arm. "Don't worry about it now. You have to rest."

"The case?" he asked.

Mantino's mouth dipped downward into a frown. "Nothing new. I took over, but for now, the case is cold. We'll keep working it though." He patted Will's arm. "Just rest up so you can come back to work."

Will gave a small nod, although the movement wore him out.

"I'll let you spend some time with your family," Chief Mantino said. "They've barely left your side since you were hauled in here."

Will swallowed again, his heart hammering as Betsy and Piper slipped up beside him again.

"I know you're upset and worried about the case," Betsy said. "But you're going to need time to recover, Will."

He did want the case solved. But most of all, he wanted his family. "I'm not going back," he said.

"What?"

"Daddy?" Piper said, her voice cracking.

He reached for her hand again. "I almost lost both of you. I want my family back. You two are more important to me than any case."

Betsy's face crumpled, tears trickling down her cheeks. "Are you sure?"

He brushed her tear away with the back of his hand. "I've never been more certain about anything in my life."

Betsy pressed a tender kiss to his lips. "Then you'll come home with us."

"If you'll have me."

"I've never stopped loving you," she whispered.

Piper leaned over him and hugged him. "I love you, too, Daddy."

It was all he could do to lift his aching arms, but he wrapped them around his daughter and his wife and hugged them tight.

Chapter Fourteen

They called him the Punisher.

He hadn't asked to do the job. The torch had been passed to him, and he couldn't deny the calling.

How could he refuse when the need for exacting justice ran in his blood?

Like his father who'd held the reigns in his big meaty hands, he now held them in his. His fists closed tightly around them, anticipation building.

Justice had to be served. Justice fitting for the sins of the sinner.

He donned his cape and hood and walked toward the cavern he created to house the new ones who needed punishing. Three of them.

Their stay would be longer than most. But it was necessary.

A smile curved his lips as an image of their terrified young faces flashed behind his eyes. They wore pretty smiles and clothes, a mask to hide the ugliness lurking beneath.

One could easily be fooled by their feigned innocence. But he knew their truth. He'd peel away the outer skin and expose the layers beneath, the vileness that had stolen their souls.

They would have to own that truth before they met their maker.

He'd experienced his first taste of blood when he was ten years old and he witnessed his father handling a problem for a local on the island.

His father's punishments were cruel. Severe. They ended in screams of terror that echoed off the ocean, blending with the waves crashing against the jagged rocky shore.

He had to live up to his father's image. Make the sinners pray for redemption. Beg for forgiveness.

Most of all, they had to suffer.

DEAD
LITTLE
DARLINGS

PROLOGUE

Pain seared Deborah Darling's abdomen. She clutched her belly and tried to breathe through it. But she refused to scream.

Because he was watching. He always watched.

Her cries of terror gave him pleasure.

Another contraction, excruciating. Sweat drenched her face and hair. The baby was coming. Now.

Tears blurred her eyes as she looked around the cold empty room. It had been her prison cell for the last few months. A tiny window allowed only a small stream of light inside. But through that window, she'd seen the ocean.

Then the lighthouse.

Home.

If she could just get out of the room, make it to the water, find a boat . . .

Fear and panic stabbed at her. She was only fourteen years old. She didn't know how to do this. Not alone.

She needed her sisters. But they were gone now.

Another pain, sharper, faster, then another and another. She bit her tongue and tasted blood. Time to push this baby out.

She clawed at the sheets covering the thin mattress, then grunted and began to push. Something wet streamed down her legs and soaked the bedding. Blood followed.

She pushed again, harder, breathing through the pain . . .

The labor went on forever. Exhausted, she cried out. She couldn't do this. She was too tired.

Then another pain. One more push. The baby slipped out. Her body trembled. Blood was everywhere.

The baby was quiet. Not crying. Something was wrong.

Cold terror washed over her. She swiped her hair from her face, then reached between her legs and scooped up the tiny infant. Blood and fluids covered the newborn. Its skin was wrinkly, sticky.

A girl.

She had a daughter.

A sob caught in her throat, and she brought the baby to her chest and patted its back. Suddenly a wail broke loose.

Tears rained down her face as she cradled her daughter closer.

"Mama's here," she whispered.

The baby wiggled and kicked, and Deborah smiled for the first time in months. Anger followed as protective instincts kicked in.

"I'm going to get you out of here," she murmured.

A noise outside the door. Footsteps.

She froze, heart pounding. Was he coming back? Would he take her little girl?

No . . . she wouldn't let him.

The footsteps faded. Relieved, she grabbed the towel on the nightstand that he'd left for her and cleaned the baby. Perfect pink skin.

She was so tiny.

She cradled her infant against her chest as exhaustion overcame her, and she dozed to sleep.

The routine was the same for the next three days. He left food and water for her through the opening at the bottom of the door. She forced herself to eat and drink. She nursed the baby as she'd seen the other girls do.

She waited and watched through the window.

The ocean was close. He kept a small boat there. And a canoe.

Finally, an opening—he took the boat and left.

Jumping into action, she wrapped the baby in a clean towel, then she dressed in one of the thin gowns he'd given her. No shoes.

It didn't matter.

She tried the door. Locked. Not surprised.

She cried out in frustration, then rushed to the corner and grabbed the nail she'd pried from a loose plank in the floor. Her hand trembled as she picked the lock. The baby began to cry.

"Hush, little darling," she whispered. "Mama's going to save us."

The door sprang open. Knowing he could return any minute, she snatched her daughter and raced through the dark hallway. The basement was cold, dank, scary. She stumbled along, feeling the wall until she found the door. Trembling, she shoved it open and rushed outside.

It was night, barely a sliver of moonlight. The sound of the waves echoed close by. Thunder rumbled. Rocks and shells dug into her bare feet as she ran toward the ocean. She ducked behind trees as she held her baby close to her.

Her legs were so weak, it seemed like miles until she reached the shore.

Thunder crackled again. She had to hurry. It was going to storm.

Her foot slipped, but she trudged on.

He'd taken the motorboat. But the canoe was wedged between the trees.

She gently eased the infant onto a bed of grass then shoved the canoe into the edge of the water. Frantic, she rushed back, grabbed her daughter and climbed inside. Her heart raced as she gently laid the infant on the canoe floor and began to paddle.

The light from the lighthouse on Seahawk Island beckoned. It would guide her to safety.

She paddled and paddled, slowly drifting toward it. Waves crashed against the canoe, making the boat bounce and sway. Wind beat at her. She imagined sharks circling the canoe, smelling her blood, anxious to feed on her.

Lightning streaked the sky and then rain began to pound down. She shivered, her teeth chattering. But determination drove her. She couldn't let him get her. He'd punish her like he had before.

She didn't know if she'd survive his cruel punishments again. No, she'd have to.

If she didn't survive, no telling what he'd do with her daughter.

Her arms ached and her lungs strained for air, but she gritted her teeth. Cold rain soaked her skin and ran down her face. She eased the baby beneath her legs to shield her from the rain.

A few more feet, she could do it. Once she reached the island, she'd find someone to help her.

She had to save her daughter from that monster . . .

THROUGH THE WINDOWS OF the lighthouse, the Punisher watched. He could see for miles and miles across the blustery sea. The minute she climbed into the canoe with the baby, he smiled.

So predictable. Just like the others.

Except this girl had been tough. A fighter.

He had to admit he admired that part about her. That and the fact that she was so protective of her child. Maybe she wasn't as bad as the others.

But still, she'd sinned. And sinners like her couldn't go free.

It was time for justice.

She was paddling and rowing with all her might. In a hurry to escape what she knew was coming.

A chuckle rumbled from deep in his gut. They all thought the lighthouse would guide them to safety.

Instead, it guided them straight back to him . . .

CHAPTER ONE

Twenty-five years later

Marilyn Ellis wanted redemption. For herself. For the victims whose stories she told.

And most of all, for the teenage girl she'd seen murdered twenty-five-years ago.

But no one knew about the girl except her mother. And she'd been so terrified the killer would come after them that she'd made Marilyn keep quiet.

But hiding the truth had eaten at Marilyn every day of her life. It also spurned her to unearth others' secrets.

The world only saw the surface side of her. That she was tough. Bull-headed. That she pushed until she peeled away layers of lies and secrets and exposed them.

They thought she had no feelings. The trouble was, she felt too damn much.

"Marilyn, aren't you coming to bed?"

Detective Ryker Brockett's gruff voice stirred her desire and made her want to forget about work. At least momentarily. "I'll be right there." She checked her schedule for the next morning on her phone calendar, then laid it on the nightstand as she slipped into the bedroom where her lover waited.

She couldn't get enough of Ryker. At least not in bed.

He was easy on the eyes, intelligent, knew exactly what to do with his hands and tongue and cock to please her.

Even better, he demanded nothing. No ties. No expectations.

Sometimes he even shared details of his cases with her, too.

Heat immediately sparked inside her at the sight of him lying naked in bed. Tall, dark and handsome seemed cliché but fit this spectacularly sexy man. He must have taken lovemaking lessons from the devil. There was no other way to explain the sinful pleasure he elicited with every kiss and touch.

"Baby, you look good tonight," Ryker said in a husky drawl.

She tossed her satin robe onto the chair in the corner, her breasts aching for his mouth, her center wet from wanting him. He reached for her, but she shook her finger playfully, then sank onto the bed on her knees and raked her finger over his broad, muscular chest. "Not yet, lover boy."

She wet her lips with her tongue and kissed him thoroughly, then slowly nibbled her way down his throat and chest to his belly. He groaned, tunneling his fingers through her hair and pulling her closer. She trailed kisses over his thick erection, circling the head of his shaft with her tongue until he growled and pulled her above him to straddle him. "I want you, Marilyn."

Her nipples tingled as he teased one then the other with

his mouth, arousing her to damn near the point of pain. She wanted more.

Outside rain hammered the roof, the sound intensifying as the storm gained momentum. Normally Marilyn hated the rain, the dark clouds, the thunder. It reminded her of that night . . .

Ryker plunged his tongue inside her mouth, and she drowned out the storm and the memories as pleasure shot through her.

It was crazy. Intense. Sometimes she thought he was becoming an obsession.. All she could think about was him.

His dark gaze met hers, heat flaring. With another sexy growl, he gripped her hips and thrust inside her. She threw her head back in wild abandon as erotic sensations splintered through her. Slowly he pulled out, then drove into her again, this time so deep she rasped his name. "Ryker, you feel so good."

"So do you, baby." He nibbled at her neck, then flipped her to her back, grabbed her legs and wrapped them around him. Quivering with anticipation, she lifted her body to take him in deeper. Titillating sensations rippled through her. Deeper, faster, explosive, he stirred her blood to a heated frenzy and drove her mad with passion.

The storm raged on. Lightning streaked the room. She cried out as colors swirled behind her eyes and her orgasm rocked through her.

Seconds later, he joined her on the ride, his rough, throaty moans intensifying her own excitement. Faster, deeper, harder, they reached the peak together, her whispering his name, him groaning into her hair.

Finally they collapsed in a sweaty, satisfied heap, arms and legs tangled, both panting from the ride.

Her phone beeped with her alarm. She snatched it from the nightstand and silenced it, then slid her legs over the side of the bed.

Ryker caught her arm. "Do you really have to go?" That sly grin had landed her in trouble the first time she'd slept with him. She averted her gaze to keep from succumbing to the temptation to stay with him and forget about work, something she never did.

But time was of the essence.

She dropped a kiss on his sexy lips. "Sorry, it's important."

He arched a brow. "A new story?"

She shrugged. "Always chasing one."

He leaned back against the pillows, his bare chest glistening with perspiration. Damn, he was so hot she didn't want to leave.

"What's this one about?" he asked.

"I can't talk about it just yet. Maybe soon." The lie came easily. She hadn't decided exactly how to expose this story. She'd been hunting the truth for as long as she could remember.

And she would get the answers, no matter what she had to do.

She laid another kiss on him, one that was wet and sensual and hopefully would keep him thinking about her all day, then slipped from bed and padded naked to the bathroom to shower.

He might be able to help.

Yeah, but then she'd have to tell him everything. Follow the rules.

Marilyn Ellis was not a rule follower.

DETECTIVE RYKER BROCKETT WATCHED Marilyn sashay to the bathroom, naked and delectably sexy, still damp with his sweat from their lovemaking.

His cock twitched and hardened as she closed the bathroom door. He was tempted to join her in the shower. Have another round with her before he headed to the police station.

But Marilyn was hiding something from him. Ryker knew it as well as he knew where to touch her to make her scream his name in ecstasy.

Unfortunately bringing her to orgasm and persuading her to confide in him were two different things. The sex with Marilyn came easily and was mind-blowing. For some reason storms tended to make it even more intense.

The conversations, the investigations, her reporting . . . that was the complicated part.

He would find out what she was up to though. Eventually.

After all, he was a damn good detective.

Pride made him smile as he climbed from bed and padded to the kitchen. He filled the water canister, then added his favorite dark roast blend and set the pot on the brew cycle.

Over the last year he'd worked with the FBI in Savannah and Seahawk Island, investigating cases involving a secret group of vigilante killers called the Keepers. Marilyn covered the investigations and had also conducted interviews with Cat Landon and Carrie Ann Jensen, two members of the group who'd been caught.

Despite the fact that some people thought Marilyn was an insensitive barracuda who'd sacrifice anyone for a story, he knew there was more to her, had known it since they'd first met. Her tough act was a cover for her own pain. Pain she refused to talk about.

But it drove her to find the truth and seek justice for others. She'd even managed to paint Cat Landon and Carrie Ann Jensen sympathetically, focusing on the emotional trauma in the women's past that had motivated them to commit murder.

He admired her tenacity.

Even if occasionally it annoyed the hell out of him. Like this morning when he wanted to know where she was going.

But she'd made it clear that she only shared when she was good and damned well ready. He felt the same way about his job. So they'd struck a balance between fucking each other and respecting the privacy necessary to protect their careers.

Still, sometimes he wanted more from her. Wanted real intimacy. For her to talk about what happened to make her so terrified of storms—and of trusting.

He removed a mug for himself and a to-go cup for Marilyn, but before he could fill them, she appeared. For a woman, she could shower damn fast. Her silky blond hair was spiked and feathered around her face, making her look sexy and . . . alluring.

She walked toward him as if wanting coffee, then glanced down at this erection and slanted him a wicked grin. He shrugged.

She knew she had some kind of hold on him. Hard to deny when his cock hardened the minute she walked into a room.

He expected her to grab her coffee and go. She wouldn't give him time to pump her for information. But he had to ask one more time.

He feathered a strand of hair from her cheek with his thumb. "Where did you say you were going?"

She chuckled. "Nice try, handsome."

He caught her hand before she lowered it to his belt. "Seriously, Marilyn, I want us to talk. I—"

She fused her mouth with his and kissed him deeply, cutting off his words. A second later, she dropped to her knees in front of him and took him in her mouth.

God . . . That woman had a vicious tongue on the job.

And a wicked one on his body.

He dug his hands in her hair and moaned, then forgot he was supposed to be unraveling her secrets . . .

MARILYN HAD BEEN KEEPING secrets all her life. Maybe one day she would confide in Ryker.

But not yet.

If anyone discovered the story she was investigating, she might lose her edge. And this one was too important to risk by sharing a single detail with Ryker.

Besides, she sensed he wanted to talk about more than work. About . . . personal things. Lately, she'd even thought he might broach the subject of taking their relationship to a deeper level. That he might even use the word . . . love.

God . . . she wasn't ready for that conversation. She might never be.

How could anyone love her after what she'd done?

Outside, the rain had temporarily ceased, but dark storm clouds rolled across the sky, gathering as if to plan an attack, a reminder that meteorologists were tracking another hurricane. Wind whistled through the windows, hurling leaves across the road, and making the palm trees sway and bend.

She shivered, wishing she was back in bed with Ryker. Or in the pool swimming laps at the gym. But she had a short window of time to visit her source before heading to the TV station. And his days were numbered.

A cold sweat enveloped her, and she clenched the steering wheel with a white-knuckled grip. The storm, the wind, the lightning . . . déjà vu of another night. That horrific evening that filled her nightmares.

Dammit. She couldn't rely on Ryker to be her safe place. She couldn't rely on anyone but herself. She had a job to do, and she would fight past the terror the storm ignited to do that job.

Dabbing away the perspiration from her forehead with a tissue, she checked the street to make certain no one was around. All her life she'd felt like someone was watching her. When she was little at school. As a teenager. And when she worked a case.

For the moment though, she didn't see anyone suspicious.

She veered into Daryl Eaton's driveway, then followed it around the side of the house to the back and parked beneath the canopy of the live oak. Shrouded in Spanish moss that hung like spider webs, it gave the dilapidated house a ghostlike feel.

The overgrown yard and dead weeds added to the morose atmosphere.

Fitting for the man who lived here.

She snagged her umbrella, then slid from the car, walked up to the back door and let herself in. Eaton no longer locked it. He didn't have the energy.

The kitchen was dark, the scent of something burnt strong as she entered. A tub of margarine sat melting on the Formica counter, a fly buzzing around it. The coffee pot was half full, the sludge thick and smelled charred as if it had been sitting for days.

A caregiver came in a couple of times a day to check on him. She must have missed this morning. Or . . . she was running late. Which meant Marilyn's visit was limited.

She bypassed the dirty counter and table, easing into the living room. It was dark, smelled of cigarettes and a musty odor that made her stomach roil, but she pushed past the queasiness.

Her shoes clicked on the battered wood floor as she made her way to the bedroom. The curtains were drawn, the air thick with despair, the man she'd come to see hunched in the bed beneath a half dozen worn blankets. His wheezing breath punctuated the dank air.

She stepped inside, hating the dreary darkness. Yet the man deserved to live—and die—like this. Alone. Suffering.

Eaton attempted to turn his head toward her then broke into a coughing fit. With a trembling hand, he reached for the bottle of pills on his nightstand.

She picked them up, then turned the bottle in her hands

and studied it for a moment. A smile curved her mouth as she looked back at Eaton.

His hair was almost gone, the few strands that were left sweat soaked and oily. His hands were thin and frail, liver spotted and wrinkled. The skin on his face sagged around deep sunken eyes that possessed evil.

The memory that had haunted her since she was six years old rose to taunt her.

Mama had to work again tonight. Waiting tables paid the bills.

"Sit in the corner and read like a good girl," Mama said.

Marilyn didn't want to sit in the corner. And she wasn't a good girl.

She wanted to explore the Village. Go to the playground. Walk the pier and see if the crabbers had their buckets filled.

The evening crowd drifted in for dinner. It was late summer, and the place was packed. Good for Mama's tips. But that meant she worked day and night and didn't have time for Marilyn.

Mama hoisted a tray of fried fish and French fries on one hand and another tray of sweet iced tea in the other and carried them to a back table. Three chubby women cackled and laughed as they dug into the food. Mama turned to take an order from a family of eight at the next table.

Marilyn slipped out the back door where the delivery trucks parked. The sky was dark, a storm brewing.

She'd sneak out and be back before it rained.

Noises from the tourists echoed around her. Kids ran and chased each other on the playground. People gathered on the benches over-

looking the ocean eating ice cream. A skinny boy with red hair stood fishing by an old man with gray hair and a cane. The man dropped his rod, and the boy picked it up. The old man smiled and rubbed his hand through the kid's hair.

She wished she had a grandpa and a grandma. But her mama didn't like to talk about that. She wouldn't talk about Marilyn's daddy either.

Marilyn played a game when she was in the Village or at a restaurant. She'd watch the daddies, and pick out one she liked, then pretend he was her father. Pretend he was chasing her at the playground or building sandcastles with her on the beach.

The ocean breeze felt cold and stung her cheeks as she passed the pier. Lightning streaked the sky.

Painted red and white, the lighthouse stood taller than the ancient trees. Mama said it had been there for almost two hundred years.

They'd climbed the steps inside together and looked out over the ocean. You could see for miles and miles. At night Mama told her stories of ships lost at sea being guided back to the island with its light.

Marilyn imagined pirates attacking boats from days gone by like the pictures she saw in the books at the library. Then soldiers from the war as they fought and landed on the island.

The wind picked up, the palm trees bending. Rain began to splatter the ground. She had to go back.

Movement from near the shore caught her eyes. A canoe. It slowly drifted near the rocks, then a young girl jumped out. The water was up to her knees, but she shoved and pushed the canoe onto the shore. She was huffing for a breath, and her thin gown was soaking wet. Her eyes darted behind her, then all around as if looking for someone.

She looked scared.

Thunder clapped. Then rain fell, harder and faster. Marilyn ducked beneath the tree for cover.

The girl scooped a bundle from the canoe floor and cradled it in her arms. A baby. The girl had a baby!

Marilyn frowned. The girl looked like a high-schooler. She was skinny and her gown was torn. She pressed the baby against her, sobbing as she ran toward the lighthouse in the rain.

Marilyn wanted to go after her. To help her. Maybe she should get her mama.

Her fingers dug into the tree bark, then she started to run toward the girl. But a big hulking man stepped into the shadows. Marilyn froze. So did the girl.

A chill went through Marilyn. Did the girl know him?

Then the man grabbed the girl and dragged her inside the lighthouse.

Rain soaked Marilyn's clothes and hair, and her feet dug into the mud. But she didn't care. She had to help the girl. Marilyn ran to the next tree and then the next until she could peak inside.

It was dark, but a streak of lighting lit the inside. Her heart pounded. The man had his hands around the girl's throat. He was choking her!

Marilyn screamed, but she was so terrified that no sound came out.

The girl spotted her and cried, "Help me."

Marilyn told herself to run at him. She could beat him with her fists. Maybe then the girl could escape.

But her feet wouldn't budge.

A second later, the girl sagged against the man.

Fear clogged Marilyn's throat. She had to get help.

But she heard the man growling. He was coming outside!

His beady eyes raked across the lawn, then shifted her way. Her body trembled. What if he saw her?

Terrified, she jumped behind a tree to hide.

For a minute, he stood there looking. He took a step toward her. His hands balled into fists. He was coming for her!

Fear gripped her.

Lightning streaked the sky. The rain came down harder.

He suddenly turned and ducked back inside. When he returned, the girl hung in his arms like a rag doll.

He threw her over his shoulder and hurried to an old car near the lighthouse. Opened the trunk and tossed the girl inside.

Then he ran back into the lighthouse and came out with the baby. He carried it to the car, put it in the front seat and then jumped inside. The glow of a cigarette lit the darkness. Then he sped off.

"Marilyn, where are you?" her mother shouted.

Mama's voice. She was mad.

"Marilyn!"

Marilyn had to tell her what she'd seen. Maybe the girl wasn't dead. Maybe she could save her and the baby . . .

The man in the bed grunted, dragging her from the memory. Eaton looked pitiful and weak, his breathing wheezy. He was knocking on death's door.

She'd been trying to glean a confession out of him for weeks, but his dementia kept interfering, and so far she had nothing.

He coughed then gave her a pleading look. "Pills . . ."

He stretched his hand toward her. An image of that same hand wrapped around the girl's throat taunted her. He was the lighthouse keeper.

She slid into the chair beside his bed, then set the prescription bottle on the nightstand just out of his reach.

"Let's go over this again. Tell me about the night you killed that girl at the lighthouse and stole her baby . . ."

CHAPTER TWO

RYKER STRODE INTO THE Savannah Police Department, adrenaline from his lovemaking session with Marilyn still charging through him. Yet curiosity was eating away at him.

Marilyn was always hush hush about her stories, but lately she'd been more secretive than ever. If he didn't know how focused she was on work, he'd think she was seeing someone else.

But he didn't think that was the case.

Not with the way she'd fucked him this morning.

She must be onto a big story. If it had to do with the Keepers, if the justice-seeking group was still active and planning more vigilante killings, he *needed* to know. While he was sympathetic to the Keepers cause, he didn't condone taking justice into one's own hands. He worked in law enforcement after all.

Rules were in place for a reason, and he followed them.

By becoming vigilantes, the Keepers became criminals themselves and part of the problem.

His commander, Captain Benjamin Henry, motioned for Ryker to meet in his office. Henry was a big man with a barrel belly and a thick beard. He was also the kind of man who demanded the best from his team.

Ryker bypassed the bullpen where other officers were busy, then made his way to the captain's office.

"Congrats on your work on the Keepers case." Captain Henry extended a beefy hand, his ruddy face breaking out into a smile. He knew Ryker's background, how far he'd come. That work was Ryker's priority.

Ryker shook his captain's hand and murmured thanks. "Do you have a case for me?"

"Actually I want you to meet with the forensic specialist and ME about those bones found in the marsh at Seaside Cemetery a few weeks ago. They finally have an ID."

"Shouldn't that information go to the Cold Case unit?" Ryker asked.

Henry grunted yes. "The FBI have an agent with their Cold Case division who's being featured on some new true crime show, Cold Cases Revisited, and are asking for our cooperation. Since you've collaborated with the feds on the Keepers investigation, I'm assigning you as the police department's liaison."

"You mean she's another reporter?" Jesus. Marilyn was enough trouble.

"No, she's a federal agent, one who's passionate about cold cases. Make my life easier and agree, Brockett."

Ryker bit back a curse. He hadn't earned his ranking by defying his superior.

Besides, he was curious about those damn bones. "All right. But if a more pressing case comes up—"

"You're on it. Like I said, you'll be working with Agent Manson so she'll assume the lead on the cold cases."

Ryker nodded. "Understood."

"Agent Manson will meet you at the ME's office."

Hopefully Manson was a professional and didn't mind grunt work. Cold cases usually meant no computer files. No social media or on-line presence back then. Old-fashioned leg-work, digging through libraries and interviewing people from the past, definitely presented challenges.

The captain's phone rang, and Ryker read it as his cue to leave. The commander was never one to chitchat. Neither was Ryker.

He left the building, glad the rain had ceased for the moment. He drove the few blocks to the medical examiner's office, parked and went inside. Maybe one day he'd develop an immunity to the smell of formaldehyde and body odors that permeated the autopsy room. But he wasn't there yet.

Today they wouldn't be looking at a recent death though. The remains found at Seaside Cemetery had been there so long they'd deteriorated to the point that nothing was left but bones. The heads had also been removed from the bodies, and stolen a few weeks ago. Thankfully, Special Agent Wyatt Camden had recovered them, which made the identification process easier.

He knocked on the chief ME's door, and Dr. Patton let him in. He shook Patton's hand, and Patton introduced him to Agent Manson.

Damn. Long, wavy auburn hair framed a heart-shaped face. He had to admit she was attractive, although she didn't spark his interest the way a certain blonde did. He didn't know what the hell was wrong with him. Marilyn had been on his mind too damn much lately.

"Nice to meet you," he said, studying the agent further. Her eyes looked pensive, pained, as if there was a story behind them that she didn't want to tell. He bet the camera loved her.

Another knock and Dr. Eve Lofton, the forensic anthropologist Dr. Patton had requested to help analyze the bones, appeared in her lab coat with a folder in her hands.

Introductions were made, and they all settled around the table. Dr. Lofton spread several pages in front of her, along with three photographs.

"The victims recovered from Seaside Cemetery are all female, ages fourteen to sixteen at the time of their deaths. Two are sisters and have been dead about twenty-five years. I'm still working on the third girl's ID."

She tapped the photographs one by one. "This one we'll call Jane Doe for now." She moved to the second picture. "This is Candace Darling, age sixteen." She moved to the third. "And Deborah Darling, age fourteen."

Agent Manson shifted. "What else can you tell us about the Darling girls?"

"Judging from the bones, the sisters suffered physical abuse for an extended period of time. A couple of the injuries appear to have happened at a young age, say three or four."

Ryker's stomach clenched.

"Cause of death?" Agent Manson asked.

Emotions darkened Dr. Lofton's eyes. "Still working on that. The numerous injuries, coupled with decomp and timing, are complicating the matter."

Dr. Lofton shifted. "But I can tell you this. Judging from the number of fractures and indentations on the bones, the girls suffered."

"Probably abuse from one of the parents or a relative," Ryker said automatically.

Dr. Lofton shrugged. "That's your department, Detective. I just examine the bones."

Ryker clenched his jaw. Yes, finding answers was his job.

This case might have happened years ago, but nothing pissed him off more than child abuse.

He'd put up with beatings himself when he was a kid. When he'd been too little to fight back or . . . leave.

Had these girls been killed by an abusive parent? Or had they run away to escape the abuse, then ended up falling prey to another monster?

MARILYN STUDIED THE BASTARD in the bed, willing him to confess his sins.

As a child, she'd imagined the man who'd killed that girl as a beast. That he was hideous and scary looking.

Instead Daryl Eaton looked like a normal old man. He'd actually been handsome when he was younger, at least in photos of him as the lighthouse keeper.

But Daryl Eaton was a cold-blooded murderer.

Although he professed to be a born again Christian. She didn't believe that for a second. "You worked as the lighthouse keeper, didn't you?"

He gave a small nod, his gaze shooting to the bottle of pain pills. His heart medication sat on the end table, just out of reach as well.

"When I was a kid, my mother worked as a waitress in the diner at the Village," she said. "I used to love going to the lighthouse. I saw you there one night."

His brows furrowed as if he might be trying to remember her. Dammit, the dementia was affecting his mind, and so were the meds, adding to her frustration. She couldn't discern whether he was lying or if he'd truly forgotten what he'd done.

He'd certainly gotten away with his crimes for years without detection.

Knowing his health was declining rapidly, she'd decided to push him to talk. God knows, she didn't want him to carry his secrets with him to the grave.

"One night when I was six, I saw this young girl in a canoe," she continued. "She looked pale and weak and terrified when she climbed from the boat and shoved it onto the shore. Then she scooped up a baby from the canoe and started running toward the lighthouse."

Marilyn paused, studying him for a reaction. He showed none. Instead, it seemed to take all his concentration to breathe.

Marilyn leaned closer to him, her voice a rough whisper. "You know what happened next?"

His gaze met hers for a long tense minute, emotions she couldn't quite read flaring in his pale gray eyes. "Pills . . ."

"You selfish bastard, I'm not giving you a pill unless you talk."

He snatched her arm, his nails biting into her skin. "Please," he said again, his tone demanding, harsh.

With her free hand, she pried his vile fingers from her arm, then shoved him back onto the bed. "You didn't care about that girl's pain. You grabbed the girl like that, didn't you? Then you dragged her inside the lighthouse and you strangled her." Anger propelled her from the chair, and she paced in front of him. "You strangled her and threw her in the trunk of your car, then you put the baby in the front seat." She paused by his bed, piercing him with an accusatory look as she glared down at his feeble body. "What did you do with the baby?"

Eaton tried to sit up, to grab her again, but Marilyn stepped out of his reach. He grunted in frustration then broke into another coughing fit.

The phone on his bedside table trilled, startling her. He glanced at it but was coughing so hard he collapsed back onto the bed.

The ringing died, and the voicemail kicked on.

"It's Gayle. I'm sorry I didn't make it this morning, but I'll be there in five minutes." Then the phone clicked silent.

Dammit. Gayle was his caregiver. Marilyn had seen her name on a note the woman had left Eaton once before.

She had to get out of here. No one knew she was questioning Eaton, and no one *would* know, not until she was ready to reveal her story.

His coughing continued, his frail body shaking with the force. "Please . . . my med . . ."

The image of the man throwing that girl's body in his trunk taunted her, and Marilyn's heart hardened.

He deserved to suffer. Then maybe he'd talk.

Still, she hesitated. If she let him die, she wouldn't get answers. And if she killed him, she'd become just like him.

A monster.

"I'll be back." She slid the pills close enough for him to reach, gathered her umbrella, then her recorder and notepad and jammed them into her shoulder bag.

His wheezing echoed in her ears as she slipped through the kitchen and out the back door.

"WHAT DO WE KNOW about the Darling family, Agent Manson?" Ryker asked as he drove toward the family's house on the island.

"First of all, please call me Caroline." She consulted her electronic pad where she'd retrieved everything she could find on the Darlings, including the family's address. "Actually, there were three girls. They disappeared twenty-five years ago on New Year's Eve."

Over two decades. The family had probably long ago accepted that the girls weren't coming home. Then again, some families never gave up the search.

When his father went missing in action in Afghanistan, his mother held onto hope for four years. She only relinquished that hope when military personnel showed up at the door with proof that he'd been killed.

A year later, she'd remarried, a bastard who'd wanted Ryker to call him Daddy. A bastard who liked to use his fists. That marriage hadn't lasted long. The moment his mother figured out what was happening, she'd thrown the man out. She still felt guilty over bringing the bastard into their lives. They'd both learned a hard lesson.

It had taught Ryker about what kind of man he wanted to be.

"The three girls were reported missing on New Year's Day," Caroline said, interrupting his thoughts. "The night before the parents attended a party and didn't make it home until around three a.m. They went straight to bed and didn't realize the girls were missing until the next morning when the mother noticed their rooms were empty."

Every parents' nightmare.

"Then they called the police?" Ryker asked.

"Not at first. They noticed the girls' backpacks were gone and assumed they'd walked to the grandmother's house. They called her, but she hadn't seen the girls. That's when they panicked and phoned the police."

Ryker turned onto the street leading to the Darling's house. Winter had taken its toll on the grass and trees, leaving them barren and dry, the yards choked with weeds. The neighborhood looked to have been built in the 1950's, and the houses were showing their age. The last hurricane had destroyed roofs and flooded homes, evident in the construction workers and repair trucks in the area.

"You said the girls took their backpacks?" Ryker swerved to avoid a pothole. "That could mean they left the house of their own accord, that they weren't abducted, at least not from their house."

Caroline made a low sound in her throat. "The officer who investigated, a detective named Willard Flagler, first speculated that the girls ran away. Neighbors had reported domestic disputes at the home, and one neighbor thought the girls were being abused."

"Which our ME just confirmed. So it's possible they ran away to escape the brutality."

"And ended up getting killed," Caroline said in a low voice.

Anger churned inside Ryker at the images the story painted. "Did Flagler suspect the father or mother of foul play?"

"His first notes say he thought the father killed the girls, but he never found any proof."

"How about the girls' friends?"

"According to Flagler, they didn't have many friends," Caroline told him. "A girl named Aretha claimed she and the middle daughter Deborah hung out, but she never went to the Darlings' house, and Deborah refused to talk about the alleged abuse. However, Aretha admitted she'd seen bruises on the sisters."

They needed to talk to Aretha.

"So Flagler never made an arrest?" Ryker asked.

She shook her head. "He had a bad accident during the time he was investigating and was forced to take a leave of absence. Then the case went cold."

"Have you talked to Flagler?"

"Yes, and to his superior at the time. Neither had anything concrete to add, except Flagler's boss suspected the accident wasn't really an accident. Flagler's car appeared to have been forced off the road. Police never found out who hit him though."

"Maybe Flagler was close to the truth and someone wanted to keep him from finding it."

"That was his boss's theory."

"How'd you end up in Cold Cases?" Ryker asked.

Caroline's mouth tightened. "Another missing child case. Never found the baby or evidence of what happened. Still haunts me at night."

Every detective had a story like that.

Still, the pained look in her eyes suggested the case was personal.

Darling's house slipped into view, silencing his questions, and he steered his focus back to the task at hand. Notifying parents of a child's death was always difficult, but news that their child, and in this case two children, were murdered made the task even more painful.

The family home was a small red brick ranch with green shutters. A black pick-up was parked beneath an aluminum carport. Mud caked the tires and rims and was splattered across the back of the cab.

"Mr. Darling's first name is Howard," Caroline informed him. "The wife was Phyllis. She left a few months after the girls went missing."

Because she'd known the father was guilty?

"Did she suspect her husband did something to the girls?" Ryker asked.

Caroline shrugged. "According to the report, she claimed he was a great father."

Hmm. Maybe she'd been too afraid to talk. Ryker parked and reached for the door handle. "What did Howard Darling do for a living?"

"Construction."

Ryker stepped from his SUV, thoughts racing. The Darling girls' bodies had been found at Seaside Cemetery, yet the graves had been unmarked. If Darling had killed them, why hadn't he buried them at one of his job sites? He could have hidden them below a house or disposed of the bodies beneath concrete and they'd never have been found.

Not that they'd been easily discovered at the cemetery. A storm had uprooted many of the graves and shifted the topography of the marsh. Carrie Ann Jensen had pulled the girls' skulls from the dirt.

He scanned the property as they walked toward the front door. The yard was overgrown and patchy with weeds, and a gust of wind caused a loose shutter to flap against the windowpane. A black cat darted into the bushes by the side of the house.

Caroline climbed the rickety steps and knocked. Ryker followed, his badge in his hand.

It took several seconds, but the door opened, and Howard Darling appeared. He was in his late fifties now, his hair wiry and graying, and a thick beard grazed his jaw. His eyes looked bloodshot, and he stank of sweat and whiskey.

Caroline identified herself and Ryker did the same.

"What do you want?" Mr. Darling asked with a scowl.

"May we come in?" Caroline asked.

The man shook his head. "I don't like cops. Say what you got to say and then leave."

Caroline exchanged a look with Ryker, and he stowed his ID. "Mr. Darling, I'm afraid we have bad news."

The man gripped the door edge. "Did you find my girls?"

Ryker gave a nod. "I'm sorry, sir, but yes, the bodies of two of your daughters were recovered."

Darling shifted, then looked at Ryker. He seemed to intentionally be ignoring Caroline.

"What happened to 'em?" Darling asked .

Ryker studied the man. "At this point, all we can tell you is that they were murdered."

The man's face paled. "Who did it?"

Caroline cleared her throat. "That's what we're going to find out, sir."

CHAPTER THREE

H OWARD DARLING'S REACTION SEEMED strange to Ryker. Then again, how was a parent supposed to respond to the news that two of their children had died? There was no right or wrong way. People often reacted to traumatic events in unusual ways.

But even after years had passed, typically the parent showed more emotion than this man exhibited. He also hadn't asked about the other daughter. That was odd.

Unless he wasn't shocked to learn the news of his daughters' tragic fate.

Because he'd been the one who killed them.

Caroline cleared her throat. "Mr. Darling, now that we have evidence of homicide, we'll reopen the case of your daughters' disappearances. If there's anything you remember and want to share with us, we'd like to hear it."

Darling rubbed a hand over his head, shifting as if uncomfortable. "The girls, you said you found two of them?"

Finally he was asking. Of course, he probably just realized that he'd be considered a person of interest.

This time for murder.

"I'm sorry," Caroline answered in a neutral tone, "but that's correct. We don't have word on your third daughter."

Darling scraped a hand over his scraggly beard. "Who did you find? Polly? Deborah? Or was it Candace? She was my oldest."

"We found Deborah and Candace," Ryker said.

"So not Polly?" The man's face crinkled. "She was my baby, you know."

"Yes, we know," Caroline replied. "Mr. Darling, can we come in and talk?"

His brows furrowed as if confused again, then he gestured for them to enter. Ryker followed the agent inside, quickly surveying the house.

Kitchen was small and closed off with ancient avocado colored appliances. A pot of coffee sat on the counter along with a box of store bought doughnuts. Yellowed newspapers were stacked in a corner in the den, and dirty clothes overflowed a laundry basket in a threadbare chair by the window.

"S'cuse the mess," Darling muttered as he gestured toward two armchairs facing the sofa. "Used to keep things clean, but after the girls and my wife were gone, didn't matter no more."

"Mr. Darling," Caroline said as she seated herself. "Please tell us about the night your daughters disappeared."

A weary resignation settled on his face as if he'd recounted his story a hundred times. He probably had, both to the police and to the press.

But after some time, people often recalled details that their shocked induced brains hadn't focused on immediately following a tragedy. On the down side, sometimes their memories became muddied and they forgot details as well.

Comparing his story to his original statement might offer insight as to whether Darling was lying or telling the truth.

"It was New Year's Eve," he began. "My wife and I went to a party at the American Legion in Brunswick. We'd just finished a big drive to gather blankets and coats for the homeless and for veterans."

A worthy project. Didn't quite fit with a child abuser, but abusers often presented themselves as respectable citizens in public to disguise the ugliness underneath.

"Go on," Caroline said with a verbal nudge.

"The girls were supposed to stay home. Candace, our oldest, was babysitting."

"Did Candace drive?" Ryker asked.

The man nodded. "Just got her license."

"Did she have a car or access to one?"

Darling shook his head. "We only had one car. We drove it to the party."

"All three girls were home when you left?" Caroline asked.

He nodded. "Watching TV and making popcorn."

"Did they have friends over?" Ryker asked.

Darling's jaw tightened. "No, teenagers didn't hang out here."

A tense second ticked by. "Not ever?" Caroline asked curiously.

Darling slanted her a dark look. "They had each other. That was all they needed."

Strained silence filled the room as they waited on the man to continue.

There were no cell phones twenty-five years ago for them to verify that the girls hadn't made plans with someone on the phone. But Flagler might have looked at phone records from the landline.

"What time did you and your wife arrive home from the party?" Caroline asked.

"Late." Darling shrugged. "Phyllis liked to drink vodka," he said, his voice cracking. "When we got home, she went to bed. My arthritis was flaring up, so I turned in, too."

"You didn't check on the girls?" Caroline asked.

Darling glared at her. "Not then. Their door was closed. I figured they were sleeping."

"What happened the next morning?" she prodded.

He squeezed the bridge of his nose and released a shaky breath. "I can still hear the tremor in Phyllis's voice." Another heartbeat of silence, and then he continued. "I told her not to panic. She thought they might have gone to her mother's, but she called her and Mamaw hadn't seen them."

"Then what happened," Ryker asked.

"I checked the carport for their bikes. Thought they might have taken a ride."

He hadn't mentioned that before. "Were the bikes under the carport?"

Darling twisted his hands together. "Yeah. So I figured the girls were on foot. I drove around for a couple of hours looking for them. Went everywhere I could think. The park, the high school, even the ice cream store. But didn't see 'em."

His voice cracked again. "I hoped they'd be home when I got back, but Phyllis was pacing and crying. Said she'd called the police. They showed up and started an official investigation." He lifted a bleak gaze to Ryker. "You know the rest. Police searched, and we put up fliers. Some of the school kids even combed the beach."

"Was there a specific reason they checked the beach?" Caroline asked.

Darling bit his lip, confusion darkening his eyes. "No. We never went to the beach. My wife was scared of the water. But I reckon the other kids like it so they thought maybe my girls went there for the day."

That made sense.

"Some officer speculated they could have snuck into a boat and rowed out to sea and the boat turned over." Mr. Darling coughed. "That freaked Phyllis out even more. One of her sisters drowned. She couldn't stand the thought of our baby girls being swept out to sea and being eaten by sharks."

Except they hadn't drowned or been attacked by sharks. And one of the girls was still missing.

Which left a lot more questions to be answered.

MARILYN SHOOK RAINWATER FROM her coat as she entered the TV station. The last damn thing this town and the island needed was another freak storm. Two hurricanes in two years was enough.

Eaton's craggy face flashed in her mind. He'd looked pale, weak. He was going downhill fast.

She needed him to talk before it was too late.

The only thing he'd admitted was that he'd been the light-house keeper during the timeframe when she'd witnessed that murder. Every time she questioned him, he started coughing up a lung, and they got nowhere.

She couldn't let the bastard die without revealing what he'd done. Then she might never know what happened to that baby.

Sometimes she woke up with the infant's cry in her head. It kept her awake at night. If only she'd done something . . .

But she'd only been six. And when she told her mother, her mom had panicked and ordered her to keep her mouth shut. She was terrified that a madman might track them down and kill them, too.

Nightmares of that happening had dogged Marilyn all her life.

Finally she was doing something about it. If she solved this crime and found the baby, dead or alive, she might be able to banish those demons once and for all.

The buzz of cameramen, the weathercaster, phones and voices filled the studio. She gave a quick glance at her boss's office. Ladd Winthrop, her coworker, exited the office with a grin. Ladd was handsome, smart, detail oriented, and driven. He was also charming and popular with the women, especially the female audience, and he wanted the lead anchor position.

So did Marilyn.

He would definitely win the popularity vote.

Her? Not so much. She had to win by bringing in the *big* story.

She headed to her office, a small windowless, boxlike space that made her feel claustrophobic with its dim lighting.

Another motivational factor driving her to impress her boss David Blakely. She wanted that corner office with a window overlooking Savannah's riverfront. There she'd have light, see the sunshine. Be able to breathe.

She dropped her computer bag and purse on her desk and was just settling into her chair when Blakely appeared.

Pasting on her professional smile, she said good morning.

Blakely looked down at her over the rim of his dark glasses. "I'm still waiting on that big one you promised."

Another twinge of nerves rippled through her stomach. "I'm working on it."

"Are you stalling, Ellis, or is there really a story?"

"Of course there's a story," Marilyn retorted. "And it *is* big. But big stories take time."

"It had better be worth the wait," Blakely warned.

She nodded. "Don't worry. It'll top the Skull story."

Instead of the smile she expected, an odd expression tightened his jaw. "There's something else we need to discuss."

Marilyn gritted her teeth. Surely to God, he wasn't going to assign her to cover a school event or garden show. "What is it?"

"Have you heard about that true crime show, Cold Cases Revisited?"

"A new one?" she asked, her eyes narrowing.

He adjusted his glasses. "Yes. Local. The star of the show is an FBI agent with the Cold Case division."

"And you're telling me this because?"

"Because the agent, Caroline Manson, is in Savannah. She's investigating those skeletal remains found at Seaside Cemetery."

Marilyn's lungs seized. Those bones might be connected to Eaton.

Damn. She couldn't let the agent break this case. This story was *hers*.

And no one would get in the way.

RYKER DIDN'T EXPECT TO find much in the Darling house. Over two decades had passed since the teenagers disappeared. If Mr. Darling had killed them, he'd had plenty of time to dispose of the evidence.

Then again, if he'd been cleared early on, he might have grown complacent and left something behind.

"Did the girls share a room?" Caroline asked.

Mr. Darling nodded. "Yeah, they fussed about it, but I wasn't made of money. Everyone had to make do."

Ryker catalogued his comment. "Mind if we take a look?"

"I don't know what good that'll do," Mr. Darling scoffed. "Police searched the place when the girls first went missing."

Caroline offered him a placating smile. "I'm sure they did, sir, but anything we learn about the girls might help us figure out where they were going when they left. The detective who first investigated thought they'd run away from home, but now that we know two of your daughters were murdered, we need to look deeper into classmates, your neighbors, any repairmen or workers around the house or neighborhood the weeks before the girls disappeared."

He pushed up from the chair with a grunt. "All right. Knock yourself out, but I doubt you find anything."

Because he'd gotten rid of anything incriminating years ago?

They followed the man into a hallway, then Darling pointed to the first bedroom. "This was the girls' room."

Caroline rubbed her arms as she entered the room. "Have you changed anything in here?"

Mr. Darling shrugged. "No. The wife wouldn't allow it. And then when she left, I didn't have the heart."

"Have you heard from her since she left?" Ryker asked quietly.

An odd look darkened the man's face. "Not a word."

"Do you know how to contact her?" Caroline asked.

Darling twisted his mouth in response. "Sure don't. She could be dead for all I know."

Ryker bit back a retort. Considering that two of his daughters had been murdered, that was an odd thing to say.

Had the police questioned the mother's disappearance? Had she left, or had Darling killed his wife—maybe to cover up the murder of their daughters?

"Mr. Darling, do you mind if I look around in your room?" Ryker asked.

The man stiffened. "Yeah, I do mind. I've been through this before."

Without his permission, Ryker would have to find enough evidence to justify a warrant and come back.

Ryker's phone buzzed on his hip. He checked the number. His captain. "Excuse me, I have to take this." He left Caroline to persuade the man to agree to the search as he stepped into the hallway and connected the call.

"I'm at the Darling house," Ryker said.

"Let Agent Manson handle it for now," his captain told him. "We have another case. I'm texting you an address. A man named Eaton."

"What happened?"

"Found dead in his home. The first responding officer said it looks like murder."

CHAPTER FOUR

MARILYN TAMPED DOWN HER nerves as she stepped into her office and punched Ryker's number. She wanted to hear his comforting voice. As much as she'd tried not to fall for the sexy man, it was growing more difficult every time they were together.

But...she had to keep it professional. He might know something about the skulls and this new agent in town.

If he knew the identity of those skulls, why hadn't he told her?

Because you're a reporter. And you both have rules.

She silently cursed. Sometimes their jobs got in the way.

But the sex made up for it. At least, most of the time.

Ryker's phone rang three times before he answered. "Ryker?"

"Marilyn, I can't talk now." His breathing sounded choppy as if he was walking or running somewhere.

"Wait," she said hurriedly. "My boss informed me that a

federal agent is working a Cold Case show here about the skulls found at Seaside Cemetery."

"Yeah, I've been assigned to work with her."

Marilyn's stomach plummeted. What if Ryker and this agent discovered the connection to her?

"Do you know the identity of the bones?"

A hesitant pause. "We'll talk later. I just caught another case." His breath rasped out. The sound of his engine starting rumbled in the background.

Her reporting instincts kicked in. "Where are you going?"

Outside her window, she saw her coworker rushing by, his phone glued to his ear. He must have a lead on a story. Dammit, she had to stay on top of things.

"Ryker, cut me a break. You know the media will get wind of this. Give me the scoop."

His breath rasped out. "It takes two to share, sweetheart," he said. "And you didn't exactly share with me this morning."

"I shared my body with you," she said in a teasing tone.

A hesitant pause. "I'm talking about more than sex," he said gruffly.

She gripped the phone with clammy hands. In spite of what people thought of her, she didn't crawl in bed with just anyone.

She had feelings for Ryker. Feelings that Marilyn never thought she'd have for anyone. But this was all so . . . complicated.

"I can't talk about the case," Ryker bit out. "Now, I have to get to work."

She started to argue, but the phone went silent. She screamed into her hand, then forced herself to calm down. He'd probably been called to a random crime. A shooting or random attack in Savannah? A domestic situation gone awry?

Nothing that affected her or was important enough to warrant her getting upset.

Ryker probably wasn't happy about being paired up with this fed either. Although he'd proven he was a team player when he worked with Special Agent Hatcher McGee and Special Agent Wyatt Camden during the investigation into the vigilante murders and the capturing of the Skull.

She checked the scanner she used for police activities and crimes. Her heart hammered in her chest at the address that appeared.

Eaton's address.

A suspected homicide had been reported.

Dear God . . . was Ryker on his way to Eaton's house?

RYKER HATED HANGING UP on Marilyn, but guarding his information was imperative. Although he hadn't liked the way she'd walked out after sex this morning.

Worse, he didn't like that it bothered him that she'd walked out.

Shit. Keeping their professional and personal lives separate was part of the job and their agreement. Although he'd definitely crossed that line during the vigilante murders and the Skull case and given her a heads up on leads.

That case and the victim, Tinsley Jensen, who'd suffered horribly at the hands of the serial predator the Skull, had gotten under his skin and everyone else's. They'd wanted to solve it at all costs.

And Marilyn was damn good at what she did. He had to play by the rules, but she had an advantage—she could skirt them.

He glanced at his temporary new partner and was glad she'd had her ear buds in while he was on the phone. He sure as hell didn't want her to hear his private conversation with Marilyn. Captain Henry had warned him multiple times about not sharing info with her.

Darling had refused to allow them to search his house, so he was going to drop Caroline off at the station so she could set up her office.

She was anxious to familiarize herself with the details of the former detective's investigation and see if Flagler had checked phone records on the landline.

She removed her ear buds with a sigh. "Judging from the tape Flagler made, his initial impression of the Darlings was that they had something to do with their daughters' disappearances."

"What did you think about Mr. Darling?" he asked.

She drummed her neatly clipped nails on her leg. "He didn't seem shocked that the girls were dead. Although after twenty-five years, he probably didn't expect us to find them alive."

"He's definitely hiding something," Ryker said. "I also wonder if his wife really left him as he claims or if something happened to her."

"I agree." Caroline made a note in her electronic pad. "That's another reason I want to review the original files. I'm interested to see how thoroughly his property was searched."

"Even if it was, I want a warrant to search it again. If Darling killed the youngest daughter and/or his wife, he could have stored their bodies somewhere else, then once the police finished conducting their original search of his property, he could have moved them, thinking that it wouldn't be searched again."

Ryker pulled up to the police precinct and parked. Agent Manson reached for the door handle. "Sounds like we're on the same page." She angled her head to study him. "You know, when I first learned I'd been assigned to work with you, I was skeptical. I'm sure you didn't ask to be partnered with me either."

"No, I didn't. And my captain agreed that if a more pressing case comes up, it takes priority."

A frown darkened her face. "These girls suffered horribly. I can't think of anything more pressing than finding out who tortured and killed them."

Without another word, she slipped out the door and slammed it.

Ryker sucked in a sharp breath, and loosened the top button of his collared shirt. Clearly, he'd hit a nerve.

He didn't have time to worry about her feelings though. And he sure as hell wasn't going to let her make him feel guilty for working another case. He answered to Captain Henry, not to her.

A chill rippled up Marilyn's spine as she skimmed the police report. A man had been found dead in his bed.

That man—Daryl Eaton.

Worry knotted her muscles. She'd known Eaton was close to death, but he'd been alive when she'd left him.

Had he died because he couldn't reach his mediation? If so, *was* she responsible?

Nausea rose to her throat. She'd walked a fine line with him, but she hadn't wanted him to die before he confessed.

Her first instinct was to ask Ryker to meet her. To tell him everything and ask for his help. But she couldn't do that without jeopardizing their relationship.

And both their jobs.

Her chest aching, she removed the photograph of her mother that she carried with her and ran her finger over her slender face. "I'm sorry, Mama. I kept the secret for so long. But I don't think I can live with it any longer."

Her mother's terrified expression the night Marilyn had run screaming to her from the lighthouse replaced her smile in the photo. "I don't care about anything but you, honey," her mother said. "You have to stay quiet. I couldn't stand it if that madman came after you."

Marilyn swallowed hard. She had kept quiet. But other girls might have died because of it. And she hated herself for being a coward.

She dabbed at the back of her neck with a tissue from her desk. Eaton's caretaker should have been there within minutes after Marilyn had left.

Had she found Eaton dead and called it in?

Considering the man's failing health, she was surprised police suspected murder.

Had they found evidence that there'd been foul play?

RYKER LEFT AGENT MANSON at the station, then sped toward the address of the crime scene. He wove through the streets of Savannah and veered onto a road leading out of town.

Ten minutes later, he parked at a small house with an overgrown yard. A police car was parked in front along with an ambulance. Ryker climbed out of his vehicle, then strode up to the door. The paramedics were waiting outside, while the officer met him at the door.

Ryker identified himself, and the officer introduced himself as Shay Finn. "What do we have?" he asked.

"Sixty-something-year-old man, Daryl Eaton, inside. Found him in bed when I arrived, wasn't breathing. I called it in, medics came, but it was too late."

"Cause of death?"

"Not sure. No signs of obvious homicide."

Ryker shifted. "But the captain said you suspected foul play?"

The officer stroked his chin. "I could be wrong. But the tip came in from a 9-1-1 call. Caller didn't identify herself. Looks like there was a struggle in the room."

They needed to track down the number of that caller.

"Any signs of a break in?" Ryker asked.

The officer shook his head.

"What about the ME?"

"On his way."

"I'm going to look around inside." Ryker surveyed the property. The house was slightly secluded, the overgrown bushes on both sides shielding it from the neighbors' sightline. "In the meantime, why don't you canvass the neighbors? Maybe someone saw or heard something."

Officer Finn nodded then headed across the yard. Ryker yanked on latex gloves as he entered the house. The musty smell of old furniture, dust, left over food on the kitchen counter, and . . . sickness assaulted him.

He peered into the kitchen and den, struck by the cluttered shelves, piles of old magazines and trash. It looked as if it had been months, maybe longer, since the place had been cleaned. The acrid odor of death guided him down the narrow hallway to the bedroom.

He exhaled sharply before entering, then noted several bottles of medication on the ancient nightstand beside the bed. A faded pea green bedspread, and dirty laundry reinforced the notion that no one had taken care of this place in a long time.

He immediately checked for signs of a struggle. The lamp had been knocked off the nightstand and lay shattered a few feet away. A bottle of pills lay on the floor, overturned and spilled out. The picture on the wall by the bed was hanging askew. A glass was shattered at the foot of the bed, an empty saucer cracked beside it. A piece of partially eaten toast and jelly was smeared on the floor.

It did appear there had been a struggle.

He inched closer to the bed, his stomach clenching at the sight of the man's feeble, gnarled hands clutching the sheets as if he'd clawed them before he died.

His face was pale and pasty looking, his skin yellow, his wiry hair sticking out, his eyes wide and staring blankly in the shock of death.

Ryker photographed the scene with his phone, capturing the way the man was lying halfway off the bed, the position of his hands, and the rumpled bedding. He also snapped pictures of the nightstand and floor, and the bottles of medication on the table.

The doctor's name was Simmons. The ME would follow up with him on Eaton's health problems and his mental status.

He stepped away from the bed for a moment and studied the scene again. Another pill bottle sat toward the back of the nightstand, not within easy reach.

Questions trickled into his mind. If Eaton was weak, could he have reached them?

Did he have a caretaker or nurse who came in? Was he on Hospice?

Ryker glanced around again, but didn't see signs that anyone else had been in the room. He started toward the bathroom, but his foot brushed something on the floor. Looking down, he scrutinized the area by the bed. Something sparkled against the dark wood.

He stooped down and spotted a small gold loop earring with a diamond chip in the center.

His pulse clamored as he picked it up and examined it.

Dammit to hell and back. It looked exactly like the earring Marilyn had been wearing this morning when she'd rushed out the door.

124

Chapter Five

Daryl Eaton deserved to die.

At one time, she had condoned what he'd done. Hell, she'd even used his services.

But the fucking bastard was about to grow a conscience on his deathbed. And that bitch of a reporter was pressuring him to talk. If she kept putting the screws to him, he might puke up details about the Keepers.

Then everyone would know the truth.

Secrets that would ruin her family would be made public. The shame . . . it had been bad enough back then when it had all happened.

She couldn't bear to live through it again.

Those Darling girls had not been the darlings everyone believed they were. Of course, no one knew that either. No one wanted to see the ugly side.

But those girls had one.

And they had needed to be punished.

If Marilyn Ellis kept nosing around, she'd have to be punished, too.

Sometimes secrets needed to stay buried. And anyone who tried to expose them had to be taken care of.

Even if it meant burying them along with the lies.

CHAPTER SIX

Ryker studied the earring, his mind whirling with questions. Had Marilyn been here? If so, why?

Could this man have something to do with the story she was so secretive about?

He removed an evidence bag from his pocket, slipped the earring inside and closed it, then stuck the bag inside his jacket pocket. He shined his flashlight along the floor and walls, searching for signs that Marilyn, or someone else, had been here.

Fingerprints, hair fibers, shoe prints.

The ERT team would have to search for forensics. But it would be a shit storm to sort out the dusty layers of grime in the room and determine what was recent and important, and what was unrelated.

A loud knock from the front brought his head up from where he was examining the bed. A couple of blood droplets darkened the sheets. The victim's, or had he scratched an attacker?

He snapped a photo then hurried to the door. Dr. Patton

stood on the stoop, his bag in hand. A crime scene van pulled up and parked beside the ambulance, and two crime investigators climbed out.

He opened the door to let the ME in. "Victim is in the bedroom."

Dr. Patton brushed past him while the evidence response team stepped up.

Ryker introduced himself. A female tech named Ruth and a male named Ken surveyed the yard and porch. "What do we have?" Ken asked.

"Man found dead in his bed. Judging from the medication on his nightstand, he had health issues, but there are signs of a struggle." Of course the overturned lamp and water glass and pills could have been the old man in the throes of a heart attack staggering to reach his meds.

"It's pretty nasty in there," Ryker added. "But pull every bit of forensics you can find and we'll sort through it."

He followed the team inside, pointing out the kitchen and layout of the small house.

Ruth gestured toward the kitchen. "I'll start in there."

"I'll dust the doorknobs and look for prints," Ken said.

Another car engine rumbled outside. When Ryker returned to the front door, Marilyn's little red sedan roared up.

Why was he not surprised?

Even without him tipping her off, she usually arrived at a crime scene within minutes of the police. Probably used a police scanner, although he'd never pushed the topic. She was doing her job and sometimes it was best he not know.

At least she was alone right now, no cameraman in tow.

The earring in his pocket taunted him. Today was a different story though. Today he had to ask questions.

She slid from the car, her gorgeous legs tempting to throw him off his game. But he banished the memory of how they'd felt wrapped around his waist earlier that morning, reminding himself that he and Marilyn had agreed to keep their lives compartmentalized.

Sex belonged in the bedroom.

In public and at work, they were both professionals. If she had information about the victim inside—and the events leading to his death—he had to push her for answers.

Still, dread filled him as she walked toward him. She was the only woman he'd ever met who'd gotten under his skin. It wasn't just her sensual mouth and body. On those long nights when she woke up with night tremors, shaking and shivering from fear, he'd pulled her in his arms. Something bad had happened to Marilyn. Something that haunted her and drove her to do her job. Something that made her vulnerable.

Her tough façade was simply an act.

There were demons she needed to deal with. Demons that he wished she'd share so he could help her slay them.

"Detective Brockett," she said as she climbed the rickety stairs. "What do you have here?"

He zeroed in on her ears. The gold earring with the diamond chip winked back from her right earlobe. The left one . . . was missing.

He considered confronting her, but decided to see if she talked first, so he hardened his jaw. "You tell me, Ms. Ellis."

Her blond brows rose, her eyes feigning innocence. "How should I know?" she asked softly. "I'm just following a lead on a call that came from this house."

Uh-huh. "So you don't know the man who lives here?"

Tension simmered between them.

She hitched out her hip. "No, should I?"

Anger shot through him. Dammit, she was lying.

He gestured toward her left ear. "Lost an earring?"

Her face paled slightly, and she lifted her hand and touched the earring in her right ear, then the left where the other one should be. He saw the wheels turning in her mind. She was retracing her steps, wondering where she'd lost it.

Wondering if she'd already been caught and if she should give up the lie.

Panic seized Marilyn as her fingers touched her earlobe.

She'd dressed hurriedly this morning after making love with Ryker. Then they'd had another round in the kitchen before she'd left for Eaton's. She could have lost it when she went down on Ryker . . .

No . . . when she'd climbed in the car, she'd checked her image in the mirror. Her job put her in the public eye, and she couldn't show up at work looking as if she'd just crawled from a man's bed. Both earrings had been in place.

"Marilyn, what do you know about the man inside that house?"

Her gaze locked with Ryker's, and her heart hammered in her chest. He knew she'd been here. How?

The earring...had she lost it inside?

Her conversation with Eaton replayed in her mind. He'd been agitated, had grabbed her arm. She'd yanked away.

Her earring could have fallen off during the altercation.

"I know his name is Daryl Eaton," she said. "I saw that on the 9-1-1 call."

Irritation, or maybe disappointment, darkened his angular face as he studied her. She fought the temptation to squirm. Ryker was a passionate lover in bed, but he was ferocious in the interrogation room.

She saw a glimpse of that man now, and it made her want to run.

"You rushed out this morning to work on a story," Ryker continued. "Does that story have to do with Eaton?"

Marilyn sighed. This question launched her back on comfortable ground. "You know I can't divulge the details of a piece I'm investigating."

"Right." He crossed his arms. "Then you should go now. Because I can't talk to you about this case either."

Marilyn tilted her head to the side. "The public deserves to know what happened here. I'm assuming Mr. Eaton died. Do you know COD?"

"The ME is doing a preliminary exam now, but as you're aware, the body will be transported to the morgue for an autopsy," Ryker said stiffly. "Cause of Death won't be determined until that's complete."

"His death must have suspicious circumstances surrounding it," Marilyn insisted. "Or else you wouldn't have been called to the scene."

He narrowed his eyes. "I have no comment." He gestured toward her vehicle. "Now, I have to ask you to leave my crime scene."

Marilyn had been thrown off of crime scenes before. Had been treated rudely, snapped at, even physically pushed away. She'd also been threatened with arrest more than once.

But for some reason it irked her more that Ryker was cutting her off. Didn't he trust her?

He rubbed a hand over his pocket, and she sensed he'd found her earring. He was waiting for her to talk.

But she couldn't reveal her suspicions about Eaton. Not yet. Not until she had proof he was the cold-blooded murderer she thought him to be.

Disappointment roiled through Ryker as Marilyn drove away. As much as he understood their arrangement, he wanted her to confide in him. And this morning, he'd even considered confessing that he wanted more from her. That he ... what? Wanted a commitment?

Hell, he didn't know what he wanted. Only that he was starting to feel discontented with their relationship.

If they worked together, they'd make a formidable team.

But when they were on opposite sides, she was a formidable enemy. Well, maybe not an enemy. An obstacle?

He didn't have time to dwell on their relationship though. He had a case to work. Technically, two cases—the Darling sisters' murders, and now Daryl Eaton's.

Ryker strode back inside, careful not to touch anything. He found Dr. Patton in the bedroom, his glasses perched on the end of his nose.

"What do you think?" he asked the ME.

"Judging from his prescriptions, Eaton had high blood pressure and a bad heart. He was also suffering from dementia." He lifted the sheet and gestured toward the man's thin, blue-veined legs and bony arms. "No visible injuries or signs he was attacked, or indication that a weapon was used against him. Of course, the man was probably so weak that it wouldn't have taken force to overpower him."

"Do you think he died of natural causes?" Ryker asked. Maybe he didn't have a case here after all.

"I'll hold off on making that call until after the autopsy. I'll run a full tox screen and let you know."

Ryker nodded. "If he was that sick, he may have had a home caregiver. Maybe a family member or nurse who came in? Hospice?"

"It's possible. I'll speak with his doctor and see what he can tell me." Dr. Patton dropped the sheet back over the man. "Did he have family?"

Ryker shrugged. "I don't know yet. The officer who responded is canvassing the neighbors. I'll look around and see if I can find any contacts or paperwork to tell us more about him."

Dr. Patton adjusted the mike he used to record his thoughts

during the initial exam. "If the CSI team has their pictures, I'll tell the medics to transport him to the morgue."

Ryker nodded confirmation, then walked over to the man's dresser, searching the top of it then the drawers. No business cards or papers with an address, name or contact information.

Inside the man's closet hung a pathetic number of worn shirts and faded pants that looked as if they were twenty or thirty years old. Dusty work boots, a gray rain slicker, and rain hat were in the corner.

Nothing helpful. No safe or even a shoebox full of papers.

He scanned the walls. An old photograph of the lighthouse on Seahawk Island caught his eye. The fog drifting across the ocean and the dark sky made the building look downright eerie.

A search of the kitchen yielded a bunch of junk mail and past due medical bills.

Ryker checked inside the desk drawers in search of a will or information on family, but didn't find anything.

In the bottom drawer along the back, his fingers brushed something hard, metal. He pulled it out and examined it. It was an old fashioned metal key that looked as if might belong to a lock box of some kind.

He hadn't found any such box in the house so far.

Hoping to find it later, he removed another evidence bag from his pocket and stored it inside. He'd keep it and see if he could figure out what it went to.

"Find anything?" he asked the CSI in the kitchen.

She shrugged. "A stray hair here and there. Fibers. More than one set of prints. We'll run them and see if anything pops."

"Keep me posted." Ryker went outside to check the carport for something the key might fit. Boxes of old junk were stacked in the corner. He plowed through them and found ceramic knick-knacks, an old cracked set of dishes, plastic funeral flowers, and other assorted junk. No lock box for the key.

Officer Finn pulled back into the drive and parked, then climbed out. He rubbed a hand over his head as he approached Ryker.

"Neighbors offer anything?" Ryker asked.

"Lady next door can't hear and doesn't drive. Said she met Mr. Eaton years ago, but she had trouble getting around and can't remember when she last saw him."

He yanked his pants up on his hips. "Fellow on the other side said Eaton used to be a hard ass, a big guy that no one wanted to mess with. Didn't have family. Years ago, Eaton was the lighthouse keeper on Seahawk Island."

That explained the photograph of the lighthouse on his wall.

"Man remembers seeing a couple of cars coming and going. One belonged to a woman with graying hair. Saw her bringing in some groceries. Thinks she was Eaton's caretaker."

Judging from the state of the house, cleaning wasn't part of her job description.

"Does he know her name or how to contact her?" Ryker asked.

Officer Finn shook his head. "She drives a beat up, dark green sedan."

He wondered if she was the person who'd called 9-1-1. If so, why hadn't she stuck around? "See if you can find that car."

"On it."

"What about the other vehicle?"

The officer heaved a breath. "A little red sporty car."

Ryker clenched his teeth. Marilyn's car.

Exactly what did she know about Eaton that she didn't want to tell him?

CHAPTER SEVEN

AGENT CAROLINE MANSON SHIVERED as she walked through the graveyard where the Darling sisters' bones had been discovered. The earth felt damp from the recent rains, her shoes sinking into the marshy ground. A breeze stirred, swirling dead leaves and brush around her feet and tossing strands of Spanish moss that had fallen from the tree across the tombstone markers, creating an eerie feel.

Months ago, the storms had uprooted the graves although the workers at the cemetery had restored the land and tombstones as best they could. A crabber had stumbled upon the bones, but sadly the skulls had been missing, which led police to connect them to their ongoing search for the notorious serial rapist/killer the Skull.

She crossed several rows of graves, her gaze drawn to the crime scene tape still roping off the area where the bones had been recovered.

The oldest Darling sisters were dead; one daughter still missing. Odds were that Polly, the youngest had also died.

But why wasn't her body with her sisters'? And who was the third girl with Candace and Deborah?

"How did you girls get out here?" she asked, as if the graves might spill their secrets. "Did your father kill you and bury you here thinking no one would ever find you?" If so, he'd been right. They had remained hidden for twenty-five years. If not for the hurricane that hit the island, they might never have been discovered.

She closed her eyes and imagined the pictures of the girls she'd seen in their school yearbooks.

The sisters had been attractive, although their clothes had been homemade or thrift store bargains, and their eyes haunted.

From being abused and hiding it?

Howard Darling. Something about the man bothered her.

His body language screamed that he was lying. Mr. Darling insisted the girls had no friends. If he'd discovered they were running away with this unidentified girl, had he gone into a rage and killed them all?

The wind whipped up again, sending another chill through her, the screams of the girls echoing in her head.

"I'll find out what happened," she whispered. "I promise."

Little girls shouldn't be afraid of their fathers or parents or fear for their lives in their own homes.

She should know. She'd grown up like that. And she'd survived because she was a fighter.

But she had scars inside. And her own secrets …

Chapter Eight

MARILYN PARKED BENEATH A live oak in the Village, her nerves on edge. If she'd lost that earring in Eaton's house and Ryker found it, he would ask questions.

Questions she wasn't ready to answer.

Although lately, she'd considered telling him about her past. But the guilt and shame kept her silent. She didn't normally care what other people thought about her. But she'd grown to respect and admire Ryker. The thought of disappointing him bothered her more than she wanted to admit.

She glanced at her hands which were shaking, then cursed. Sunlight glinted off a droplet of blood on the cuff of her blouse.

Cold dread enveloped her, and she pushed up her sleeve and saw the marks Eaton had left on her wrist when he'd grabbed her. His rough fingernails had pierced her skin enough to draw blood.

What if he had her blood on his fingers or her DNA underneath his nails? Or on his bed somewhere?

She slapped her forehead in disgust. She had been in such a rush to leave before his caregiver arrived that she hadn't noticed the blood or missing earring.

A rookie mistake.

She yanked on her jacket to ward off the winter chill and hide the bloodstain, then climbed out of her vehicle and walked across the parking lot toward the shops and restaurants, struggling for an explanation in case Ryker asked. But she drew a blank. If she was the last person to see Eaton alive, she would be considered a suspect.

Stop panicking. He was a sick old man and probably died of heart failure or respiratory distress. Natural causes.

It wasn't as if she'd poisoned him or strangled him. He'd been alive when she left.

She needed to talk to Gayle, Eaton's caregiver. Find out what she knew about him. Maybe he'd talked to her while he was ill. Even confessed his sins . . .

But first, she wanted to question Agnes Stanley, the owner of the Treasure Chest antique store. Agnes had been around Seahawk Island for as long as anyone could remember. She knew the history of the island and had served on the town council when Eaton had been the lighthouse keeper.

Maybe she could fill in the blanks about the man's activities twenty-five years ago.

Marilyn crossed the parking lot then turned onto the sidewalk, the January wind rolling off the ocean whipping through her. In the summer the park, stores and restaurants were packed with tourists and locals, but today the area was practically deserted. A few people lingered over lunch at the café, and the coffee shop was busy.

She ducked inside the Treasure Chest, and wove through the mixture of furniture, local artist's work, beach décor and handmade jewelry. Customers browsed the store while an older couple stood debating over a selection of farmhouse clocks. A middle-aged woman with graying hair stood studying several prints of the lighthouse and pier.

Marilyn feigned interest in a silk shawl draped over an antique armoire in the corner while the owner rang up purchases and then assisted the couple. Finally when all the customers left, she approached the owner.

Judging from her gray bun and wire rimmed glasses, Agnes Stanley looked past retirement age although she seemed energetic and agile. Sunspots dotted her hands, a sign she'd worshipped the sun in her youth.

Marilyn offered her a smile and introduced herself.

"I know who you are," Agnes said with a scowl. "I've seen you on the news."

Marilyn shrugged off the woman's disapproving tone as a lady with dark brown hair entered the store holding her daughter's hand. Recollections of her own mother and how hard she'd worked to take care of Marilyn taunted her.

Her mother had been so terrified for her that she'd made her keep quiet about what she'd seen.

But that memory tormented Marilyn every day. And no one was going to stop her from uncovering the truth.

RYKER HAD TO TALK to Marilyn. Dammit, they'd danced around the same case before and gotten through it, but he had a bad feeling about this investigation.

If Marilyn had been the last person to see Eaton alive, learning what they'd discussed might be key to solving this murder.

If it was a homicide.

The ruling wouldn't be official until the autopsy, so no need to jump the gun.

Still, he pressed Marilyn's number. Her phone rang three times, then a fourth, and then rolled to voice mail.

"We need to talk," he said curtly, then hung up.

While he waited on the ME's ruling and the crime team's report, he'd meet with Agent Manson. The Darling case was definitely homicide. Whoever killed the girls had gotten away with murder for over two decades.

That didn't sit well in his gut.

If Mr. Darling was responsible, the case had been personal and an isolated event.

If not . . . if other girls around that age had disappeared over the past two decades, they might be dealing with a serial predator.

He needed to interview people who'd known the girls and their family before the teens went missing. He was tempted to start digging around on his own, but it would be a waste of time to interview people Agent Manson had already questioned.

Heaving a weary breath, he phoned Caroline. "Have you found other cases similar to the Darlings?"

"You mean, are we dealing with a serial killer?"

"That crossed my mind."

Her breath rasped out. "I have looked for similar cases, but so far haven't made any connection." She paused. "What was the case you caught?"

He relayed what he knew so far. "Will wait on the autopsy report and forensics before proceeding." And he'd talk to Marilyn. But he didn't plan on sharing that with Agent Manson. At least not yet.

He owed Marilyn that much.

"Anything new on the Darling case?" Ryker asked.

"I've done some research on Deborah and Candace Darlings' classmates and teachers. According to the original police report, the school counselor made some interesting comments. I'm on my way to talk to her now."

"Text me the address and I'll meet you there."

"That's not necessary, Detective," Agent Manson replied. "I can handle it."

"Listen," Ryker said, annoyed. "Neither of us asked to be paired, but two heads are better than one."

A heartbeat passed. "All right. Let's meet."

Ryker almost chuckled. She was prickly, but she probably had pressure from her boss to accept help from the locals.

Hell, he didn't care. Working the Darling investigation would distract him from the other woman in his life. The woman who drove him crazy. The one who'd gotten under his skin.

God, he wanted to trust her. To work with her, not against her.

But she'd crawled from his bed this morning, then lied to him two hours later about being at a possible crime scene.

And she could jeopardize his career if he didn't listen to that voice in his head warning him to push her for the truth.

His gut told him that if Marilyn was investigating Eaton, there was a reason.

A big one.

MARILYN FORCED A CONGENIAL smile. Intimidating Agnes Stanley was not going to work. She needed her cooperation and trust, not her animosity. "Ms. Stanley, I'm researching a story about the island and its history, specifically the lighthouse. I was told you served on the town council twenty five years ago, and that you knew everyone on the island."

Agnes peered at her with steely gray eyes. "That's true. But a history lesson doesn't seem like the kind of story you usually cover."

Marilyn chuckled softly. "True. You must be referring to the series about the Keepers that aired. I tried to do the victims and their families justice. It's hard for us to know what we'd do if one of our loved ones was a victim of a violent crime."

The woman picked up a stack of hand embroidered handkerchiefs and began folding them. A ploy to avoid eye contact?

"That's true, I suppose."

"I'm interested in information regarding the man who used to run the lighthouse, Daryl Eaton. Did you know him?"

Agnes pressed the scalloped edge of a handkerchief with her thin finger. "I met him a few times, but I wouldn't say I really knew him." She gave Marilyn a pointed look. "I don't think *anyone* really knew that man."

"What do you mean?"

Agnes leaned closer, her voice a hushed whisper. "Mr. Eaton kept to himself. Didn't make friends. Now why are you asking about him again?"

Marilyn waited until the woman and little girl walked to the rear of the store to examine a display of music boxes before speaking. "I think he may be connected to an unsolved murder that happened twenty-five years ago."

Agnes emitted a soft gasp, her thin fingers shaking slightly as she hurriedly folded another handkerchief.

"Agnes, please talk to me."

"I don't know anything. "The shopkeeper blinked rapidly as if struggling to control her nerves.

"I think you do," Marilyn said.

Agnes closed her eyes for a moment, then exhaled and finally looked up at Marilyn. "I heard he was dangerous."

"Go on."

Her eyes darted around nervously. "Good folks stayed away from him. Word was he was a charmer with the ladies when he was young. Then he turned mean. Some thought he was a killer, but others said he just took care of problems."

Marilyn frowned. "What kind of problems?"

The bell on the door tinkled, and a robust man with a beard strode in. Agnes's eyes widened in something akin to panic, then she began hurriedly stacking the neatly folded handkerchiefs into a basket on the counter, this time haphazardly, ruining the effects of her careful handiwork.

Marilyn touched Agnes's arm. "It's important, Agnes. If Daryl Eaton was dangerous and hurt someone, the truth about him needs to be exposed."

Agnes shook off her hand. "If I were you," Agnes whispered. "I'd find another story. Asking questions about Daryl Eaton could get you killed."

The hair on the back of Marilyn's neck prickled. She wanted to know more. But Agnes slipped from around the corner of the glass case and hobbled toward the man who'd just entered. He said something to the woman in a low hushed voice, and worry flashed across her face.

Marilyn smiled sweetly then tossed a wave to Agnes. "See you later, Agnes. Have a nice day."

The man glared at Marilyn, his eyes boring into her as she left the store.

If Agnes said people had gossiped about Daryl Eaton, someone else on the island might know something.

Someone who might be willing to talk . . .

Ryker met Agent Manson at the Sugar Shack, a new little café that served coffee, pastries and deserts.

"Evelyn Morris seemed reluctant to talk," Agent Manson said as they entered. "But once I explained that two of the Darling girls' remains had been identified, she agreed to meet us."

The scent of coffee and chocolate croissants assaulted Ryker, a potent combination that made his mouth water. He followed Caroline past several tables packed with patrons to a booth in the back corner.

Evelyn, a woman with short, wavy brown hair who looked to be in her late fifties, was the sole occupant. She kept running her finger around and around the rim of her coffee mug. An uneaten powdered scone sat waiting, but she hadn't touched it yet.

He watched as she dipped one finger into the powdered sugar on the ceramic saucer and licked it off, her gaze wary.

Agent Manson gestured toward the booth. Ryker slid in next to the wall, and she claimed the aisle seat.

"Thank you for agreeing to talk to us, Ms. Morris." Caroline removed an envelope from the inside of her jacket and laid it on the table.

The former school counselor fidgeted, her face paling. "I'm sorry they found those girls dead," she said in a low voice. "But I suppose I'm not surprised."

Ryker raised a questioning brow. "It is a tragedy," he murmured.

"Why aren't you surprised?" Agent Manson asked directly.

"Well, look how long it's been and no word. The people on the island and the teachers, all thought—hoped—those girls just ran away," Evelyn mumbled. "But back then, it was impossible not to be afraid that something bad had happened. The town was in a panic. Everyone started looking at everyone suspiciously. Wondering if it was the family or if a pedophile or rapist was stalking the girls in their neighborhoods and at school."

Ryker remained still, letting the woman work off her nervous energy as she continued to dab the powdered sugar with her finger.

"So far, we've only recovered the skeletal remains of two of the girls." Caroline gestured to photos of Deborah and Candace that she laid on the table. "These are the oldest two. Polly, the youngest, is still missing."

Tears blurred the woman's eyes. "I've thought about that family over the years, wondered if there was more I could have done."

Ryker gave her a sympathetic look. "What do you mean?"

Her eyes widened as if she thought she'd said something wrong.

"I'm not judging," he said softly. "We simply want to hear what you knew about the family. That might help us piece together what happened to the girls."

"You think there's a chance Polly might still be alive?" Evelyn asked hopefully.

Caroline gave a small shrug. "We can't say. But learning what happened to Deborah and Candace might lead us to Polly."

Evelyn reached for the scone and tore it into several pieces.

"Tell us about the family," Ryker said. "According to the original police file, neighbors suggested that Mr. Darling was abusing the girls."

A shaky sigh escaped the woman. "The girls never admitted that he did. But there was something going on in that house that wasn't right."

Dammit, they needed details, not just speculation. "Did the girls come to you for counseling?" Ryker asked.

The woman gave a sarcastic laugh. "No, as a matter of fact, I had to call them into the office. There were a couple of instances where . . ." She paused, indecision on her face. "I hate to talk ill of the dead—"

"But you want to help find their killer," Agent Manson prodded. "So please go on."

Emotions colored her face. "The Darling girls . . . well, a student in gym class claimed they were bullying her."

Ryker hadn't expected that.

Caroline drummed her fingers on the table. "Isn't it common that abused children sometimes mimic the behavior of their abusers? That they in turn become violent or hurt others?"

Evelyn released another breath. "Yes, that's true. That's probably what was happening."

Ryker contemplated her statement. So the Darling girls hadn't been so darling after all.

If the allegations were true, this case might be more complicated than an abusive father.

CHAPTER NINE

Anger stirred deep in her belly as she read the text.

Marilyn Ellis is at the Village now. She's asking questions about the Darling girls and the lighthouse keeper.

A cold wave of fear washed over her. She glanced around the hallway near the door to Marilyn's condo, careful to keep her head ducked, her face directed away from the security cameras. She'd never broken into anyone's place before, but she was desperate.

It was a damn good thing she knew people. People who didn't mind crossing the line. People who could circumvent security systems. Sure, it had cost her, but it was well worth the price to have access to Marilyn's home.

She checked the code she'd confiscated, punched the numbers into the keypad, then eased inside the foyer.

Surprise flitted through her at the clean lines. This was Marilyn Ellis's home?

Her condo seemed sterile. Everything was neat and orderly. Nothing out of place. Sleek furniture.

Except for the handful of personal photographs on the mantle, it was almost as if no one lived here.

She itched to run her finger along the glass surface of the coffee table, to touch the perfectly lined up photographs of the woman who must be Marilyn's mother that sat on the stone fireplace. Yet, she couldn't leave fingerprints.

She'd come here to learn more about the reporter. To find out exactly what Marilyn knew about the Darling girls' murders.

Now two of those teenagers' bodies had been found, the police were back on the Darling case like hound dogs who smelled blood. And Marilyn was right in the mix.

She couldn't allow them to find out the truth. Especially about what she'd done.

She had her reasons. Good fucking ones. And she had no regrets. Well . . . maybe one.

But she couldn't think about that right now.

She paused to stare at the face of the little girl in the picture. Marilyn. She must have been around four years old. She was running on the beach with the wind blowing her hair. She looked happy and carefree as she chased a rainbow colored kite.

Then another photo, a couple of years later. In this shot, Marilyn's eyes looked sad and terrified as she stood on the pier facing the lighthouse.

Stop it. You can't care about that nasty woman. She could expose you.

Although she couldn't help but wonder what drove the

tenacious investigative reporter. Why was she so interested in the Darling case, a case that was closed a long time ago.

Nerves tightened her muscles as a noise sounded outside the condo. She froze. There was no way Marilyn could have gotten home so quickly.

But she might stop in soon. Which meant she had to hurry.

Bypassing the photos, she checked the kitchen and desk drawer in search of a computer or files Marilyn might have on the case.

Nothing.

Irritated, she strode to the bedroom and searched the dresser drawers and closet. A beautiful wardrobe of dresses, skirts, suits and casual clothing. But no safety deposit box or safe.

She studied the bedroom again. Something seemed off. Everything was in place. Dresser and mirror and bed and nightstand, yet near the closet there was a bank of bookcases. She walked over and studied the neat rows of books. A book featuring lighthouses in the South looked out of place because it was facing the wrong way.

On the front of the shelf, a small knob was protruding. She twisted the knob and gasped as two doors opened. Inside the bookcase was a built in desk with a wall above it.

Photographs of the lighthouse, Daryl Eaton and the Darling sisters covered the interior along with articles about the missing sisters.

Sheer panic seized her. Marilyn was looking at all angles. She might be getting close to the truth.

Trembling with anger and fear, she ripped the pictures

and articles off the board then shredded them into pieces. But shredding them wasn't enough. She had to stop Marilyn.

She ran to the bathroom, grabbed a lipstick from Marilyn's vanity, then stared at herself in the mirror. She looked wild and crazed.

But she was just a normal woman. She'd done what she had to do back then.

She'd do the same now.

She raised her hand and began to write Marilyn a message in her own bold red lipstick.

Stop asking questions, or you'll die just like the Darlings.

CHAPTER TEN

MARILYN HAD ONE LAST person to question about Daryl Eaton. Lloyd Willing used to oversee the grounds at the Village, which included the park and lighthouse.

He'd retired years ago and lived on the east beach side. Many of the homes were older, small bungalows or ranches built in the sixties. Investors and homeowners interested in renovating were flocking to the area.

Willing's property was an older A frame that desperately needed a facelift. Even the yard looked unkempt, indicating the retired groundskeeper had lost interest in maintenance or wasn't physically able to keep up the property anymore.

The wind picked up, bringing the scent of the marsh and salt water as she approached the house. Marilyn knocked on the door and waited but no answer. She tried the doorbell, but got the same result, so she walked around the side of the house facing the marsh. An older man in jeans and boots stood at the edge with a crabber's net.

"Mr. Willing?"

He didn't respond, but the wind was howling, so she moved closer. "Mr. Willing?"

His head jerked toward her, and he pulled the hood of his jacket down, then fiddled with his ear. She realized he was wearing a hearing aid, so crossed the distance.

"My name is Marilyn Ellis," she said.

He shifted his ball cap. "I seen you on the TV."

She sighed inwardly. Her Keeper series had definitely garnered her recognition, both positive and negative.

"What you want with me?" he barked.

Marilyn forced a smile. "You used to take care of the grounds at the Village, didn't you?"

He studied her for a minute, his craggy face weary. "Yeah, had a small landscaping company back in the day."

"I'm doing a story on the island and the lighthouse and wondered what you could tell me about Daryl Eaton, the lighthouse keeper." She shaded her eyes from the midday sun. "Were you friendly with Mr. Eaton?"

He went still, his gaze dropping to his crab net. "Eaton didn't have friends."

That fit with Agnes's description.

"Why you asking about him?"

Ryker wouldn't approve if she spread the news that Eaton was dead. But she wanted answers. "His name is connected to a murder investigation. Was Mr. Eaton violent?"

Willing began winding up the rope to his net. "If you're asking if I saw him hurt anyone, no. But word was he was dangerous. He held up in that lighthouse like a hermit and rarely came out, especially during the day."

"I was told he took care of problems," Marilyn said. "Do you know anything about that?"

His face blanched. "Look, Miss, I don't want to get involved in anything to do with Eaton."

"Mr. Willing, if you're afraid of Mr. Eaton, you don't have to be."

His bushy gray eyebrows climbed his forehead. "Why would you think I'm afraid?"

"Because you don't want to talk about him," she said "But Mr. Eaton has been ill for months."

Willing wheezed out a breath, then seemed to relax slightly.

"Tell me what kind of problems he took care of?" Marilyn pressed.

Willing shrugged. "It was just rumors."

She was tired of everyone dancing around the truth. "Tell me about it."

Willing rubbed his leg as if it ached. "They called him the Punisher. Word was that if you wanted someone taken care of, he'd do it."

The Punisher?

"What kind of punishments?"

"That's all I know. Now go away, lady, and leave me alone." He pinned her with a warning look. "And don't go telling anyone what I said or plastering my face and name on the news, or you'll be sorry."

Anger shot through Marilyn. "I believe Daryl Eaton killed a young girl and kidnapped her baby. If I learn you hid the truth,

I'll be back. And I will expose him and what he did, and anyone who covered it up."

Panic flared in the man's eyes. She understood the motive behind the Keepers's actions. They were vigilantes who'd targeted perps who'd escaped justice the legal way.

But killing a young girl and kidnapping her child were not the same thing at all. The Keepers had killed truly heinous people.

She turned and walked back to the driveway, but when she glanced back, Willing was lighting a cigarette. Smoke curled into the air as he watched her.

Déjà vu struck her. The cigarette, those menacing eyes . . .

The man in the lighthouse who'd strangled the girl . . . it had been dark, she hadn't seen his face. But she'd seen the embers of his cigarette glowing when he drove away.

Willing had access to the grounds and lighthouse. Could he have been the man inside the lighthouse that night, the man who'd strangled that young girl instead of Daryl Eaton?

RYKER WRAPPED HIS HAND around his coffee mug. "Evelyn, who was the girl who reported the bullying?"

Evelyn twisted her hands in her lap. "I don't understand how this can help you. She was only fifteen. She couldn't have kidnapped and murdered two teenagers her own size and age."

"Maybe she knows what happened to them," Agent Manson cut in. "Any detail about where they were going that night could help."

Evelyn sighed. "Her name was Libby Barrett."

"Does Libby Barrett still live around here?" Ryker asked.

"Actually she's a librarian at the public library." Evelyn sipped her latte. "There was another girl though who was friends with Deborah and Candace. Her name was Aretha Franton."

Ryker cleared his throat. "Did you talk to Aretha or Libby after the Darling girls went missing?"

Evelyn nodded. "Libby was nervous, but her parents insisted she was home with them that night." She massaged her temple in thought. "Aretha wouldn't talk. Her mother was upset, too, and told me and the sheriff to leave her daughter alone."

Ryker and Caroline exchanged looks.

"The Frantons moved away three weeks later." Evelyn snapped her fingers. "Oh, and there was another girl named Mellie Thacker who hung out with them. Mellie and her mother left town the week before Christmas and never came back."

Ryker's mind raced. "Didn't you think that was suspicious?"

"Not really," Evelyn replied with a shrug. "Mrs. Thacker's landlord said she left a note saying her mother was ill so they moved to Ellijay to take care of her."

Could be nothing. But both girls leaving town around the same time as the Darling girls' disappearance was too coincidental to ignore.

"Did you meet Mr. Darling?" Ryker asked.

Evelyn's eyes fluttered downward. "Yes, he seemed angry, especially at his wife. The girls acted as if they were afraid of him. But ... that wasn't all."

"Go on," Caroline said

159

"The wife . . . she had a drinking problem."

Howard Darling had mentioned that she liked her liquor, and that she was drunk on New Year's Eve.

"The girls wouldn't talk about it," Evelyn added. "But I sensed she lost control when she'd had too much."

Had she become violent enough to hurt her daughters?

MARILYN CHECKED HER MESSAGES as she parked at the public library on Seahawk Island. Another one from Ryker asking her to call him.

She jammed her phone back into her purse. She would talk to him. Later.

But research had to come first.

Although she had pulled photos and articles of the original investigation and studied them, hoping she'd see something the police had missed. She slung her shoulder bag over her arm, then hurried up the steps of the library building.

A woman who looked to be about forty with red hair, freckled skin and glasses stood behind the front desk. Marilyn approached her with a smile, hoping she didn't recognize her from TV. According to her nametag, she was Libby Barrett.

But the wariness in the woman's eyes indicated she did in fact recognize Marilyn.

Still, she introduced herself. "I'm looking for old articles about the missing Darling sisters from twenty-five years ago."

Libby's eyes widened. "Why do you want to know about them?"

"Because that case was never solved." Marilyn hesitated. "Did you grow up here on the island?"

Libby chewed her bottom lip. "Yes, and I attended school with those girls. Then you probably already know that or you wouldn't be here." She grabbed several books from the return bin and began sorting them.

Actually she hadn't, but she'd lucked up. "Were you friends?" Marilyn asked.

Libby shot her a scathing look. "Hardly." She gestured toward her wiry red hair and glasses. "They called me Four-eyes."

"Kids can be mean," Marilyn said in an attempt to win Libby's cooperation.

The librarian nodded, then stacked the books on a rolling cart. Marilyn followed her toward the shelves. "Do you have any idea what happened to them?"

Libby swung around, anger making her freckles look blotchy. "No, but I hope they got what they deserved."

"Why do you dislike them so much?" Marilyn asked.

"That's none of your business," Libby snapped. "Now, I have to work so leave me alone."

Marilyn's pulse hammered. The woman was definitely hiding something. Deciding to give her time before she pushed her again, she headed toward the microfiche room. Although microfiche were becoming obsolete, this small town still kept an archive of articles and documents on file and hadn't yet updated everything to the digital age.

She found a set of film for the year the Darling girls disappeared, skimmed through the articles chronicling the original search and police efforts, but found nothing new.

The murder she'd witnessed had occurred in late summer. The sisters had disappeared on New Year's Eve nine months before.

The girl she'd seen killed might be one of the Darlings. The police had always assumed the sisters would be found together, but the girl she'd seen was alone, except for the baby.

Candace was sixteen, Deborah fourteen when they'd gone missing.

She accessed photographs of the Darlings from the news coverage. First she perused the class photo of Deborah. She was pretty with long, golden blond hair and green eyes, her head tilted sideways in a cocky pose that didn't fit with the image of an abuse victim.

Marilyn massaged her temple, struggling to recall the face of the girl she'd seen murdered. But it had been late and dark and stormy. Was her hair golden blond like Candace's?

Her memory was foggy.

She scrolled through the yearbook until she located a photograph of Deborah. These pictures were definitely clearer images of the girls. The ones she'd pulled before were grainy and discolored, and taken from a distance.

Deborah had wavy brown chin-length hair. A plain face, big dark eyes. Not quite as pretty as her older sister, and a deep sadness haunted her expression.

Marilyn retraced her steps that night. She'd been at her mama's diner, had snuck out to the playground. Kids had packed the play equipment, tourists strolling the pier. She'd cut across the grassy lawn to the lighthouse, hidden behind that tree.

Then she'd seen the canoe in the water. The girl paddling for her life. Her dark, brown hair was wet and tangled around her face in the wind and rain.

She studied Deborah Darling's face again, and her stomach clenched.

The girl she'd seen climb from the canoe with that infant . . . it was Deborah. Deborah who was fourteen years old. Deborah who'd tried to shield a baby—her baby?—from the elements.

Why had she been out in the canoe? Where had she come from?

Marilyn located a map of the area dating back two and a half decades and spotted a couple of tiny islands a mile out to sea. Could she have been on one of those islands?

A dark chill engulfed her. If the baby was Deborah's, then it was possible the girl had been raped.

By whom? Daryl Eaton?

The baby's scream had echoed in the wind as the light keeper had carried it to his car. That baby's cry taunted her now.

Had Eaton killed the baby, too?

If so, and one of the skeletons recovered at Seahawk Island belonged to Deborah, had the baby been with her?

Her lungs strained for air. She had to question Ryker about those bodies.

But how could she probe him for information without divulging her own secrets?

CHAPTER ELEVEN

S HE EXITED THE SECRET chat room for the Keepers where she'd been lurking for hours. The police and FBI thought they'd shut down the Keepers, but they could never stop them.

They were too clever. Too secretive. Too determined.

Too necessary.

They had tentacles reaching into places no one knew about or ever would. Tentacles that went higher up.

Hearing the plans and thoughts of the others gave her comfort. They were caring, loving women determined to exact justice.

Just like her.

She felt a sisterhood with Cat Landon and Carrie Ann Jensen. And with those poor victims of the River Street rapist and the Skull. Those bastards had deserved to suffer.

The sound of Daryl Eaton's last breath kept echoing in her head, tapping at her sanity. She poured herself a glass of vodka and tossed it back, then crossed the room to her prized wall and ran her finger over the photographs.

Pictures of the Keepers' victims. Pictures of Cat and Carrie Ann.

And articles on the deaths and the deals the police had made with both women.

They were like sisters to her.

Her hand shook as she poured herself another drink.

She would not feel guilty about killing Daryl Eaton. And she sure as hell didn't intend to go to prison for his murder.

Why that reporter had latched onto the story of his death and those Darling girls' disappearance escaped her. But the trail the reporter was following would eventually lead her into the dark world that hid *her* secrets.

Sooner or later, Marilyn would figure out the connections. Sooner or later, she'd find out everything.

She guzzled her drink, then snagged her keys and hurried outside to her car before she lost her courage. The warning message she'd left on Marilyn's mirror earlier wasn't enough.

Marilyn had to die just like Eaton.

CHAPTER TWELVE

RYKER TRIED TO FORMULATE a possible scenario around the Darling girls disappearance, but there were too many missing pieces.

"Something strange was going on with that foursome," Caroline said as Ryker parked at the library.

"I agree. Mr. Darling said his daughters didn't have friends, but the counselor contradicted that. And two of their friends moved away around the time the sisters disappeared. Maybe Libby Barrett will shed some light on the situation."

Ryker checked his messages to see if Marilyn had returned his call, but nothing from her.

His mother had called though, wanting him to come to dinner soon. She'd been bugging him lately asking if he had a girlfriend. So far he hadn't told her about Marilyn. But he'd been thinking about introducing them.

He gritted his teeth. He'd talk to Marilyn tonight. And he wouldn't let her get away with lies.

A text from the ME appeared, saying he had information. "I need to call Dr. Patton."

Caroline opened her tablet. "I'll see if I can find contact information on Aretha Franton and Mellie Thacker."

Ryker murmured okay then quickly pressed the ME's number.

"Daryl Eaton's tox screen came back," Dr. Patton said. "He died as a result of an overdose of heroine."

Ryker drummed his fingers on his thigh. "I didn't see any hypodermics or a syringe on his nightstand or in the house, did you?"

"No. And he didn't have track marks indicating he was a user."

"I'll check with the ERT and see if they found evidence." Ryker hung up, more questions plaguing him. Why would someone kill a man who was on his deathbed?

Caroline glanced up from her phone. "I can't seem to find Mellie Thacker, but the analyst is working on it. I tried Aretha's number and left a message. She lives in Florida."

Ryker relayed the ME's findings regarding Eaton. "Looks like he was murdered."

"Someone must have really hated him to kill him when he was so ill."

Marilyn's earring taunted Ryker. She had been there. But she had no reason to hate Eaton.

Did she?

THE THOUGHT OF EATON raping a fourteen-year-old girl, holding her and her child hostage, then killing her and taking the baby made nausea rise in Marilyn's throat.

Lloyd Willing's face materialized behind her eyes.

She searched the articles for any mention of Willing or Eaton in the investigation, but neither of them had been interviewed by the police. The police had concentrated on talking to students for background on the girls, then focused on the father.

Howard Darling had been their primary person of interest. Although one neighbor suggested he abused his children, and the police had visited the house twice for domestic violence, the police hadn't arrested Darling. They hadn't had enough evidence.

According to Mrs. Darling, her husband adored the girls. Yes, they argued, even spanked them when they were younger, but she insisted parents needed to discipline their daughters or they'd turn into whores.

Marilyn stiffened as she read that last line. Did Mrs. Darling have reason to worry her girls were experimenting with sex, or had she been overreacting? Had she covered for her husband because she was afraid of him?

In more than one interview, Mrs. Darling had been drinking heavily. Police assumed she was simply distraught, but what if her drinking had been problematic in the marriage?

What if . . . what if *she* had been the one who'd hurt the girls?

If so, it explained why she defended her husband. But why wouldn't Mr. Darling have done something to stop her?

Marilyn ran a hand through her hair and sighed. It was just a theory.

If the girls were being abused, they could have run away out of fear. Where had they been going?

She skimmed the articles again, searching for names of classmates who might have answers, but the articles hadn't printed the teens' names.

They would be listed in the official police report.

She returned the microfiche, then stood and stretched. Ryker had access to that report.

RYKER'S PHONE BUZZED AS he and Caroline climbed the steps to the library. He glanced down at the screen.

His captain.

"I have to get this," he said.

"No problem. I'll try calling Aretha Franton again." Caroline stepped aside.

Ryker connected the call.

"What the hell is going on?" Captain Henry bellowed.

Ryker tensed. "What do you mean?"

"Listen, Ryker, I know you're seeing that damned reporter, but you can't let her interfere with the Eaton case."

He bristled. There was no way the Captain could know about Marilyn's earring. "What makes you think I am?"

"I just received a call from Lieutenant Granger, head of the ERT. They found the Ellis woman's prints at Eaton's. They're running the blood sample they collected from his sheets against her DNA now."

Why the hell had they called the captain instead of him?

He pinched the bridge of his nose as the truth slammed into him. *Because they know you and Marilyn are hooking up.*

Dammit to hell and back. He liked being with Marilyn. She was gutsy and strong, vulnerable and soft, sexy and mysterious. If she'd only open up to him . . .

But he couldn't risk his career for her. Could he?

"I haven't seen or talked to Marilyn since I left the crime scene," he said. "But trust me, Captain. I'll find out why she was at Eaton's."

He glanced up and saw Caroline watching him. Shit. She'd overheard his side of the conversation.

"Ryker, stop thinking with your dick. Marilyn will do anything for a story. She's been defending the Keepers. If she's somehow involved in this murder, she could feed you false information and intentionally lead you astray."

Ryker inhaled a deep breath, striving for calm. Would Marilyn really distract him from the scent of a killer to get the scoop?

"Don't worry, Captain," Ryker said. "Nothing will keep me from finding the person who murdered Eaton."

"Bring Ms. Ellis in for questioning," Captain Henry ordered. "I want to hear what she has to say."

Ryker hung up, his pulse pounding. His association with Marilyn was already costing him.

But hell . . . it was worth it. *She* was worth it.

"What's going on?" Caroline asked.

Ryker jammed his phone in his pocket. "It's about the Eaton case."

"Let me guess. The reporter you're seeing was at the crime scene?"

He didn't like her smug tone.

He replayed the morning in his head. Marilyn making love to him, then rushing out the door. Marilyn showing up at Eaton's after he'd arrived, then pretending she didn't know the man.

Marilyn . . . all lies.

"I'll handle it. Let's talk to Libby Barrett," he said.

"You aren't going to share inside information on this investigation with her, are you?" Caroline asked.

Ryker glared at her. He didn't need her on his back, too. "I know how to do my job, and I'm damn good at it. So don't question my integrity."

Her dark eyes studied him. "I don't trust her."

"Maybe not," he said. "But if you're going to work with me, you have to trust me."

Ryker didn't wait for a response. He strode inside, the wind beating at his back as thunder rumbled and rain began to pour.

Marilyn was headed toward the exit when she spotted Ryker and a tall, attractive auburn-haired woman approach Libby Barrett at the desk.

She ducked behind one of the dividers separating the research books from fiction, but stayed close enough to hear the conversation. Ryker introduced himself and the federal agent, Caroline Manson.

Marilyn's stomach tightened. Damn. She was pretty.

She needed to talk to Ryker, but she'd speak to him in private, not in front of the agent.

"I'm sure you heard about the skeletal remains recovered from Seaside Cemetery," Ryker said to the librarian. "Two of the bodies have been identified as Deborah and Candace Darling."

Marilyn inhaled a deep breath. She'd only seen one of the girls that night, Deborah. But their bodies had eventually been dumped at the same graveyard.

"The third body hasn't been identified yet," Ryker continued. "The high school counselor from Seahawk High said you had some trouble with the Darlings, that they bullied you."

Libby touched her throat, her face paling. "There really wasn't anything to it. They just teased me, you know, kids' stuff."

"But you were upset enough to see the counselor about it," Agent Manson said.

Libby fidgeted. "Yeah, but I got over it."

A heartbeat of silence passed.

"Students talk," Agent Manson went on to say. "Did you happen to hear the sisters mention running away from home?"

Libby shook her head no. "I stayed away from them and their friends."

"And those friends were?" Ryker prodded.

"Mellie Thacker and Aretha Franton. The four of them used to meet up and whisper. They made fun of those of us who weren't popular. And they flirted with the jocks."

"Anyone in particular?" Agent Manson asked.

Libby shrugged. "Two football players. Jeremy Linchfield

and Preston Richway." An odd smile tilted her mouth as if she was lost in a memory. "But those guys didn't want anything to do with the Darlings."

"Why not?" Ryker asked.

"Because they could have anyone they wanted." Libby blew out a breath. "I mean *anyone*."

"How did the girls handle that?" Agent Manson asked.

"Not well," the librarian replied. "Deborah and Candace had a mean streak. Mellie said they'd get revenge. That Jeremy and Preston would be sorry."

"What did they do?" Agent Manson asked.

"I don't know what they planned." She raised a brow. "Jeremy had a bad wreck the last day of school before Christmas break. Rumor was that he was drinking and driving."

"Does he still live in town?" Ryker queried.

Libby nodded. "The wreck tore his leg up. Couldn't play football his senior year and lost out on a scholarship. Think he works with computers now."

Marilyn rubbed her temple. If the Darling girls had something to do with Jeremy's accident, he had motive to hurt them. But . . . she hadn't seen a young guy with Deborah.

She'd seen Eaton.

Libby pushed her glasses up on her nose. "If you want to know what those girls were up to, you should look in Deborah's diary," she told them. "She was always writing in it."

Marilyn bit the inside of her cheek. The police never mentioned a diary. Had Deborah taken it with her when she'd run away?

Or if she hadn't run away and Darling had killed her, it might still be at his house.

Libby stepped from behind the desk and glanced around. "I don't want my name involved in this," she said. "That's why I didn't talk to that reporter a while ago. You won't tell her what I said, will you?"

Marilyn's stomach tightened.

"A reporter was here asking about the Darlings?" Ryker asked.

"Yeah, you know that lady who covered the vigilante murders." Libby hesitated. "She went to the back to look through old microfiche."

"Really?" Ryker's voice rose an octave, and Marilyn knew she had to leave.

She inched along the divider until she reached the opposite end and peeked around the corner. The coast looked clear. She stepped from her hiding spot, but a second later Ryker's voice stopped her.

"Marilyn, imagine seeing you here."

She squeezed her eyes closed and took a deep breath, then squared her shoulders and turned to face him. Anger darkened his beautiful brown eyes, eyes that had looked at her with passion this morning.

Eyes that now held distrust.

He snatched her arm. "You haven't been returning my calls."

"I've been working."

He ushered her into the hallway near the restrooms and blocked her from leaving. "You were at Daryl Eaton's house before I arrived this morning."

She opened her mouth to argue, but he silenced with a stern look.

"Don't even think about lying to me," he said. "Your fingerprints and blood were found in Eaton's bedroom. My captain wants me to bring you in for questioning."

Marilyn gritted her teeth, then offered him a smile. "Ryker, it's me, Marilyn. You can't possibly think that I killed Daryl Eaton."

CHAPTER THIRTEEN

RYKER SHIFTED. THE WHEELS were turning in Marilyn's head. He knew every delicious inch of her body—and every nuance of her body language. And he could tell when she was hiding something.

She was doing both now.

"What's going on, Marilyn?" he asked. "Why were you at Eaton's this morning?"

She had the audacity to give him a sexy smile. "Ryker, I don't like to discuss my story until I get it right."

"So you were investigating a piece on Eaton?"

She blinked, a sign she was stalling. "I thought he might be a source."

Ryker raised a brow. "A source for what? What's your angle?"

"I'm doing a story on the history of Seahawk Island and the lighthouse. He used to be the lighthouse keeper."

Ryker chuckled. "He did. But you and I both know you don't cover routine pieces." He leaned closer, so close he inhaled the scent of her body wash. Lavender.

Dammit, that scent always aroused him.

He sharpened his tone. "If you won't talk to me here, I'll take you down to the station."

Her eyes widened. "You wouldn't!"

He reached for the handcuffs inside his jacket. "I don't have a choice. You're officially a person of interest. And my boss thinks I'm feeding you information."

Worry flickered in her expressive eyes for a second. For him or for herself?

"Come on, Marilyn, why were you at Eaton's?"

Her gaze shot over his shoulder as if she was looking for someone. He quickly glanced backward and saw Agent Manson watching. Her body was rigid, a deep frown marring her face.

She folded her arms. "Detective Brockett, you aren't sharing details of our investigation with *her*, are you?"

She made Marilyn sound like a piranha.

"No," he said between gritted teeth. "I'm trying to find out why she was at my crime scene this morning and what she knows about my victim."

Agent Manson gestured toward Marliyn. "How did she know we'd identified two of the Darling girls' remains?"

Ryker dropped his hands by his side and stepped away from Marilyn. "I don't know. I didn't tell her."

"Ms. Ellis, why were you asking Libby Barrett about the Darling girls?" Agent Manson pierced Marilyn with an accusatory look. "And why were you looking at microfiche about the girls' disappearance?"

Ryker searched Marilyn's face. "How *did* you know about them?"

"I am investigating the girls' disappearance, but I didn't know for certain that you'd identified their remains until I heard you two talking to Libby."

Ryker didn't like the way Marilyn went ramrod straight. She had her back against the wall, literally and figuratively, and was clearly trying to figure a way out.

"The mystery of those girls' disappearance has plagued the island for over two decades," she continued. "I thought if I broke the story, I'd earn a promotion."

Her explanation held a ring of truth. Marilyn was competitive. If she'd heard Caroline was doing a true crime show about the Darling case, she probably wanted to beat her to the scoop.

"And what about Eaton?" he demanded.

"I answered that already," Marilyn said curtly.

He wanted to ask about the blood droplets found on Eaton's sheets, but didn't intend to discuss it in front of his new partner. Her animosity toward Marilyn was palpable. Why he wasn't sure, but she seemed to instantly dislike her.

"I have to go." Marilyn clutched her shoulder bag and pushed past him.

Ryker grabbed her arm to keep her from escaping, but she winced slightly. The sight of her bruised and scratched wrist surprised him. He instantly released her.

He searched her face again. "What happened this morning?"

She pulled her arm away and yanked her sleeve over the bruise. "I thought Eaton might have seen the Darling girls at the pier the night they went missing. I asked him, but he didn't remember them."

Then she lifted her chin and turned to Caroline. "Good luck with your show, Agent Manson. I hope you find what you're looking for."

Without another word, Marilyn strode toward the exit and hurried out the door.

Agent Manson was scrutinizing his every move, but he didn't care. He chased after Marilyn and spotted her near the exit. But he halted when he saw her talking to a young woman with an infant.

The woman was struggling with an unruly toddler who was begging for a lollipop. Marilyn knelt to speak to the child, then offered to hold the baby while the mother strapped the toddler into the stroller. To his surprise, the mother handed over the baby, and Marilyn rocked the child in her arms and began to sing to the infant.

Ryker's lungs strained for air. He'd never imagined Marilyn as a mother, but the sight of her comforting that baby seemed right.

She glanced up and saw him watching her, and he could have sworn tears blurred her eyes.

"We have to talk," he mouthed.

Her gaze latched with his, the wealth of emotions in Marilyn's eyes ripping at his heart. "I know," she whispered in return. "Later. I promise."

The woman reached for the baby, and Marilyn gently eased the infant back into her arms.

Ryker wanted to go to her then. Go hug her and make her tell him about the bruises and everyone who'd ever hurt her. But she pressed her fingers to her mouth then blew him a kiss and walked out the door.

He watched her leave with a mixture of awe and a sense there was a lot more to Marilyn Ellis than anyone knew. The enigma of a woman was stealing his heart.

And he would do whatever he had to do to find out her secrets.

MARILYN PAUSED OUTSIDE ON the stoop of the library, shivering as the storm clouds unleashed a deluge of rain on the ground.

A moment later a streak of lightning zigzagged across the dark sky. She hugged her arms around herself, struggling to remain calm. But emotions clawed at her like a heavy undertow trying to drag her out to sea.

Sometimes lying came with her job. But she hated lying to Ryker. He'd been good to her, understanding about her work. And he'd consoled her so many nights when the nightmares came.

But he was so angry now that she couldn't gloss over the truth much longer. She had a lot to answer to. And she would tell him everything. Soon.

But she refused to share her motive for pursuing Eaton and the Darling case in front of that female agent.

Thunder boomed outside, and she startled. Shit, shit, shit. She didn't want to run out in the storm.

But she glanced back and saw Ryker and Agent Manson talking to Libby again, and knew she had to escape.

Something about that agent had unnerved her. When she'd looked into her eyes, a chill had rippled up her spine.

Marilyn wasn't the only one keeping secrets.

She was a pro at investigative reporting, at asking questions and putting others on the spot, at hiding things she didn't want divulged.

Agent Manson was evidently a master at the same thing. It was easy to see why she'd earned the lead on Cold Cases Revisited. With her striking good looks, direct attitude, interrogation skills, and cool facade, she would have viewers glued to her every word.

The agent hadn't liked *her*.

It had seemed immediate. Or hell, she'd probably seen her on TV and criticized her methods.

Or ... maybe she was intimidated by you.

No ... that woman wasn't intimidated by anyone.

Ryker and the agent started toward the door, and Marilyn cursed again. She'd never been possessive of a man, but seeing Ryker with Caroline Manson disturbed her. What if he decided he enjoyed working with her? What if he wanted to make it a permanent arrangement?

What if he gets fed up with you and tosses you away?

Her father hadn't wanted her. And until Ryker, no other man had either.

Sure, the two of them had simply been fooling around. Had kept their relationship physical and friendly, both in and out of the bedroom, but not serious.

But she liked having Ryker around. He made her feel safe. Cherished. Desired.

Sometimes she thought she might even be falling in love with him . . .

She'd felt vulnerable though when he'd seen her with that baby. Had he sensed how much she secretly wanted a child of her own?

Guilt slammed into her again. She didn't deserve a child because she hadn't saved Deborah Darling's baby.

Ryker cut his eyes toward the door, and she inched away from the glass so he couldn't see her. They would be leaving soon. She had to make a run for it.

She buttoned her jacket, wishing like hell she'd thought to bring an umbrella, then clutched her shoulder bag and dove outside into the downpour. The steps were slick and she nearly slipped, but managed to make it to the landing. Water soaked her hair and clothes, and her wet shoes sucked up an inch of rainwater as she sprinted toward her car.

A truck flew past, and she had to jump back to keep from getting sideswiped. It was raining so hard she could barely see. She checked the street again. Satisfied it was clear, she darted across the two-lane road and hit the pavement in the parking lot running.

Several other cars were parked in the lot, and she darted between two rows, but just as she reached the clearing, a dark sedan flew at her.

She threw up her hands to warn the car in case he didn't see her.

But the car barreled straight toward her. Marilyn screamed and dove to the side to avoid getting hit, but the front bumper skimmed her leg and she pitched forward onto the wet pavement.

"You're aware she's lying to you," Caroline said curtly.

Ryker maintained a neutral expression. "Let's just focus on the case."

She studied him for a long minute, then folded her arms. "All right. What Libby said about the Darling girls getting back at those guys might not be anything, but—"

"It might lead us to the truth. If they were responsible for Jeremy's accident and hurt Preston Richway, those guys had motive for murder."

Caroline frowned. "Which would mean that Howard Darling is innocent."

Darling was anything but innocent. Ryker removed his phone from the clip on his belt. "Let me see if I can locate Jeremy."

"I'll see what I can find on Preston Richway." Caroline settled her tablet on a table by the window and began to search.

Ryker phoned the precinct, and asked their information specialist to research Jeremy Linchfield. She texted him Jeremy's home address which doubled as his office.

He gestured to Caroline that he had it, and she closed her tablet. "My associate is searching for Richway."

Ryker checked the address in the text. "Jeremy doesn't live far from here. Let's go."

They walked together to the exit, and Ryker ran through the rain to his car, then pulled up to the curb to pick up Agent

Manson.

He couldn't help but think about Marilyn as the dark clouds rumbled. More than once, she'd awakened him screaming during a storm. He'd encouraged her to confide in him about what had happened to traumatize her, but she'd completely shut down.

Was she okay now?

Annoyed with himself for worrying about her when she was keeping secrets, he drove in silence to Jeremy's house. It was a small bungalow outside of Savannah but in close proximity to the cultural events, restaurants and bars the town offered.

The rain collected in puddles on the tiny lawn, but the white wooden house looked in decent shape. A beige van was parked in the driveway, and a handicap ramp on the left led to the front porch.

He and Caroline climbed the front steps, and she knocked on the door. Water streamed down the gutters and dripped off the porch roof. A minute later, they heard a lock turning and the door opened.

A man about Ryker's age with sandy brown hair and a short beard greeted them from his wheelchair.

Caroline introduced the two of them. "We'd like to talk to you about the disappearance of the Darling sisters."

A frown deepened the lines around Jeremy's mouth. "That was a long time ago. Why are you asking about them now?"

Ryker gave him a deadpan look. "Because the skeletal remains found at Seaside Cemetery belonged to the oldest two sisters, Deborah and Candace."

Jeremy's fingers tightened around the arms of his chair. "That's too bad. But like I told the sheriff back then, I wasn't friends with those girls. And I don't have any idea what happened to them."

"We realize you weren't friends," Caroline said. "That's why we're here." She gestured toward his wheelchair. "We heard the sisters wanted revenge against you and Preston Richway because you rejected them."

A muscle ticked in Jeremy's jaw. "That was high school stuff."

"Maybe," Caroline said. "But it raises questions about your accident."

A haunted look passed across Jeremy's face. "I don't want to talk about my accident. Now, please leave."

Ryker tried to inch his foot inside the door, but Jeremy slammed it in their face. The sound of the lock clicking indicated their conversation was over.

Ryker's gut tightened. He wasn't finished with Jeremy though. They'd hit a nerve with the man.

And Ryker intended to uncover the truth.

As soon as he got in the car, he phoned the captain and updated him. "I need a search warrant for the Darling property."

"I'll see what I can do," Captain Henry said. "About Marilyn—"

"I'm on it," he said, then hung up.

As soon as he dropped Caroline at her car, he intended to find the woman and make her talk.

MARILYN SHUDDERED AS THE car raced from the parking lot, tires spewing rain. For a second, she was in so much shock she couldn't move. She'd landed on her hands and knees, and lost one shoe as she'd fallen. Drenched in rain, she pushed herself up to her feet and stared after the car, wishing she'd seen its license plate, but the car careened away.

She scanned the parking lot for witnesses, but didn't see anyone walking or near their vehicles. Trembling, she snatched her shoe and hobbled to her car. Her leg throbbed, and her shoulders ached from the impact of the fall.

Her hand shook as she aimed her key fob at the car and hit the unlock button, and she kept her eyes peeled in case the car returned. When the lock clicked, she opened the door and collapsed inside.

That hadn't been an accident. The car had driven straight toward her.

Dear God. She dropped her head against the steering wheel, struggling to breathe. Someone had just tried to kill her.

Chapter Fourteen

Marilyn had made a lot of enemies on the job. She'd received threats before, but no one had actually tried to murder her.

Did the attempt on her life have to do with the Darlings or Eaton? Or had someone she'd angered over the Keepers' stories decided to come after her?

She considered calling the police to file a report, but she hadn't seen the driver or gotten the license plate of the car. Besides, Ryker was the police.

If she talked to the cops, it would be him.

She'd tried to redeem herself by painting Cat Landon and Carrie Ann Jensen in a sympathetic light. They'd both suffered and had been desperate for justice. Their victims had deserved what they'd gotten.

Some protested that no one had the right to play God or dole out punishments for personal reasons. But after covering those stories, she'd realized there were shades of gray.

She was still trembling as she started the engine and veered onto the street. The rain had slackened, although deep puddles stood along the road, slowing drivers.

Nerves on edge, she searched the streets for the vehicle who'd nearly hit her, but fog made it difficult to see more than two cars in front of her. Shivering from her wet clothing, she flipped on the defroster and heater, blending in with the clogged traffic.

She needed a hot shower and some hot tea—or something stronger. She turned to go home, but at the moment, all she could think about was being in Ryker's arms.

Besides, if someone wanted her dead, they might know where she lived. She wasn't ready to face another attack, not today anyway.

Horns honked as a truck pulled in front of another car, and her tires ground through the water on the streets as she made the turn toward Ryker's. Night was setting in, the sky darker because of the storm. She blinked against oncoming headlights.

It took her over ten minutes to reach Ryker's place, but she used the time to calm herself in case he was home. He hadn't been happy with her at the library. She dreaded facing the distrust in his eyes.

But she couldn't imagine being with anyone else tonight but him. She wanted to crawl into his arms and curl up against him, and forget what had just happened.

Ryker dropped Agent Manson at the precinct with the agreement they'd resume the investigation the next day. Hopefully by then, they'd have contact information on Preston Richway, and he'd have the search warrant for Mr. Darling's house and property. The forensic team might have details to share as well. Maybe they'd located the syringe or a needle in the garbage outside or on Eaton's property. And hopefully they'd found someone's prints besides Marilyn's.

He texted his mother that he'd call her later about time for a dinner. Tonight he had too much on his mind.

Itching to talk to Marilyn, he drove by her apartment. Confronting her in person would give him the advantage. He parked on the street in front of her building, climbed out and hurried to the entrance. The lofts had been built in an old warehouse and blended brick, industrial elements and reclaimed wood to create a modern yet historic feel that fit with Savannah.

Ryker liked the style, but couldn't quite swing it on a detective's salary, so he rented an apartment a few blocks away. He entered the security code for the building, then rode the elevator to the second floor and hurried down the hall to her unit.

As he rang the bell, he replayed their conversation at the library, trying to pinpoint anything he'd missed.

No answer.

Dammit, she was probably avoiding him. Or hell, maybe she'd caught a lead and was onto something.

Irritated she wasn't including him, he punched her number, but the phone rang and went to voice mail.

Body taut, he rode the elevator to the first floor. He checked the streets for her car, but nothing.

The wind picked up, rainwater trickling off the awning of the building as he jogged to his car. Tired and hungry, he drove to his apartment, parked in the deck and climbed the stairs to his floor.

Night had fallen, more storm clouds rumbling as if they'd set in for the night. He'd make a quick dinner, grab a shower and call Marilyn again.

His instincts jumped to alert as he unlocked his door. The light in the bathroom was on.

He hadn't left it that way.

He reached for his gun, visually sweeping the room. A raincoat and purse were on the side table by the door. Marilyn's.

She was here?

The sound of the shower running echoed from the bathroom. Surprise fluttered through him along with arousal. Just thinking of Marilyn naked and wet made his body harden.

But anger hit him.

He balled his hands into fists, tamping down his libido. Did she plan to seduce him in hopes that he'd forget she was lying to him?

Jaw clenched, he hung his wet jacket on the coat rack by the door, then crossed the room to the bathroom.

He'd turn the tables on her and prove he was immune to her ploy. Or at least partially immune.

Resolve made, he left his gun and holster on the nightstand, then opened the bathroom door and stepped inside. Steam from the hot water drifted through the interior, coating the mirror and glass shower door.

She must have heard him because suddenly the shower door swung open. His heart hammered at the sight in front of him.

Marilyn was naked and wet all right. But she didn't look as if she'd come to seduce him.

Her eyes were red and swollen from crying. Fuck.

Not only did she have that bruise on her wrist, but bruises and bloody scrapes marred her legs, knees and her hands.

What the hell had happened to her?

MARILYN HAD HOPED TO regain her composure before Ryker arrived. She hated being vulnerable.

But emotions had overcome her in the aftermath of the attempt on her life, and once the tear gates opened, they flooded.

Ryker's dark eyes raked over her, quickly assessing her, and his jaw clenched. She grabbed a towel and hurriedly wrapped it around herself. Being naked made everything worse.

She'd planned to hide the bruises and scrapes, but now he'd seen them.

Ryker exhaled sharply, started to reach for her, then seemed to think better of it as if she might push him away.

"What happened?"

She swallowed hard to control the tremor in her voice. "Someone tried to run me down in the library parking lot."

"*What?*" Anger exploded in that one word, and he rushed forward and tenderly touched her cheek. "Are you okay?"

She nodded. She was alive but far from okay.

His look softened. "God, Marilyn." He tilted her hands up to examine them, then stooped and looked at her knees and leg. His jaw clenched. Then he removed his robe from the hook on the wall and gently helped her into it.

Tears blurred her eyes again at his tenderness. He didn't speak again until he'd led her to the den, turned on the gas logs in his fireplace and poured them both a drink.

Her hands trembled as she cradled the highball glass and lifted the bourbon to her lips. The first taste of the whiskey soothed her throat which was raw from crying.

Ryker fingered her damp hair from her face, then tossed back his own drink. His gaze met hers afterward, a myriad of emotions playing in his dark eyes. Eyes she could get lost in.

"Tell me exactly what happened."

She strove for a steady voice. "Right after I saw you, when I left the library and crossed to my car, I heard an engine, then this car drove straight toward me."

Silence, thick with tension, stretched for a minute. He stood, went to the bar, grabbed the bottle of bourbon and brought it to the coffee table. He poured himself another shot, then set it on the table and looked at her again, his eyes filled with questions.

He'd first reacted like a lover. Now the detective in him was taking over.

"What kind of car was it?"

She sighed. She'd never understood how victims claimed they didn't see anything or didn't remember what happened, but she understood now.

"Marilyn, close your eyes and think."

She did as he instructed. The memory of the incident returned, choking her with fear again. "A dark sedan with tinted windows, but it raced away before I could get the license plate."

"Did you file a police report?"

She shook her head. "The car was gone. What could they do?"

Disapproval flickered in his dark eyes. "They could issue an APB for the fucking car."

"But I didn't get a good description," Marilyn said. "And I . . . just wanted to get out of there and go home."

Except she hadn't gone home. She'd come to Ryker's.

His look softened, and he finally did what she'd wanted all along. He drew her up against him, wrapped her in his embrace, and held her tight.

RYKER HAD VOWED NOT to allow his personal feelings to interfere with his job, but Marilyn could have died today. He closed his eyes and savored the feel of her in his arms.

He faced danger every day. Marilyn had made enemies, had been threatened before, too. But she'd always held her own.

Tonight was different though.

She sighed against him, her breathing raspy, and he rubbed slow circles around her back to soothe her. "Shh, it's okay, I've got you," he murmured.

Outside, the storm heated up again. Thunder crackled and rain pounded the roof.

Marilyn startled, then shivered and burrowed into him as if she wanted to crawl inside his skin and hide. He'd let her if it were humanly possible.

She felt small and vulnerable, nothing like the strong, gutsy woman who stood up to tough criminals and refused to back down when she wanted an interview or the truth about a story.

He leaned back against the couch, and cradled her in his arms, then dropped kisses into her hair and whispered more nonsensical assurances that everything would be all right.

But he would find out who'd hurt her and make him pay.

"Do you have any idea who did this?" he murmured against her ear.

She pressed her hand against his heart, and he was sure she could feel it thumping erratically.

"I don't know, I've pissed off a lot of people," she finally whispered.

He chuckled wryly. "That's for sure. But have you received any threatening phone calls or emails or texts?"

"Nothing recently."

Another clap of thunder cracked outside, and she jumped. He stroked her arm and shoulder, tightening his hold on her. "Was there anything that sticks out?"

"Not really," she said quietly. "I received hate mail during the Keepers stories, but I also received support."

He nuzzled his cheek into her hair. She smelled like lavender. He'd suggested she keep some toiletries at his place, but she was so damn stubborn and independent she'd refused. It was as if she thought leaving a toothbrush at his place meant a commitment.

As a compromise, he'd bought her favorite lavender body wash and kept it in his bathroom for her visits.

Her body quivered, drawing him back to what happened to her.

It was time to address the big white elephant in the room, their earlier confrontation. "Then today's incident was about the story you're currently working on?"

"Maybe." She rubbed his chest with her hand. He was tempted to wipe away the memory of the attack on her with lovemaking, but he wanted answers. It was the only way to protect her.

They sat for a long time simply holding each other, and he continued to stroke her hair with his fingers. "I can't protect you if I don't know the truth, Marilyn. You have to talk to me. Tell me what's going on. Why you were at Eaton's and what happened there this morning."

She didn't reply. Instead he realized her breathing had steadied, and she'd fallen asleep in his arms.

Frustration knotted his insides, but he didn't have the heart to wake her. He'd let her sleep tonight.

But in the morning, he'd demand she come clean.

MARILYN WRESTLED WITH NIGHTMARES of storms and murder all night. Every time she awakened, she curled closer to Ryker. It was so easy to hide in his arms in the dark that she wanted to stay there forever.

Tomorrow though she'd have to face realty. Talk to him. Look him in the eye and . . . do what?

Confess everything?

That she believed Eaton had murdered a fourteen-year-old girl and kidnapped her baby? That she knew that because she'd witnessed it and never told anyone?

Tears of shame clogged her throat. She'd kept the secret for so long that it was eating up her inside.

She choked back another crying fit. Damn it. She wasn't usually so emotional.

But it wasn't every day a car tried to run her down.

Shuddering, she welcomed Ryker's arms as he tightened them around her.

Could she finally break the silence she'd kept for twenty-five years and trust him with her secret?

CHAPTER FIFTEEN

Ryker held Marilyn all night. He woke to her dropping sweet kisses on his chest. His body instantly hardened, but he rolled to his side and tilted her chin to look at him.

"I don't want to hurt you," he whispered.

"You could never hurt me." She pulled his face toward her and kissed him hungrily, her lips melding with his. Her husky voice, laced with desire, stirred his arousal, and he deepened the kiss, using his tongue to tease her lips apart so he could taste her.

Seconds later, they were naked and writhing against each other. He slowly ran his fingers over her naked body, then trailed kisses over her bruises, his anger churning, intensifying his passion for her.

When he thrust inside her, she cried out his name, and he closed his eyes and silently told her that he loved her.

The words would come one day. When she was ready. But for now, he didn't want to scare her off.

Hell, he'd been scared himself for a long time. His parents had a good marriage. But his mother's second marriage was a disaster, and he'd shut down from thinking about family or love after that.

Only today, seeing Marilyn hold that baby roused images of Marilyn in a long white gown at their wedding, then Marilyn holding their son or daughter . . .

"Ryker, I need you," Marilyn whispered against his neck.

He buried his head against her. "You've got me as long as you want me," he whispered.

Her body trembled with her release, drawing him back to the present and he thrust deeper. Her soft sensual sounds of pleasure triggered his own orgasm, and he gripped her hips and held her tightly as he pounded himself inside her.

Their erratic breathing punctuated the air as they lay entwined, and rode out the sensations.

His phone buzzed, but he ignored it. He had to get to work, but he wasn't finished with Marilyn yet.

He kissed her on the nose. "I'll make coffee."

She murmured yes, and he slipped from bed, yanked on a pair of gym shorts and a t-shirt and strode to the kitchen.

He brewed a pot of coffee and carried her a cup. He didn't intent to let her sneak out without an explanation.

While she leaned against the pillows and sipped her coffee, he returned to the kitchen to make breakfast before he crawled back in bed with her and kissed her senseless.

When she appeared in the kitchen a few minutes later still wearing his robe, regret darkened her eyes. Regret for coming here? For breaking down in front of him?

He sat two plates filled with eggs and bacon on the table.

She patted his robe self-consciously. "My clothes are wet and torn," she said softly.

His stomach clenched at the reminder of the attempt on her life. "I can probably find a pair of sweats and a sweatshirt you can wear home."

"Thanks, that would help."

She sank into the chair and eyed the eggs as if she was starved. If she'd come straight here from the library, she'd skipped dinner and crashed without eating.

Their conversation could wait a few more minutes. He dove into his food and gave her time to do the same, hoping the silence would encourage her to open up.

She devoured the meal then poured herself another cup of coffee, but she was moving slowly and limping slightly.

He gestured toward her leg. "We should have taken you to the hospital."

She shook her head. "I'm just bruised, nothing broken."

He gritted his teeth. She didn't deserve to be bruised or battered. No woman did.

Marilyn slid back into the chair across from him with a sigh, then ran a hand through her hair. Without makeup and in his robe, the choppy layers made her look even sultrier.

He leaned back in his chair, studying her. Waiting. It was a technique he'd learned in beginner's interrogation class.

"I guess I owe you an explanation," she finally said.

Ryker's lungs squeezed for air. Why was it so hard for her to confide in him? Because of the case, or was it personal?

"I told you I'd protect you, Marilyn, but I need to know from what."

That self-defiant chin lifted. She looked as if she was going to insist that she could protect herself, but he gave a pointed look at her bruised wrists and hands, and she hesitated.

"I don't know who tried to run me down," she said. "Or if that attempt on my life has to do with the story I'm investigating."

"But that story involved Eaton, a man who was murdered yesterday. Assuming you didn't kill him, you may have been the last person who saw him alive."

Her gaze swung to him. "He was alive when I left."

He gestured toward her wrist. "But he did that?"

She looked down into her coffee, then took another sip. "Yes. He grabbed my arm before I left. I thought he was going to say something, but he . . . didn't. A call came in from his caregiver, and I left before she arrived."

Ryker narrowed his eyes. "What do you know about the caregiver?"

"Just that her name is Gayle," Marilyn told him. "That's what she said on the message. So if she arrived right after I left, *she* was the last person to see Eaton alive, not me."

He sat his coffee mug onto the table. "I'll find her. Now, why were you questioning Eaton?"

Marilyn resisted the urge to squirm. Last night she'd contemplated confiding everything to Ryker. But in the light of day, she wanted answers first. Right now all she had were hunches.

She felt raw and unhinged this morning, as if her outer layer of skin had been peeled off and Ryker could see all the way to her soul.

"Marilyn, don't lie to me," Ryker said. "For God's sake, you could have been killed last night. And who knows when this person might try again."

A chill slithered through her. He was right. "I think Eaton had something to do with the disappearance of the Darling girls. Or at least with one of their deaths."

Surprise flickered in Ryker's eyes. "What makes you think they're connected?"

Marilyn traced a finger around the rim of her coffee mug. She really liked the seashells in the design. Ryker had bought it for her one day when she commented on it in a store window. She'd told him then that it reminded her of collecting seashells with her mother on the beach on her days off. He'd also insisted she keep it at his place.

He wanted more from her. She wished she had more to give. But if he knew the whole truth about her, he would never look at her the same way.

Still, she'd been alone so long, ever since her mother had died. She wanted to be close to him, to have someone in her life she could count on.

"Marilyn?" he said. "Go on."

"A source told me." She raised a finger. "And don't ask for

the name of my source. You know I can't divulge names."

Irritation oozed from his grimly set mouth. "All right. But why does this person think Eaton is connected to the Darling case? The girls' father was the primary suspect, and still is."

"Eaton was the lighthouse keeper," she said. "My source believes that Eaton saw the girls at the Village after they left home. That would mean that Mr. Darling didn't murder them."

His phone buzzed with a text, and he checked it. "The captain. I have a warrant to search the Darling property."

"Good," Marilyn said. "Maybe you'll find something indicating the girls' plans when they left home."

He attached his phone to his belt. "But we're not finished. What else have you dug up?"

She breathed out. "A woman in town claims Eaton was known as the Punisher, that he eliminated problems for other people."

Interest flared in Ryker's eyes. "What kind of problems?"

"I'm still working on that." She leaned forward. "Now, you answer me something, Ryker. The ME identified Deborah and Candace Darling's remains. Did he mention that either of them delivered a baby?"

Ryker had an incredible poker face, but a slight widening of his eyes indicated he was surprised by her question.

That he hadn't known about the baby.

Perhaps she was wrong, and the infant hadn't belonged to Deborah. But if it hadn't, who was the mother?

RYKER'S MIND RACED. EATON had been known as the Punisher? One of the Darling girls might have had a child?

Questions ticked in his head. If Mr. Darling had discovered one of his daughters was pregnant, he might have gone into a rage and killed her . . .

Or perhaps fear of severe repercussions was the reason the girls ran away.

"What makes you think one of the girls was pregnant?" he asked.

Marilyn sighed. "Again, that came from my source."

"What if this person is just feeding you misinformation to lead you astray? What if he or she is the one who tried to kill you?"

Marilyn shrugged. "Whoever was driving that car doesn't want the truth to be revealed."

"You're saying the driver might have been Mr. Darling?"

Marilyn seemed to consider that possibility. "I guess it could have been. I also spoke to the groundskeeper who worked at the lighthouse twenty-five years ago. He warned me not to keep asking questions."

"A name, Marilyn?" Ryker asked impatiently.

She hesitated. "Lloyd Willing."

"I'll look into him and see if Darling has an alibi for last night," Ryker said,

"Is there anything else?"

"That's it," she said. "Now that I've shared, tell me where you are on the case."

Ryker's phone beeped with another text, and he checked it.

"I think you may be onto something regarding the Darling teens. Agent Manson and I talked to a guy named Jeremy Linchfield who had a bad accident shortly after the girls said they would get back at him and his friend Preston for ignoring them."

"Does Jeremy believe the girls caused his accident?" Marilyn asked.

"He refused to talk to us, but his animosity toward the Darlings was clear."

"Maybe he'll talk to me," she said.

Ryker frowned. "Let me do the investigating, Marilyn."

A devious smile flickered on her lips. "Then I can go with you to the Darlings to execute that warrant?"

He mumbled an obscenity. "You can go home and stay there and rest."

She simply nodded, and he knew good and goddamn well going home and resting would be the last thing she'd do.

Still, she'd unearthed information he hadn't.

She stood, then leaned over him and kissed him deeply. "Thank you for taking care of me last night."

He held her tight. "Thank you for trusting me enough to talk to me this morning."

She clung to him for another minute, and he knew she was still holding something back. But pushing her wouldn't get him anywhere.

Hopefully, in her own time she'd tell him everything.

If she didn't get herself killed first.

MARILYN BORROWED A PAIR of sweats and one of Ryker's sweat-shirts, tugged on her raincoat and drove to her loft.

The fact that he'd held her and comforted her last night without question humbled her—and made her feel closer to him than she ever had before.

She scanned the parking deck to make certain no one was watching her, then hurried up the back staircase of the building to the main lobby. A noise down the hall startled her, and she swung around and dropped her keys.

Voices . . . just her neighbors. She was safe.

A mother pushed her infant in the stroller toward the ele-vator, giving the little girl a running play of their plans for the day. For a brief second, something tugged inside Marilyn.

The yearning to have a little one of her own?

She quickly pushed aside the feeling that her biological clock was ticking as she entered the elevator. She'd seen the hardships her mother faced as a single parent. Her life was too complicated for a child. She wasn't married.

Ryker might not want kids.

She halted, wondering where those thoughts had come from. She'd never experienced maternal instincts before. Or thought about marriage.

Except even as a little girl, she'd wanted to save that baby from that monster.

She made a mental note to research infants who'd been abandoned around the time of Deborah Darling's death.

After exiting the elevator, she hurried to her unit and un-locked the door. As she stepped inside, she checked the security alarm and visually scanned the living area. A relieved breath escaped her. No one was inside.

Senses still alert, she hurried to her bedroom, and flipped on the light. But she froze in the doorway, her lungs straining for air.

Someone had been here. The articles and photos she'd tacked on her desk wall had been ripped into pieces. Fear pulsing through her, she scanned her room, then stepped to the closet and looked inside. The intruder wasn't there.

She slipped her phone from her purse to call Ryker as she inched toward the bathroom.

Lipstick . . . on her mirror. A warning.

Unable to breathe for a moment, she simply stared at the scrawled angry message.

Then she slowly backed away. Back into the bedroom. Her mind trying to process what she was seeing.

The torn pieces of her research, the message written in red lipstick that looked like blood.

Hand shaking, she pressed Ryker's number.

He answered on the second ring. "Hey, sexy," he murmured. "I didn't expect to hear—"

"Ryker, someone broke into my condo."

A heartbeat passed. "Is the intruder still there?"

Marilyn frantically glanced around the bedroom, then hurried back to the living room. "No, I don't think so."

Ryker's breath rushed out. "Keep the doors locked. I'll be right there."

CHAPTER SIXTEEN

RYKER RACED TOWARD MARILYN'S, his stomach knotting with every mile. Someone had tried to run her down yesterday. And now an intruder had been in her house.

He didn't like it one damn bit.

He careened into the parking lot, raced to a stop, jumped from his vehicle and jogged up the steps to the entrance to Marilyn's. Inside, he took the elevator, then raced to her unit and knocked on her door.

"It's Ryker, Marilyn!" he yelled through the door.

The buzz from the security system sounded as Marilyn opened the door. One look into her frightened face, and he dragged her into his arms.

"You okay?"

She nodded against him, but clung to him, a sign she was truly shaken. He stroked her back, soothing her, but held her tightly just to assure himself she was safe and alive.

Her heart was pounding, her breathing unsteady, but as they cradled each other close, slowly her breathing and heart rate steadied.

He tucked a strand of hair behind her ear and lifted her chin so he could see into her eyes. "What happened?"

She licked her lips, her bottom lip quivering. "When I got home, I went into the bedroom. Someone had been in there. They . . . ripped up articles and pictures of the story I was working on."

"Show me."

She inhaled sharply, then took his hand and led him to her bedroom. He'd been in this room a dozen times, but nothing prepared him for the sight of the room being trashed. Just as she said, bits of torn paper and ripped photographs littered her desk and floor.

She shuddered then pointed toward her bathroom. "Whoever broke in left me a message on the mirror."

Careful not to touch anything, Ryker clenched his jaw as he stepped to the door of the bathroom. The red lipsticked writing made his blood run cold.

Stop asking questions, or you'll die just like the Darlings.

He glanced at Marilyn. Her face was ashen, the violation of her home and the attempt on her life the day before taking their toll.

"I'm going to call a crime team to process your place," he said. "Maybe we'll get lucky and find some prints."

"I'll need a new security system, too," Marilyn said. "Somehow the intruder hacked my code and got in without breaking a door."

He slipped his arm around her and rubbed her back again. "We'll find out who did this, Marilyn. I swear we will."

"I know," she said with a tilt of her chin. "You're good at your job."

"You're more than a job," he said in a husky whisper.

Her eyes glittered with emotions as she looked up at him. She parted her lips as if she was going to say something, then her breath caught, and she glanced at the shredded articles and pictures in her room. "I must be onto something," she said. "Someone knows I'm investigating the Darlings' and Eaton's death."

"We can set you up in a safe house until this is over," he suggested. God, he wished she'd take him up on the offer.

She shook her head no. "I'm not running from this story, Ryker. I'll do whatever I have to in order to expose the truth."

He'd expected no less.

Still, he was worried about her.

He couldn't help himself. He kissed her again just because he needed to feel her lips against his.

He'd do anything necessary to keep her safe.

WHILE MARILYN WATCHED THE ERT search her condo for prints and collect forensics, she drew on her anger to replace her fear. Someone had invaded her private sanctuary. Someone who wanted to scare her.

She refused to give in to scare tactics and let them win.

Ryker made some phone calls, one to his mother. She didn't

mean to eavesdrop, but she heard him promising to come by for dinner the next week.

"I'll try to bring my friend," he murmured. "But she's a busy lady and works a lot."

Marilyn's pulse jumped. Was he planning to invite her to his family dinner? To meet his mother?

Was she ready for that?

One of the investigators paused by the table where she'd set her laptop after they'd dusted the table for prints.

"The lipstick—"

"It was mine," Marilyn said. "Take it. Maybe you'll get DNA off of it."

The young man bagged it just as Ryker returned to her side.

His phone buzzed again. He checked the number, then murmured it was Agent Manson and stepped into the kitchen to take the call.

She booted up her computer then ran a search for abandoned babies during a three-week time frame before and after the week she'd seen Deborah murdered.

She found one article about a kidnapping, but the infant had been found with its father in Tennessee. She phoned her friend Piper from the SPD and asked her to dig deeper into the adoptions and reports of missing/found babies.

Piper was the daughter of William Flagler, the detective who'd originally investigated the Darling case. When she and Piper first met, Piper confided that her father had been haunted by the case ever since he'd been forced to retire. Piper felt guilty herself for that decision because she and her father had fought before his accident.

Piper wanted to give him closure.

She was also intrigued by the Keepers and offered to help Marilyn in any way she could, as long as Marilyn kept their relationship confidential.

Ryker's comments about the teens who attended school with the Darlings replayed in her head. When she hung up with Piper, she decided she'd talk to Jeremy Linchfield today. She googled his name and learned he was a computer programmer who worked from home.

Just as she closed her computer, the crime team finished and left. Ryker returned with a puckered frown. "We have a warrant for the Darling house. I'm meeting Agent Manson there in a few." He glanced at her computer. "I can send a uniform over to guard you until we tie up this case."

"I don't need a bodyguard," Marilyn said. "I have work to do."

Ryker's eyes darkened, and he paused beside her and traced his thumb over her arm. "I don't want you going around alone asking questions, Marilyn. You saw that message."

She forced herself not to shudder. "If it were you, you wouldn't let someone terrorize you into hiding out." She placed her hand on his jaw. "I'm not going to do that either, Ryker." She gestured toward the locked kitchen drawer. "I have a pistol. I'll take it with me and I'll be fine."

His jaw tightened. "I don't like it," he said, his voice thick with worry.

"I know, but I'm going to finish my story." It was too important to abandon.

She stood on tiptoe and kissed him. "I promise I'll be careful. You need to be careful, too."

Their gazes locked. His breath rattled out. Finally he sighed as if he knew he had no chance of convincing her to stay put. "When this is over, we have things to discuss."

Her breath stalled in her chest. But she nodded. She owed Ryker a conversation.

"I'll call your security company while you shower," he offered. "I want to find out how someone got your code."

"Thanks."

She hurried to take a quick shower. By the time she emerged from the shower and was dressed, he'd questioned the people at her security company, fired them and arranged for a different company to install a new system.

"They have no idea how someone got your code," Ryker told her. "But they're going to question their staff. It's also possible that someone hacked into their system."

"Thanks for doing that."

He squeezed her arm. "I'd do anything for you, Marilyn. You know that by now."

And she'd do anything for him. Except confess about what she'd seen. She wasn't ready yet. Maybe she never would be.

His phone buzzed again. "It's Agent Manson. I have to go."

They kissed again, and he left, but made her promise to check in regularly.

She retrieved her gun from the drawer and ran her fingers over the smooth metal.

If someone came after her, this time she'd be ready.

CHAPTER SEVENTEEN

Marilyn headed out to her car, anxious to talk to Jeremy. As she drove, she scanned the road and side streets for the vehicle that had tried to hit her yesterday.

When she arrived at Jeremy's, she pasted on a smile as she knocked on his door. A noise sounded inside, then locks turned and the door opened.

Jeremy frowned at her from his wheelchair. "I figured you'd show up sometime."

So he knew who she was. "Why is that?" Marilyn asked.

"Cause the cops stopped by yesterday."

She softened her tone. "I'd like to talk to you about the Darling girls."

"I already told that detective I don't know anything," Jeremy said bluntly.

"Maybe so. But I have reason to believe those girls weren't so sweet, that they were bullies and that they might even be responsible for your accident."

He made a low sound in his throat. "You're a reporter. Don't you read the news?" He barked. "I was drunk."

"Were you?" Marilyn asked.

Jeremy's look flattened as if he hadn't expected her to challenge him.

"That's what the tox screen said."

"Maybe so, but I'm interested in your side of the story." She offered him a smile. "If you were wronged, it's time you spoke up."

"It won't make any difference." Jeremy gripped the arms of his wheelchair.

"You're right, it won't change your condition, but justice needs to be served. For you . . . and if the Darling girls hurt your friend, Preston, he deserves it, too." She inched closer, wedging one foot inside the door. "Tell me what happened the night of the accident," she said. "They say telling the truth will set you free."

Jeremy glowered at her. "Some secrets aren't ours to tell."

"And some destroy you if you keep them bottled up inside." She should know. Sometimes she felt as if she was going to explode.

"I'm not going to talk about Preston," Jeremy said. "All I can say is that you're right about justice. Sometimes that means stepping outside the law like the Keepers."

Marilyn's heart hammered. Was he implying the Keepers had taken care of the Darling girls?

How could that be true? They'd only formed their group recently . . .

Unless the man they called the Punisher had been a Keeper and the Keepers had been exacting their own brand of justice for years without being discovered.

Or . . . another possibility: Jeremy and Preston had conspired to make the Darling girls pay.

RYKER'S NERVES WERE ON edge. Damn, he wanted Marilyn with him. Wanted to protect her.

But he understood her tenacity. Hell, he admired her for it. But he wished he could keep an eye on her all the time.

Not going to happen. Smothering Marilyn would only make her run.

He swung by the station to pick up the warrant for the Darling house, then called the ME.

"Dr. Patton, it's Detective Brockett. I have a question about the bodies of Candace and Deborah Darling."

"Yes?"

"Did either one of the girls give birth?"

A heartbeat passed. "As a matter of fact, yes. With bones this old, I had to consult the forensic anthropologist for verification. Dr. Lofton confirmed that Deborah Darling had given birth. She's still working on Candace's remains."

A chill engulfed Ryker. If Mr. Darling had known his daughter or daughters were pregnant, that provided motive.

On the other hand, they didn't have definitive time of

death, so the girls could have run away because of the pregnancies, stayed with someone else, then been murdered later.

Questions assailed him. What happened to the baby? And where had Deborah been during the months she carried the child?

He pressed the accelerator and sped toward the Darling house, his mind racing with more questions. How had Marilyn known about the pregnancy?

More dark clouds rolled in over Seahawk Island, the winter wind beating at the marsh grass. He slowed as he passed the Village, and glanced at the lighthouse where Marilyn said Eaton might have seen the girls.

If the sisters had been at the pier, they could have taken a boat over to one of the smaller islands a few miles out to sea. But if so, where had they stayed? Had someone given them housing until Deborah delivered?

Then what? Sometime later she'd fallen prey to the man who'd killed her? Or her father had found her?

The pieces were still scattered.

Agent Manson's car was waiting on the side street in front of Darling's house when he arrived. She followed him to the drive and parked behind him.

Warrant in hand, they walked up to the door together.

"Any updates on the Eaton case?" she asked.

Marilyn's state of emotional upheaval came to mind. But a fierce wave of protectiveness swelled up inside of him. He didn't want to discuss Marilyn with Caroline. "It's possible there's a connection with Eaton to the Darling case, but it's too soon to tell."

She rang the doorbell. "Why do you think they're connected?"

The door opened, saving him from having to respond. "Mr. Darling, we have a warrant to search your house and property."

The older man's face paled, but he stepped aside as if he'd been expecting them.

MARILYN NEEDED JEREMY TO open up. "Just because you weren't friendly to a girl doesn't mean you deserved to be handicapped for life."

He wheeled himself across the room and gazed out the window into the back yard. The wind shook the trees, rattling the windowpanes.

"I appreciate the way you handled the Keeper stories," he finally murmured. "Most people see the law as black and white. You found a way to show both sides."

"Sometimes the law protects the accused more than the victims," Marilyn agreed.

Jeremy rubbed a hand through his thick brown hair. He was a handsome guy, but pain lined his face. "You're right. The Keepers, they're just victims trying to take back their lives."

"You seem to have done that yourself," Marilyn said.

He made a sarcastic sound. "If I could go back and change things, I would. I understand what it's like now to have people judge you from what they see on the surface."

"You were only teenagers," she uttered softly.

"We should have at least been kind," he said. "Tried to

understand where those girls came from. But we were jocks and into being popular and had big plans for college." He ran a hand through his hair again. "I'd just been offered a scholarship," Jeremy added. "Preston threw a party for me at his mother's beach house. We snuck in beer and cheap wine, and all our friends showed up."

"You were all drinking," Marilyn said, urging him to continue.

Jeremy murmured that they were. "But I hadn't told my folks about the scholarship offer yet, and wanted to surprise them that night. So I only had a beer. Preston had a few and passed out in the back room before I left."

Marilyn studied him. "Earlier, you said you were drunk when you had the accident?"

Bitterness edged his tone, "I said the tox screen showed that. I think someone drugged my water bottle," he admitted. "I remember chugging it before I started home. Then on the way, I got dizzy and . . . started swerving. That's all I remember. I woke up in the hospital a week later and couldn't move my legs."

Marilyn contemplated his statement. "Was your water bottle in your car?"

Jeremy nodded.

"Was the car locked?"

He shook his head no. "It was an old clunker. I never locked it."

"So someone could easily have put something in your water bottle?"

"Yeah." He heaved a breath. "But everyone saw me with a beer at the party, and assumed I was drinking and driving."

Marilyn squared her shoulders. "Did you have an altercation with anyone that night? Was someone there jealous of your scholarship, maybe another player?"

"No. Preston was excited for me, and Cade, my other friend, had an offer from another college so he was celebrating, too."

"Did you see anyone outside?" Marilyn asked. "Maybe near your car?"

He shook his head no again.

"Jeremy, were Candace and Deborah Darling at the party?"

"I didn't see them, but . . . later, Preston said they showed up with a couple of their friends."

She narrowed her eyes. "What friends?"

"Mellie Thacker and Aretha Franton."

"I thought Preston passed out."

"He did." A dark look crossed Jeremy's face. "He didn't tell me till weeks later that they were there. That's when he admitted what they did to him."

Marilyn's heart stuttered. "What happened?"

His jaw tightened. "You'll have to hear that from Preston. It's not my story to tell."

RYKER INSTRUCTED MR. DARLING to remain in the den while he and Agent Manson searched the house. He didn't know what he expected to find after all this time, but if they located Candace's diary, it might hold valuable details as to the teenager's plans, possibly even the name of the father of Deborah's baby.

Odds were though that if the girls had run away, Deborah had taken the diary with them. Unless Mr. Darling or his wife had confiscated it.

Ryker searched the kitchen while Caroline began in the girls' bedroom. For the next hour he examined the drawers and cabinets, the desk, pantry, and closets. He ran his fingers along every nook and cranny searching for loose boards that could have been pried far enough apart to hide evidence, and did the same with the wood flooring.

The laundry room held towels, cleaning supplies, household items, shoe polish, cleaning rags, and a couple of duffel bags that smelled like fish and mildew.

He shined a penlight along the wall in search of a hiding spot, but found nothing helpful.

Ryker moved to the man's bedroom and searched his drawers and closet. Nothing inside but clothing and personal items that had seen their better days. Either the wife had taken her belongings with her, or he'd disposed of them.

He checked inside the closet and felt along the top shelf. His hand brushed a picture frame, and he pulled it down. It was an eight-by-ten of the Darling family, all three girls and their mother, standing beneath a live oak tree, shrouded by dripping Spanish moss. The branches of the tree were thick and curved inward as if they were arms wrapping themselves around the family.

Polly was nestled next to her mother, but Candace and Deborah stood far away, as if they didn't want to be close to her. Typical teenage rebellion, or was the other daughters' relationship with their mother strained?

Ryker thoroughly searched the rest of the closet, and found a box holding mementos of Darling's daughters when they were little. Tucked inside were a stuffed bunny rabbit with worn ragged ears, a crocheted baby cap, a baby blanket imprinted with teddy bears, and three bronzed baby shoes.

Darling had either forgotten about these things or hadn't been able to part with them.

Ryker set the box back where he'd found it, walked to the window and glanced outside. That tree . . . it looked like the tree in the picture. Except two small beds of flowers were planted beneath the tree now.

Dread curled in Ryker's belly.

Deborah and Candace had been found, but not their baby sister. Polly had been closest to the mother. What if Darling had killed her and his wife discovered her death?

Pulse pounding, Ryker strode from the room, and walked past Darling. He was still sitting in his chair, his hands cradling his head as if he knew his day of reckoning had come.

CHAPTER EIGHTEEN

S HE CLENCHED HER CELL phone with a white-knuckled grip, nerves pinging in her stomach as she paced her kitchen. That blasted reporter and the cops were asking questions all over the island.

Her threats to Marilyn Ellis hadn't made a difference. Damn the bitch, she'd survived the incident in the parking lot like she was a cat with nine lives.

She poured herself a shot of vodka then opened her special hidey-hole where she kept the photographs.

Pictures of each of the Darling girls. First school pictures she'd cut out of the high school yearbook. Then candids she'd snapped the month of December.

Sluts.

She should have asked him to paint that on their foreheads when he left their bodies in the ground.

She took a red lipstick and drew S's in red on their foreheads in the pictures. S's for sluts. Double S's for justice just like the Keepers had.

Then the picture of Marilyn Ellis. She'd been sympathetic to the other Keepers, Cat Landon and Carrie Ann Jensen.

Would she be sympathetic to her?

It didn't matter. Some secrets weren't meant to be exposed.

She tacked Marilyn's photograph on the wall with the others. A red lipsticked S came next. The bitch was screwing that cop. She was a slut, too.

She added a set of double S's next for what was to come.

Chapter Nineteen

Marilyn needed to talk to Preston Richway. Although Jeremy appeared regretful over the way he'd treated the Darling sisters, his physical injuries would have prevented him from committing murder.

But it was possible he hired or conspired with someone else to do the job . . .

"Do you still keep in touch with Preston?" Marilyn asked.

A faraway look settled in Jeremy's eyes. "We haven't talked in years. He and his mother moved away after graduation."

Mellie Thacker and Aretha Franton had left town, too.

They were all running from something. Maybe from what happened that night at the party?

"Do you know how to reach him?"

Jeremy shook his head. "All I know is that they moved to Florida."

Florida was a place to start.

"Are we done here?"

Marilyn folded her hands together. She couldn't be certain

of the timing, but she'd seen Deborah and the baby about nine months after Deborah disappeared. "There's one more thing, Jeremy. It's possible Deborah Darling was pregnant when she disappeared. Did you know anything about that?"

Jeremy's face blanched. "What? No. God. She was only fourteen."

Marilyn nodded. "I know. Do you have any idea who she might have slept with?"

He looked down at his hands and knotted them into fists. "It wasn't me, if that's what you're asking."

A sick knot tightened Marilyn's stomach. Eaton again. If the girls ran away, he could have picked them up then raped them and fathered the baby.

Or . . . if Darling had abused his daughters, he might have sexually molested them.

Then he might be the baby's father—another motive for murder.

RYKER FOUND CAROLINE SEARCHING the girls' closet when he entered the bedroom.

"Any luck?"

She lifted an empty bottle of rum. "Found this in the closet. But no diaries or anything to indicate that the girls planned to run away or that there were problems in the home." She sighed. "Of course, Mr. Darling had ample time to dispose of evidence before he reported the girls as missing."

Ryker gestured toward the window. "I found a photograph of the family in Mr. Darling's room. In the picture, the youngest daughter is standing close to the mother, but Deborah and Candace are distant. The picture was taken by the tree in the back. Flowers are planted there now."

Caroline stepped from the closet, her eyes widening as she followed his train of thought. "You think Mr. Darling killed Polly and buried her in his yard?"

Ryker shrugged. "I think we should consider that possibility."

"That would explain why the other two girls ran away." She worried her bottom lip with her teeth. "Did you find any guns in the house?"

Deborah and Candace hadn't been shot. But he understood her concern. If Darling knew he'd been caught and was armed, he might attempt suicide. "No. You?"

She released a breath. "No."

Darling was pacing in front of the window, staring out.

"I'll stay here while you search outside," Caroline offered.

Ryker nodded, then left the room. He walked the perimeter of the house in search of a crawl space but didn't find one. Pulse hammering, he crossed the yard to the tree, then stooped and raked his hand over the ground.

If Darling had buried someone here, the ground had settled over the decades. But the flowers, set in two patches, were what drew his attention. He retrieved a shovel from his SUV and strode back to the tree. He rammed the shovel into the dirt beside the flowers and began to dig.

Thunder rumbled again, and the sky darkened. He dug

faster, hoping to finish before another rainstorm hit. In spite of the chill in the air, perspiration beaded on the back of his neck as he tossed dirt aside.

"What the hell are you doing?"

Ryker glanced over his shoulder to see Mr. Darling barreling across the back yard toward him. He was shaking his fists in anger. Caroline was on his tail, her hand on her weapon in case things went south.

"Get away from there!" Mr. Darling shouted.

The man's reaction raised Ryker's suspicions, and he jammed the shovel deeper into the dirt. He was a good three feet down now, still shallow, but he didn't intend to stop.

A second later, the shovel hit bone.

"Please go now," Jeremy said. "I have work to do."

Marilyn sensed he'd revealed all he would. But the fact that Deborah Darling had been pregnant disturbed him. Because he was lying and he could have been the biological daddy? Or . . . perhaps his friend Preston fathered the child?

Even if Deborah had consented to sex, she'd been underage. Whoever slept with her could have been charged with statutory rape.

"All right, just one more question. Did you ever hear of a man called the Punisher?"

A puzzled expression creased Jeremy's brows. "No. Who's that?"

"That's what I'm trying to find out," she answered matter of factly. "I heard he took care of people's problems."

"You mean he was a *hit man*?"

Marilyn chewed over that possibility. Or he could have been a Keeper long before the Keepers organized themselves. "Like I said, I don't know. That's why I'm asking."

"Sorry, but I can't help you." He angled his wheelchair toward the door. "Now, I really do have to work."

"Thank you for your time." Marilyn removed a business card from her pocket. "If you think of anything else that might be helpful, please call me. And if you talk to Preston Richway, tell him I'd like to speak to him."

She dropped the card on the end table by the sofa, then walked to the door. As soon as she made it back to her car, she drove to the nearest coffee shop. She snagged her laptop, hurried inside to a table in a back corner, ordered a coffee, then began searching on-line for Preston Richway.

RYKER LAID THE SHOVEL on the ground, dropped to his knees and raked dirt away from the bone. If this was a body, he didn't want to disturb it or any forensics left behind.

"You have no right," Mr. Darling growled.

Ryker gritted his teeth. This was a skeleton. A small skeleton.

Anger churned through him as he raised his head and stared at Darling. Caroline stood beside the man, her face ashen.

"Call the ME and a forensic team to excavate this grave," Ryker told her.

She jerked her eyes away from the bones, pulled her phone from her jacket pocket and made the call.

Ryker stood and faced Mr. Darling. "Who did you bury here? Your daughter Polly? Your wife?"

His face crumpling with emotions, Darling fell to his knees and began to sob.

Unmoved, Ryker removed his handcuffs and yanked the man's arms behind his back.

MARILYN FOUND TWO PRESTON Richways. The first had just celebrated his hundredth birthday surrounded by his children, grandchildren and great grandchildren. Pictures on social media documented the party.

The second Preston Richway took a little longer to research. No personal Facebook, Twitter or Instagram accounts. However, she finally found his name associated with a rehab center in Delray Beach, Florida. The center focused on drug and alcohol addiction and residential programs and counseling.

She clicked on the site, found a list of employees, and scrolled to Preston Richway's bio. He was from South Georgia, Seahawk Island.

It was him.

Dammit, Delray Beach was a five-six hour drive, although it would only be a short flight. She'd rather interview him in person, but calling him would be faster.

She sipped her coffee, then dialed the number for the rehab center. When the receptionist answered, she asked for Richway.

"Who may I ask is calling?" the receptionist asked.

If she revealed she was a reporter, she'd get nowhere. "I'm an old friend from his hometown. We're having a reunion and want to make sure he has all the details."

"He's with a group therapy session right now. Leave me your name and number and I'll have him return your call."

Marilyn hedged. "Actually I'd prefer to call him directly if you'll just give me his cell number."

"I'm sorry, Miss, but we can't release that information."

She clenched the phone tighter, struggling to refrain from losing her temper. "Oh, right, I understand." She gave the woman her cell. Odds were that if Preston was hiding something, he wouldn't call back.

If he didn't, she'd hop a plane to Florida and confront him in person.

The waitress stopped at the table, and she ended the call and ordered a chocolate chip muffin.

While she nibbled on the muffin and sipped coffee, she searched for Mellie Thacker and Aretha Franton. Nothing on Mellie Thacker, no social media accounts, address or phone number. No driver's license issued or renewed for Mellie since she was sixteen.

That was odd.

She perused death records, but found nothing on Mellie. But she did locate a death certificate for a Theresa Thacker.

A few minutes of searching birth records, and she connected Theresa Thacker with Mellie. Theresa was Mellie's mother. More research revealed that the mother died in a car accident three weeks after she'd moved from Seahawk Island. There was no mention of any surviving family or of Mellie.

The timing seemed coincidentally soon after the Darling girls disappeared. Her mind began to shift the puzzle pieces to create a picture.

Mellie had been with the Darling girls the night of that party at Preston's. Mellie also hadn't been heard from since, and there was no record of her anywhere.

A chill swept through Marilyn. Two bodies had been identified from the three skeletal remains found at Seaside Cemetery. The third hadn't yet been identified.

Was the third victim Mellie Thacker?

RYKER SCRUTINIZED HOWARD DARLING's reaction as the team excavated the bodies buried in the man's yard.

He'd sobbed at first, but soon lapsed into a bewildered, stunned silence. As if what—he hadn't known they were buried there? Could he have repressed the memory?

Or perhaps he'd never imagined after twenty-five years his crimes being revealed?

The ME lifted his glasses onto the top of his head. "There are two skeletons here. One appears to be a child, well, maybe a teenager. The other, a female. Adult."

Polly and her mother? So Mrs. Darling hadn't run off and abandoned Howard Darling as he'd claimed.

"We'll transport the bones to the morgue for analysis," Dr. Patton said.

Caroline and a uniformed officer were waiting beside Mr. Darling at the police car. Ryker relayed his conversation with the ME, but he couldn't quite read Caroline's expression.

A pale-faced Darling glanced up from the back seat with tears in his eyes. Ryker braced himself. A man who'd killed his family didn't deserve sympathy.

"I'm having him transported to the station for booking and interrogation," he told Caroline.

"I'll follow you. I definitely need to document this interview."

Ryker spoke to the head of the ERT, then left them in charge of collecting evidence.

Twenty minutes later, he and Caroline were seated at a metal table that had been bolted to the floor in an interrogation room at the police station. Darling sat slumped across the table from them, looking shaken and confused, but resigned.

Ryker had Mirandized him, but Darling hadn't yet asked for an attorney.

"Mr. Darling, you know we found the remains of two females in your back yard," Ryker began. "They belong to your wife and daughter Polly, don't they?"

The man rubbed a hand over his eyes, then gave a weak nod.

Disgust clawed at Ryker. "When we notified you that we found Deborah and Candace, you already knew Polly wasn't with them, didn't you?"

The man released a weary breath. "I . . . I didn't know what else to do."

Caroline leaned forward with both hands on the table and glared at Darling. "You had to lie to cover up what you'd done," she hissed. "First you abused your daughters, maybe even your wife, then you killed Polly and your wife?"

He shook his head no.

"Don't deny it, teachers and neighbors stated that the girls were abused. What happened? Did things get out of hand after the party? Maybe you hit Polly and your wife stepped in to defend her?"

"That's not the way it happened," Mr. Darling said in a low, pained voice.

"We just dug up their bodies in your back yard," Ryker cut in. "You put them there."

"I did," Mr. Darling said. "But . . . you've got it all wrong."

Caroline scoffed. "How do we have it wrong, Mr. Darling? We know you abused the girls—"

He shot up from his seat, eyes fuming. "I didn't abuse them," he snarled. "It wasn't me."

Ryker stood, ready to tackle the man if he became physical. "Sure it was. You have a temper. The girls did something to make you mad and you snapped."

"No, that's not true," Mr. Darling insisted, his voice shaking with fury. "My wife was the one who hit them, not me. She drank too much, and when she got drunk, she flew into a rage. She jumped all over the girls and . . . I couldn't stop her."

Tension vibrated through the room. Caroline went still. Ryker stared at the older man, contemplating his accusation.

"It's easy to blame your wife when she isn't here to defend herself," Ryker said in a low, lethal voice.

Darling raked his handcuffed hands over his head. "It's true though. She hurt the girls. She was always sorry the next day, but then she got drunk again and the same thing happened."

Ryker scrutinized Darling's reaction. The man had twenty-five years to practice his story. Was Darling a killer, or was his emotional reaction a ploy to convince Ryker he was innocent?

Chapter Twenty

"You've lived with this guilt for a long time," Ryker said to Mr. Darling. "You'll feel better once you get it out. We have your wife's body and all three of your daughters' remains. It's only a matter of time before we prove everything you did."

The fight seemed to drain out of the man. He laid his cuffed hands on the table, looked at his fists as if he was remembering strangling Deborah and Candace. They didn't have COD on Polly or the wife yet.

"I buried Polly, and then my wife, but I didn't kill them," he said in a voice filled with such calm that Ryker and Caroline exchanged a look. "I swear I didn't."

Either the man was in serious denial, and he thought they couldn't prove what he'd done or . . . he was telling the truth.

Caroline cleared her throat. "Then what did happen?" she asked in a quiet tone.

Mr. Darling heaved a shaky breath. "The night of the party when we got home . . . it was . . . awful. The girls . . . they'd had a big fight."

Ryker narrowed his eyes. "Go on."

Darling cut his gaze toward him. "It was a bad one. They were mad and were pushing and shoving, and . . . Polly was . . . dead."

Caroline slapped her hand on the table. "You expect us to believe Candace and Deborah killed their little sister."

"They said it was an accident. That she fell and hit her head." Tears trickled down the man's ruddy cheeks. "My wife was drunk and went at the girls."

He'd heard of children from abused families abusing their younger siblings. Was that what had happened here?

"What was the fight about?" Agent Manson asked.

Mr. Darling rubbed his cheeks with the palms of his hands. "Candace and Deborah had made some kind of pact with two other girls. Polly didn't want to go along with it. She threatened to tell."

Ryker's mind raced. "What kind of pact?"

Mr. Darling lifted his head, his expression anguished. "To get pregnant." His voice cracked. "They said they wanted to have babies, that they'd be better mothers than their own mama. They called her a drunk, and she was intoxicated that night, cussing and screaming like a lunatic." His body shook with emotions. "I had to drag her off of Candace and Deborah. I thought she was going to kill them right then and there."

Another tense moment stretched. Agent Manson's eyes widened. "Your daughters were pregnant?"

Mr. Darling nodded. "They were bragging about it. Said they were going to live in a house with their friends and raise their babies together."

A tense minute passed, then Caroline spoke. "What happened next?"

Mr. Darling scrubbed at his face with the back of his hand. "Phyllis was so enraged she screamed at the girls to get out, said she wouldn't let whores live under our roof. They were crying and yelling at her, then they threw some clothes in their backpacks and ran off." He choked on a sob. "That's the last time I saw my daughters."

The school counselor mentioned that the girls were troubled. Ryker had heard of pregnancy pacts before, concocted by hopeless teenagers who thought having a baby was a way to escape their own dysfunctional families and fulfill their need for love.

"You never heard from the girls after they left?" Caroline asked.

"I didn't. The next morning when my wife woke up, she was hysterical and ashamed of what happened."

"Your wife buried Polly?" Agent Manson asked.

Mr. Darling studied his fingernails as if he could still see the dirt beneath them. "We both did, that night."

Caroline's jaw hardened. "Then the next morning your wife called the police and you both acted as if the girls disappeared, and that you had no idea where they were."

"That part was true, I didn't know where they were," Mr. Darling said. "And I did go looking for them. I was hoping to convince them to have an abortion and to come home. I . . . just lost Polly. I didn't want to lose them, too."

"Do you know who fathered your daughter's babies?" Ryker asked.

"No, they didn't tell me."

Caroline crossed her arms. "Let's say we buy your story. That still doesn't explain how your wife's body ended up in the ground with your daughter's."

Mr. Darling closed his eyes and pinched the bridge of his nose. Either he was fabricating another lie or reliving what happened.

"You claimed she left you," Ryker reminded him.

"She did," Mr. Darling said in a tormented whisper. "She blamed herself for what happened to the girls, for Polly's death and that damn pregnancy pact, and for running Candace and Deborah off. One night she got drunk again and swallowed a bunch of pills. I . . . found her dead out in the yard, slumped over the grave where we buried Polly." He gulped back another sob. "That's when I decided to bury her with our little girl. So Polly wouldn't be alone."

Ryker cleared his throat. "Or maybe you felt guilty for not protecting your daughters from an abusive drunk mother, and you snapped and killed your wife?"

Mr. Darling shook his head. "She killed herself. I swear it."

"Why should we believe you?" he asked.

Darling released a shaky breath. "She wrote a note before she died."

"Where is this alleged suicide note?" Caroline demanded, tapping her foot.

The man wiped at his cheeks again. "I put it in the back of a photograph in the bedroom."

Ryker straightened. "The family photograph."

Mr. Darling nodded.

"I'll be right back." He gestured toward Caroline. "A word outside."

She shot Darling a look of disgust, then followed Ryker into the hall. "I'm going to call the ERT to look for that note."

She nodded, but her face looked ashen.

"What is it?" he asked.

She leaned against the wall, visibly trembling, her complexion as white as a ghost. "What's wrong, Caroline?"

Her legs slackened as if she was going to faint, and she reached for something to steady herself. The damn woman had been so cold and professional before that her reaction seemed odd. Perhaps she was sick. He rubbed her arms, soothing her. "Talk to me. What's wrong?"

She started to stay something, but footsteps clattered behind him. Dammit. He glanced to his side. Marilyn was staring at the two of them.

WHAT THE HELL WAS going on?

Marilyn was ready to confess everything to Ryker. Her mother had insisted she keep silent out of fear, but if Preston Richway had enough courage to talk, so did she.

It was long overdue.

But seeing Agent Manson in Ryker's arms made her turn cold inside. Once before, in the beginning of their relationship, she'd screwed up so badly that he'd turned to another woman. He'd sworn it was just for a night. And it had been her fault. She'd practically thrust him into the other woman's arms by pushing him away.

She hadn't liked it then. And she'd vowed to do better. To try to open up her heart and let him in . . . It was just so hard for her . . .

Ryker gently eased the other woman from his arms and asked her, "Do you need to sit down?"

The agent's face looked pale.

When she spotted Marilyn, she straightened as if she hated looking weak. "I'm sorry. Excuse me. I wasn't feeling well." She darted down the hall toward the restroom.

Marilyn folded her arms. "What happened, Ryker?"

He shrugged, although he looked confused. "I don't know. We were interrogating Howard Darling and I came out to make a phone call. She looked as if she was going to faint."

"Is that all there was to it?" Marilyn asked, a hint of jealousy edging her voice.

Ryker raised a brow, then seemed to realize that she was bothered by the other woman. He leaned closer and brushed his hand against her cheek. "Yes, Marilyn. That's all." His look softened. "Are you okay?"

Her stomach fluttered, and she silently chastised herself. She was supposed to be tough. Independent. But this case—and seeing Ryker touching another woman—had shaken her up. "I'm fine."

"Are you sure? I know yesterday was hard, honey."

His husky voice sounded so intimate that she wanted to curl in his arms and kiss him. But Agent Manson might return any minute. "Don't worry about me, Ryker. I'm a survivor."

"Even survivors need someone to lean on occasionally."

The urge to tell him nagged at her, but she thought she heard footsteps, so bit back a response and gestured toward the ladies room.

"Do you think the interview upset her?" Marilyn asked.

For a moment his jaw tightened as if he realized she'd intentionally changed the subject. Then he sighed. "It's been a disturbing few hours." He explained about finding the graves in the back yard, and Mr. Darling's statement. "This is off the record, Marilyn."

"Understood." Marilyn rubbed her hands with her arms. "Do you believe Darling?"

"I don't know yet. I came out here to call the crime team to search for the suicide note." Ryker removed his phone from his belt. "Darling does seem genuinely distraught. It's possible he's telling the truth about the pregnancy pact."

"The pregnancy pact fits," Marilyn said, then relayed her conversation with Jeremy about the party. "Does Darling know who fathered his daughters' babies?"

Ryker shook his head. "Claimed he didn't."

"Do you think Darling molested Deborah and Candace?" Marilyn asked.

"I don't." He exhaled roughly. " I think he's finally telling the truth."

"Preston Richway could be the father," Marilyn suggested. "When Jeremy left the party, Preston was drunk. Later, he told Jeremy that the Darling girls showed up along with two other girls, Mellie Thacker and Aretha Franton. Maybe one or all of them hooked up with him."

Ryker clenched his phone. "That makes sense. The school counselor mentioned those girls. Preston could have moved away so he wouldn't have to accept responsibility for the babies."

Marilyn nodded. "There's something else."

Ryker arched a brow. "What?"

"I think Mellie Thacker and Aretha Franton were in on the pact. I couldn't find any information on Mellie after she and her mother left town. No driver's license, nothing."

Ryker shifted on the balls of his feet. "What about her mother?"

"She was killed in a car accident three weeks after she and her daughter left town."

Questions flickered in Ryker's eyes. "Jesus," he breathed. "You think Mellie is the other body found at Seaside Cemetery?"

"I think that's a distinct possibility," Marilyn said.

Agent Manson exited the ladies room and walked toward them, her confident air back in place.

"I'll call the ME." He glanced at Agent Manson. "Do you feel better?"

"I'm fine," she said curtly. "What is she doing here?"

Marilyn clenched her jaw at Agent Manson's disapproving tone.

"She had some helpful information to share," Ryker said.

"And I suppose you reciprocated," Agent Manson snapped.

Marilyn lifted her chin. "Ryker and I have an understanding," she told the other woman. "We've worked together long before you entered the picture."

Agent Manson's cold gaze met Marilyn's.

Ryker raised a hand. "Listen, ladies, I don't understand what's going on between the two of you, but we all want the same thing."

Yes, she and Agent Manson wanted the same thing. Ryker. And Marilyn wasn't about to give up the fight.

"My show has an exclusive on this story," Agent Manson said. "And she is not to interfere or report a word on the Darling case without my permission."

Marilyn bit the inside of her cheek. So much for sharing information. She turned to Ryker. She'd planned to ask him if he wanted to go with her to question Preston Richway. But not now, not with this haughty agent glaring down at her, ordering her to stay out of the way.

Marilyn didn't take orders.

"I have to go." She didn't wait for a response. She wheeled around and stormed down the hall.

Ryker caught her just as she reached the exit, and snagged her arm. "Marilyn, wait. Please don't run away from me."

The vulnerability in his tone made her heart squeeze. "I'm not," she said. Hadn't she promised herself to try harder with Ryker?

"It feels that way," he said. "Last night . . . I was worried about you." He shifted and tilted her chin up with his thumb. "I with I could keep you with me every minute so I could protect you."

Her breath caught. She wanted more than protection. She wanted intimacy. "You might not feel that way if you knew everything about me."

His eyes darkened, skating over her. "Try me."

Her heart melted as she searched his face. Would he understand?

"You can trust me. I won't run." Then he cupped her face in his hands and closed his mouth over hers. Marilyn succumbed to the passion strumming through her, ran her fingers through his hair and deepened the kiss. Lost in the moment, she forgot everything but being in Ryker's arms.

Until a voice interrupted. "Detective Brockett?"

Damn that federal agent.

Ryker pulled away, his breathing choppy, desire heating his eyes. "We'll finish this later." He squeezed her arm. "Call me if you need me."

Without another word, he turned and strode back down the hall toward Caroline Manson.

Marilyn pressed her fingers over her lips. She could still taste Ryker. She wanted to taste him again tonight.

Agent Manson might get her story.

But Marilyn would get hers, too. She wouldn't lose Ryker either.

Still, the story came first. She wanted to know about that missing baby. And no one, including Cold Cases Revisited star Agent Caroline Manson would stop her.

"Good fucking grief, Caroline," Ryker said. "Why do you have so much animosity toward Marilyn?"

"I know how pushy she can be working a story, and this one is mine."

"Caroline, I can't ignore when a good lead is handed to me."

"So what is this lead?" Caroline asked.

Ryker relayed what Marilyn had told him about the party at Preston Richway's, and about Mellie Thacker and Aretha Franton.

Running a hand through her hair, Caroline huffed, "I've tried repeatedly to reach Aretha, but she hasn't responded."

"Because she's hiding something, or she's scared. And if Marilyn is right, we can't reach the Thacker girl because she's dead." Ryker gestured toward the interrogation room. "Now, if you want to talk to Darling again, I'll call the crime team and Dr. Patton."

She worked her mouth from side to side, then stalked back into the room.

Dammit, he didn't like playing referee between these two spirited women. At least he'd driven his point home with Marilyn with that kiss. Hopefully he was hacking away at her distrust and she'd talk to him soon.

If she didn't . . . he didn't know if he could continue their relationship the way it stood now.

He phoned the ME first and explained his suspicions.

"I'll see if I can dig up the Thacker girl's medical and dental records," Dr. Patton said. "And I'll keep you posted."

Ryker thanked him and called the head of the ERT at the Darling house. "Darling claims his wife killed herself, and that she left a suicide note. He put that note in the back of a family picture in his room. I saw the photograph when I was there. I'll hold while you look."

He tapped his foot on the floor while he waited. Seconds ticked by. A minute, then two, then three.

"I found the photograph," Lieutenant Granger said. "I'm removing the back now."

Another minute passed. Then another. Ryker had been so certain Darling had killed his daughters and wife. Was he wrong?

"It's here," the lieutenant said. "It's definitely a suicide note."

"Read it to me."

The lieutenant sighed. *"Dear Howard, I can't bear to go on in this world any longer. All my children are gone. Three daughters. I was not a good mother to them. I know that now, and I'm so ashamed. I drank too much and took my temper out on them. That's the reason they came up with that crazy pregnancy pact.*

Poor little Polly. She was the sweet one. The one who didn't go along. And Deborah and Candace got into a fight with her because of it. A fight that ended so badly.

That's my fault, too. I should have taught the girls how to handle their problems without using their fists.

The grief and regret have eaten me alive. I'm so sorry for failing my girls. I don't know where Deborah and Candace are, or if they have had babies of their own by now. That would make me a grandmother.

But I'll never know. I don't deserve them anyway.

I can't stand the thought of my sweet Polly being alone. I'm going to be with her now.

Howard, please put me in the ground beside her.
Phyllis

"That's it," Lieutenant Granger said.

Dammit. "Then Darling may be telling the truth. Bag the letter and we'll have the handwriting analyzed to verify that it's Mrs. Darling's handwriting."

"Will do."

Ryker hung up and scraped a hand over his chin. If Darling was telling the truth, what happened to Deborah and Candace after they'd left their house? And who had killed them?

Chapter Twenty-one

Marilyn's body tingled from that heated kiss with Ryker. She'd sensed he was hungry for more than just sex. She recognized it because she craved it herself.

She'd been alone for so long. Guarded her heart and tackled her life all alone.

What would it be like to truly have a real partner? One who understood and loved her in spite of her faults?

She wanted to find out.

"Promise me you won't go asking questions about what you saw that night," her mother had asked on her deathbed.

Marilyn was breaking that promise now. But she had to know what happened to that baby. How could she even consider a relationship or a family of her own when an infant might have died because of her silence?

Riddled with guilt again, she left the hospital more determined than ever to crack the case.

During her research into the Keepers stories, she'd made enemies, but she'd also gained friends. Some people, especially women, supported the Keepers and their devotion to rid the world of men who preyed on women and children.

Cat Landon and Carrie Ann Jensen were two of them. Liz Roberts, the counselor she'd been working with, was another. Even Laura Austin, Rachel Willis and Kendall James had vented their frustrations with the system.

Another was Piper.

She explained that she needed all she could find on Aretha Franton and Preston Richway. "I'll get back to you in a few," Piper said. "And about the adoptions/missing babies reports—I'm still digging."

Marilyn thanked her, then hung up and stopped by the Village café. She made notes on the investigation as she sipped her coffee and polished off a salad.

She listed the names of everyone she'd questioned and other persons she needed to interview, then drew lines to the possible connections she'd made to date.

Mr. Darling and Daryl Eaton remained at the top of the suspect list—with a question mark beside their names. Had they met or known each other?

She added Jeremy's name but didn't like him as a suspect.

Preston Richway was a possibility. A phone call from him to Candace or Deborah might have lured them from their home on New Year's Eve. Perhaps they'd planned to discuss Deborah's pregnancy and things had gone sideways.

That theory also raised other questions. Either Preston

would have had to arrange for Deborah to stay somewhere until the baby was delivered—or he'd held her hostage.

Although Preston had only been what? Seventeen or eighteen at the time. Holding Deborah hostage without anyone realizing it would have been near impossible.

Her phone buzzed on the table, and she snatched it up.

"It's Piper. Aretha Franton lives in Jacksonville, Florida. She works at a Planned Parenthood clinic."

Interesting. Jacksonville was only an hour away. She started repacking her notes so she could get on the road. "Is she married? Children?"

"No to both."

Hmm, perhaps she hadn't fulfilled the pregnancy pact. Or she worked at a Planned Parenthood clinic because she'd had an abortion?

"I'm texting you her phone number and address."

"Thanks. Preston Richway works at a rehab center in Delray Beach, Florida. Did you get his phone number and home address?"

"I'm sending it now. Do you want to fill me in?" Piper asked.

Marilyn tossed her computer bag over her shoulder. "I will after I finish my interviews. I want to see if my theory pans out first."

Piper murmured that she understood, then ended the call, and Marilyn hurried outside to her car. The light from the lighthouse at the Village flickered, shining across the ocean, still leading boats back to shore.

An image of Deborah Darling dragging that canoe onto the

land and carrying that infant haunted her. The poor girl had been terrified. Even at fourteen, maternal instincts had driven her to protect her child.

Yet someone had robbed her of her baby and her future.

Her cell phone buzzed with a text. Marilyn's blood ran cold as she read it.

You should have left the past alone. Now you have to die like the others.

RYKER STUDIED HOWARD DARLING, determined to make the man confess everything. He was sick and tired of the man dancing around the truth. "Mr. Darling, you said your daughters didn't have friends, but others claimed they were close with Mellie Thacker and Aretha Franton. Did you know those girls?"

Darling went still, his face contorting in anger. "No. I told you my daughters didn't have friends over to the house."

"Because of your wife's drinking?" Agent Manson cut in.

He gave a pained nod. "They said they were embarrassed by our family," Darling said. "It all came out that last night."

"When they told you about the pregnancy pact," Ryker said.

Another nod of confirmation.

"Both Deborah and Candace were pregnant?" Ryker asked.

Darling tugged at the loose skin around his neck. "That's what they said."

"And you have no idea who fathered the babies?" Agent Manson said.

He jerked his gaze to hers. "They refused to say. Said it was none of our business."

"Maybe you were so angry that you hired someone to get rid of them and their unborn children?" Ryker suggested.

Darling vaulted up from his seat, his face reddening. "God dammit. How many times do I have to tell you that I did not kill my daughters? And I sure as hell didn't hire someone to do it!"

Ryker and Caroline exchanged looks, then she gave him a pointed look. "Sit down, Mr. Darling."

He shot her a venomous look, then dropped into the chair, his jaw clenched in rage.

Ryker cleared his throat. "Help us piece together what happened after Candace and Deborah left your house."

Darling muttered a sarcastic sound. "I told you I don't know where they went. My wife was furious and yelled at them to get out, and they did. I figured they went to their grandmothers or to the park for the night. That they'd let the dust settle then come back."

"But they didn't?" Agent Manson said.

"No."

"And you didn't hear from them after that? Not even a phone call?" Ryker asked.

Darling shook his head. "If they had called, I would have gone after them."

Ryker intentionally used a sympathetic voice. "Maybe you did go after them. Or if you didn't, you sent someone else."

Darling fisted his hands on the table. "What are you talking about?"

Ryker leaned forward and pinned the man with an accusatory look. "I'm talking about a man called the Punisher."

MARILYN PHONED PIPER ABOUT the text, and Piper agreed to trace it. She'd tell Ryker about it later.

Memories of that car running her off the road haunted her, and she checked over her shoulder and the streets as she left the island. Just as she left town, she sensed someone was following her.

A dark sedan eased up on her tail. She tried to see the driver's face, but the windows were tinted. Nerves tied a knot in her belly, and she slowed and made a turn, hoping she was wrong. The car turned as well.

Was it the same vehicle that had struck her in the library parking lot?

Body wound tight with tension, she sped up and maneuvered around a slower car. The sedan didn't immediately follow, but two miles down the road, it passed the other vehicle and crept up behind her again.

This time she slowed, and veered into a gas station parking lot. She drummed her fingers on the steering wheel and waited. The sedan crawled by as if watching her. She stretched to see the license plate of the vehicle, but then it sped up and drove on.

She breathed out in relief, then went into the convenience store, bought a bottle of water and waited a few more minutes before she returned to her car. But she kept an eye out for the sedan as she pulled from the parking lot and drove to Aretha Franton's.

Who was driving that damn car? Was she being paranoid or had it been following her?

She checked the streets for the sedan as she parked at the Franton woman's house. A gust of wind whipped the palm trees back and forth, and brought the hint of impending rain as she walked to the door and knocked.

The southeast coast was under a tropical storm warning due to the hurricane in the gulf moving their way.

Marilyn shivered and knocked again. She wanted to see Aretha and Preston before the storm hit the next day. Her flight for Delray Beach left in three hours.

Footsteps echoed from the inside of the townhome, then the door opened. A short curly-haired brunette in her early forties answered with a surprised look. She must have been expecting someone else. "What are you doing here?" she asked without waiting for an introduction.

"You're Aretha Franton?"

The woman eyed her warily. "Yes."

"Can I please come in and talk with you?"

Aretha shifted from one foot to the other, then gestured for her to enter. As she followed Aretha to the living room, Marilyn noted contemporary furnishings, but there were very little personal photographs or decorative décor.

The woman sank down onto a cream-colored leather couch, and Marilyn settled on the loveseat. "I know who you are and the stories you cover," Aretha said. "Why are you here to see me?"

Marilyn decided to cut to the chase. This woman was direct. She might as well be, too. So she explained about the bodies of

Deborah and Candace Darling being recovered. "At this point, I know you, Mellie Thacker and the sisters created a pregnancy pact. We also know that the night they disappeared, they told their parents about the pact and that a big fight ensued. Apparently Mrs. Darling was inebriated and ordered the girls to leave."

Aretha cut her gaze away from Marilyn, but the guilt streaking her face confirmed Marilyn was on the right track. "Did you see or talk to Deborah or Candace after they left their parents' house on New Year's Eve?"

The woman released a weary sigh. "No, my mother learned about that pact the week before and made me cut all ties with the others."

"So you *were* in on the pact?"

Aretha nodded. "I'll tell you the truth, but you cannot print this or repeat my story without permission."

Marilyn was desperate for answers. Even if she never recorded a single word, she wanted to know who killed Deborah and kidnapped her baby.

She raised two fingers in a symbol of an oath. "You have my word."

Aretha studied her for a moment, then twisted her fingers together. "I was in on the pact. We were all young and stupid. I suspected the sisters were being abused by their father because I'd seen bruises, but Deborah and Candace denied it. When they suggested the plan to get pregnant, they started badmouthing their mother, saying she was a mean drunk. They didn't know how their father put up with her."

So Mr. Darling had been telling the truth.

"They were mad at him for not defending them," Aretha continued. "Candace insisted that if we had babies, we'd have someone to love us."

Such sad, twisted logic.

"Did you get pregnant?" Marilyn asked softly.

Aretha gave a wry laugh. "I was the only who didn't. My mother forced me into a counseling program at a Planned Parenthood center. That counselor saved me."

"That's the reason you work with Planned Parenthood now?"

She nodded. "I realized how foolish we all were, that it was selfish to have babies when we were kids ourselves and had no way to take care of them. I decided to help steer girls into making better decisions than we did."

"That's admirable," Marilyn said.

Pain wrenched Aretha's face. "Not really. Ironically though, I've never been able to conceive. I figured it was God's way of punishing me for what we did."

Marilyn gave her a sympathetic look. "For trying to get pregnant?"

Aretha's lower lip quivered, and she dropped her gaze to her lap where she knotted her hands together. "No, for the way we did it."

This was her opening to ask about Jeremy and Preston.

"Go on."

"You won't air this on TV?" she asked again. "Because it's not just me that was involved. It would hurt others. People who don't deserve to have all this dredged up again."

"I gave you my word and I always keep it."

Aretha released an agonized sigh. "As I mentioned, the four of us were determined to get pregnant," she said. "But none of us were dating or had boyfriends. And we didn't want to just have some geek's baby." She wiped at a tear. "I know how awful that sounds, and it *was* awful. I can't believe I ever thought like that."

"You were a teenager," Marilyn said softly.

"I know, but it doesn't excuse it, "Aretha blurted. "But the four of us had low self-esteem and fed off of each other. It's a dangerous combination."

True. "So you went to Preston Richway's party?" Marilyn asked.

Aretha's eyes widened. "You know about the party?"

"Not details," she admitted. "But I spoke with Jeremy Linchfield. He said he was there but he left. Then he had an accident."

Another tear slipped down the woman's cheek. "He and Preston wouldn't give us the time of day at school. We wanted them to get drunk," she said in a choked voice. "We thought if they did, they'd sleep with us."

"So you put something in Jeremy's water bottle."

"It was so stupid," she lamented. "We didn't think about him driving. And then he had that horrible accident." A sob broke free and the tears started flowing. "We never meant for that to happen. Poor Jeremy. We ruined his life."

And still could go to prison for what they'd done.

But Aretha was talking, and Marilyn wasn't going to stop

her. She sensed the woman had wanted to come clean for some time. "What about Preston?"

A strained silence stretched through the room. Somewhere a clock ticked off the hour. Outside the wind howled, and a tree branch slapped the windowpane.

Marilyn clutched the arm of the loveseat in a white-knuckled grip to fend off a panic attack at the volatile weather conditions. "Tell me the rest."

Aretha swiped at her damp cheeks. "Preston was so drunk that he passed out," she said. "The four of us, we shook him enough to rouse him, then we climbed on him and we . . . took turns."

They had raped Preston Richway. Meaning he was the father of Deborah's baby.

Rape and unwanted pregnancies gave him motive for murder.

Chapter Twenty-two

Ryker battled sympathy for Howard Darling. The man had suffered. But if he'd protected his daughters from their mother and forced her to seek help, his children might still be alive.

"Mr. Darling," he repeated, "did you know of a man they called the Punisher?"

Darling gave a low groan. "I heard rumors about him, but I didn't know who he was."

"You didn't contact him to punish your daughters for the pregnancies?"

Darling flattened his hands on the table. "No. A real man doesn't need to hire someone to discipline his own family."

"What about your wife? You said she was angry with the girls. Could she have contacted him and asked him to punish her daughters?"

Darling's eyes filled with questions that seemed to be tormenting him. "I . . . don't know. Sometimes she went to bars . . . I guess she could have met him somewhere. But . . . my wife loved our daughters. She just couldn't control her temper."

Ryker let that statement linger for a few seconds. "I'm going to ask you again. Do you have any idea who fathered Deborah's or Candace's babies?"

Darling shook his head. "We asked. My wife was sure our girls were seduced. She demanded to know the boys' names, but Candace and Deborah refused to tell us. That was the last straw and pushed Phyllis over the edge. She slapped Candace, and Deborah, then told them to get out. Everyone was screaming, and I . . . I didn't know what to do. I was in shock seeing poor little Polly lying there in a pool of blood, not moving." He dropped his head into his hands again and started to sob once more.

Ryker glanced at Agent Manson, but her expression held a mixture of contempt and some other emotion he couldn't quite define.

Maybe she was feeling ill again.

She barely gave him a minute, then continued, "In all the chaos that night, are you sure that the girls didn't mention a boy's name? Someone they knew from school? Or a boy one of them had a crush on?"

Mr. Darling groaned. "They didn't tell us anything. I didn't even know they were interested in boys."

The man had buried his head in the sand. They were teenage girls. Of course they were interested in boys.

"We heard that Deborah kept a diary," Ryker said. "Are you sure you don't know where it is? She may have written the name of the baby's father in it."

"I swear I don't know. If I'd found it and the boy's name was in it, I would have talked to him myself."

Agent Manson's heels clicked as she stood. "If you think of a name or anything else that can help us, let us know." Then she left the room.

Ryker left Darling alone to be escorted to a cell. He still wasn't sure what to charge the man with. He needed more details and forensics to confirm his story.

Agent Manson was pacing the hall. "You okay?" he asked.

She whirled toward him, and he realized she was hanging onto her temper. For some reason, this case was getting to her.

"You seem awfully upset," Ryker said. "As if this case is personal to you."

She straightened her shoulders. "I . . . just can't stand the thought of these girls' killer going free. And now one of them may have had a baby that no one was even aware of."

Ryker remembered her comment about the other case where she hadn't found a missing child. There was probably more to the story, but he didn't want to press at the moment. "The father of the baby may know where the child is. It's possible he wanted Deborah to have an abortion."

"And he killed her because she refused," Caroline said. "Still, what happened to the child?"

"That's what we're going to find out," Ryker said firmly.

He needed to call Marilyn. So far, she'd dug up vital information.

Maybe she had something new to add.

THE THREATENING TROPICAL STORM made the landing at the airport in West Palm Beach rough. Marilyn was grateful to have her feet on land again. Battling a storm was always difficult for her, but being in the air with the plane bouncing around intensified her fears.

Her phone buzzed with a message as she departed the plane, and she paused to check the message. Ryker, asking her to call him. "I'm sorry for the way we left things Marilyn. Would like to have dinner tonight and talk."

Perspiration beaded on her neck, and she stepped into the ladies' room, then phoned him. When he didn't pick up, she left a message. "Just landed in West Palm Beach. Am going to interview Preston Richway. Will keep you posted."

Her phone rang a second later. "Marilyn, what the hell are you doing flying to Florida by yourself? Have you forgotten that someone tried to kill you?"

Marilyn smiled at his protective tone. "No, but I told you I'm not running scared, Ryker. We must be getting close to the truth." She paused. "And I'd love to have dinner when I get back."

A tense heartbeat passed. "When will that be?"

"Tomorrow," she said. "I'll fly back after I talk to Preston."

"You have to be careful," Ryker said. "If he fathered Deborah's baby, he may have killed her to keep it quiet."

"I know that," Marilyn said. "But I want to know exactly what happened. If she gave birth, she was alive for months after she disappeared. Where was she all that time?"

"Good question," Ryker muttered. "If you'd told me you were going to see him, I would have gone with you."

Marilyn bit her lip. "I'm sorry, Ryker. I guess I'm so accustomed to working alone that I didn't think. Besides, you have your new partner now."

A hiss from Ryker. "Yeah, well, I don't think that will last once this case is done."

Marilyn checked her watch. She hoped not. "I'd better go. I need to get a rental car tonight."

Ryker's breath rattled out. "Jesus, Marilyn, please watch your back."

Another smile. "I promise I will. And you'll be the first to know what I find out from Richway." She hung up and hurried to the rental car desk.

A few minutes later, she plugged the address for Preston Richway into the GPS and followed it. The rehab center where he worked was a residential treatment center, but he should be finished for the day.

A slow drizzle of rain fell from the sky, a sign of what was to come. Delray was a hip little town that seemed to draw young people with its restaurants, bars, parks, and public beach. Snowbirds flocked to the area for the winter and its pleasant temperatures, but with the impending inclement weather, the streets were nearly deserted tonight. At this point, residents weren't evacuating. That should give her some comfort, but the trees thrashing back and forth made worry knot her stomach.

Forget the storm. You're so close to the truth. Find it and maybe you can sleep without that baby's cry echoing in your head.

Marilyn drove through the heart of the town, then veered onto a side street that led to a condominium development built between Delray and Boynton Beach. The older looking high rise offered a view of the water and was set back from the road for privacy. She parked, then checked Preston's address, and battled the wind gusts as she made her way to the front door.

Stepping inside the building, she walked to the desk and asked for Preston Richway.

The woman behind the counter buzzed Preston's condo. Marilyn held her breath, half expecting him to tell her to get lost, but was surprised when the woman pointed for her to go up. "Third floor. Unit 31 A."

Marilyn nodded, then rode the elevator, anxiety and hope mingling as the doors opened, and she stepped into the hallway. She found Preston's door and rang the bell. Seconds later, he responded and invited her in.

"Thank you for seeing me," she said.

"Jeremy called. I've been expecting you."

So he knew the reason she'd come. Was he ready to talk?

He led her through a small entryway to a living room which was open to the kitchen. The furnishings were contemporary gray and white, although the dark gray sofa and recliner looked inviting and gave the room a cozy feel.

She quickly surveyed him while he retrieved bottles of water and set them on the glass coffee table. He was early forties, tall with an athletic build, his dark hair short and neat, a heavy five o'clock shadow adding an aura of mystery about him. She imagined him as a cocky teenager and could see why he'd been so popular with the girls. He was still handsome, although a dark sadness permeated his eyes.

He sat down on the sofa and studied her. "Jeremy said they found Candace and Deborah Darling's bodies."

"Yes."

He screwed the lid off his water and took a deep drink, then wiped his mouth with the back of his hand. "They were both murdered?"

"Yes."

He released a sigh. "Was it the father?"

"I don't know," she answered. "The police are looking at more than one person of interest."

"Who do they suspect?"

Marilyn hedged. "It's early in the investigation. They're talking to everyone who knew the girls and their family."

Preston leaned forward, his elbows on his knees, his jaw clenched. Her gut told her that he wanted to say something but was holding back.

"Preston, I won't print or report anything that you tell me without your permission."

He swallowed hard, then stared at her as if he'd placed her under a microscope.

She spoke softly, hoping to earn his trust. "Jeremy told me there was a party at your house the night of his accident."

"That was supposed to be such a fun night," he said, his voice cracking. "But everything went wrong."

Pain and regret laced his tone, stirring Marilyn's sympathy. But she refrained from showing it. Preston might be involved in the girls' deaths . . . although he was not the man she'd seen strangle Deborah. That man had been much older. Eaton's age.

"Tell me what happened, Preston."

A heartbeat of silence, then he released a wary breath and leaned back against the sofa. "You promise you won't go public with this?"

"I promise. I want to know who killed the girls. I don't think it was you, was it?"

Preston shook his head. "I . . . hated them, but I didn't kill them."

"Why did you hate them? What happened?"

He shifted, then ran a hand over his face before looking back at her. "I had the party. Jeremy and our other friend had scholarship offers, and we wanted to celebrate. We got a bunch of beer and our friends showed up and it was all fun. I didn't think I'd had that much to drink, but I was young and stupid, and must have had more than I thought. I passed out on the bed in the back room."

Marilyn waited quietly, hoping he'd continue.

"Sometime later, I woke up and . . . they were there."

"You mean Deborah and Candace?"

"All of them," Preston said in a choked voice. "Deborah, Candace, Mellie and Aretha." A far away look settled in his eyes as if he was lost in the memory. "They were all over me. I was so weak and dizzy that I tried to tell them to go away, but they shoved my pants down and . . ."

"They raped you," she said softly.

Emotions clouded his eyes. "I know that sounds ridiculous. I was a guy. I was stronger than them."

"Except that you were inebriated."

"Yeah."

Compassion for him broke through her resolve. "Preston, Jeremy said that he only had one beer, then he chugged water from his water bottle before he started driving. Have you considered the possibility that he was drugged? And that you were too? That that's the reason you were so dizzy that you couldn't stop the girls?"

His gaze jerked to hers. "My counselor suggested that," he admitted. "I just felt so ... ashamed. Like who would believe four teenage girls raped me? I was bigger than them. An athlete for God's sake."

"That's the reason you didn't come forward and file charges?"

He nodded. "Our friends saw me and Jeremy drinking. We were both players back then. Everyone would have assumed I got drunk and slept with the girls. I could hear the teasing, that I'd had an orgy."

"You never told anyone what they did?"

He hesitated, then cleared his throat. "Not for a while. But it ate at me, and I finally told Jeremy. He was a mess though, working through physical therapy, dealing with being paralyzed."

"That was a tragedy," Marilyn agreed.

"I became seriously depressed. I started drinking and doing drugs, anything to dull the pain." His voice grew gruff. "Finally my mother found me passed out over the toilet one night. I almost OD'd."

"And you admitted what happened."

He nodded.

Marilyn clasped her hands together. "How did she handle it?"

He muttered a sarcastic sound. "Not well. She went ballistic, blew up at me, blamed me for being so stupid I let it happen."

Female victims faced accusations and guilt all the time. It was one reason they didn't come forward or testify. Prosecutors shredded them on the stand.

No justice there.

"That must have been difficult," Marilyn said quietly.

He made a low sound in his throat. "It made me more ashamed. So I drank more. Finally I was spiraling out of control, and she made me go to rehab." He looked up at her. "I was angry and resented her for it, but it was the right thing for me, the best thing. I got counseling and learned to accept what happened and to forgive myself."

"You know it wasn't your fault, Preston, don't you?"

He gave a grave nod. "On some level, yeah. But they picked me because I was rude to them."

"They chose you because you were popular and they were troubled," Marilyn pointed out.

He shrugged. "Rehab saved my life. Literally. I decided to turn that bad incident into a driving force to help others."

"That's admirable," Marilyn said. "Your mother must be proud of you now."

Another pained look crossed his face. "Not really. My mom . . . she was so filled with rage and bitterness. She never looked at me the same after that. Eventually we just stopped talking."

Being estranged from his mother was obviously a sore spot.

But while he was opening up, she had to press on. "Did you have any contact with the Darling girls or Mellie Thacker or Aretha Franton after the rape?"

He shook his head no. "I missed a lot of school because I was so depressed and because of the drinking and drugs. Then Mellie moved away and so did Aretha. And then the Darling girls disappeared."

"So you had nothing to do with their disappearance?"

"I told you I didn't talk to them after the night of the party," he said, his tone hardening. "But I was glad they were gone."

She gave him an understanding look. "There's one more thing," Marilyn said. "The Darling girls and Mellie and Aretha made a pregnancy pact."

Preston jerked his head up, his eyes widening. "What?"

"You didn't know?"

"Hell, no, that's sick."

"It's also the reason they raped you," Marilyn said. "They thought if you and Jeremy were drunk, you'd sleep with them."

Preston's face twisted with emotions as the implication sank in. "What exactly are you saying?"

His shock seemed so genuine that her heart ached for him. "Preston, Deborah and Candace were both pregnant when they disappeared."

CHAPTER TWENTY-THREE

CAROLINE STUDIED HER FACE in the bathroom mirror. Sometimes she didn't know who she was anymore.

She hadn't been with the agency long enough to be burned out. But this case had gotten under her skin just like the stories of the Keepers had.

She identified with them. Had spent hours talking to Carrie Ann Jensen and Cat Landon and visiting the secret Chat Room where the Keepers gathered.

Although as a federal agent sworn to uphold the law, she couldn't show her sympathy for the group. Or her alliance.

But she had wanted to help them. Had wanted to take up their cause herself.

Her own secrets haunted her.

In that room with Harold Darling, she'd come close to losing her cool as if her demons had gathered in that room to bait her. She stared at her hands which were white from clenching them into fists. As she'd listened to Darling, the temptation to snatch him by the neck and choke the truth out of him taunted her.

But . . . some inner voice screamed at her to wait out his story. To get to the truth first. Judging and doling out sentencing on her own without irrefutable proof that he was a vile man who'd battered and killed his daughters would be wrong.

And now . . . what?

She was beginning to think that he might be telling the truth.

For some reason, his anguish had actually seemed sincere as if he was truly mired in grief.

She'd been drawn to that grief and anguish. Had even felt a tug of compassion for him.

She splashed cold water on her face, then straightened and looked at her reflection again.

When she'd first decided to tackle this case, in her mind the Darling girls had simply been victims. But the more she learned, the deeper the ugliness ran, like rotting floorboards underneath a house that eventually made the entire structure crumple down.

Her phone buzzed with a text. One of the Keepers wanting to be filled in.

She quickly texted back. *Not yet.*

The other woman would know what she meant.

She pasted on her professional mask, turned and went to meet Ryker.

CHAPTER TWENTY-FOUR

Ryker fought irritation that Marilyn hadn't asked him to go with her to Florida. If she got herself killed, he'd never forgive himself.

Caroline was another stubborn lady. She'd ducked into the ladies room, claiming she was getting a migraine. But something else was going on with her. She didn't seem to want to share with him any more than his girlfriend did.

While he waited, he checked in with the analyst about the search for that dark sedan.

"There are dozens and dozens," the analyst said. "I'm trying to narrow it down."

"How about Lloyd Willing? Did you find anything on him?"

"He was the groundskeeper at the Village and lighthouse for twenty years. Married with three kids and five grandchildren. Nothing suspicious."

"Keep looking for the car." He hung up and phoned the ME. "I know you barely received the bones of Phyllis and Polly Darling, but wondered if there's anything you can tell me."

"The forensic anthropologist says that Polly did sustain a blow to the head which most likely caused her brain to bleed and led to her death. It's hard to say at this point whether she was struck intentionally or if she was pushed or simply fell."

A blow to the head was consistent with Darling's story.

"How about Mrs. Darling?"

"That's more complicated. Dr. Lofton is still working on her. But there were no signs of physical abuse, strangulation or gunshot wounds."

So she could have mixed pills and booze like Darling claimed.

Ryker's phone was buzzing with another call so he thanked the ME and connected.

"It's Lieutenant Granger from the crime lab. We've been processing the forensics found at Eaton's place. There were three sets of prints. Eaton's. Marilyn Ellis's. And another set belonging to a different female."

"Have you identified those last prints?"

"No, they aren't in the system. But we found the name of Eaton's caregiver. Prints could be hers."

She might have been the last person to see Eaton alive. "Send me her name and contact information. I have to talk to her."

"On its way."

Ryker hung up and saw the message come in. Gayle Burton, 225 Pebble Drive. Seahawk Island.

He rushed toward Caroline as she exited the ladies room. "I have a name and address for Daryl Eaton's caregiver."

"What does that have to do with the Darling case?"

"I'll explain on the way."

They hurried out to his car. On the drive to the island, he relayed Marilyn's theory.

"She thinks Daryl Eaton was the man people called the Punisher?"

"Yes," he said. "She suspects he's connected to the Darling sisters' deaths."

Ryker sped over the causeway, then turned down a side road leading to an older group of apartments near the Village.

"Do you think she's onto something?" Caroline asked.

Ryker shrugged. "You may not like her, Caroline, but Marilyn is damn good at her job. And as tough as she seems, she really wants justice for victims."

Agent Manson simply studied him, her lips pressed into a grim line.

He noted the numbers of the buildings and that the parking lot was half empty. These apartments were run down and needed a significant facelift before the hurricane. Since then, they'd fallen into serious disrepair.

He parked near Gayle's building, cut the engine and climbed out. Caroline joined him, and they walked to the door together. The blinds were closed, the place dark.

She rang the bell, and when no one answered, he tried the door. To his surprise, it squeaked open. He and Caroline exchanged looks and drew their weapons.

In the entry, he paused to listen for sounds that someone was inside, but there was only silence. The interior was dark, so he pulled his penlight and shined it across the foyer, then he inched inside the living area. The place was empty.

"Looks like no one is here," Caroline murmured.

Ryker refrained from comment as he paused to listen again. Silence. He eased across the room then glanced into the kitchen. Empty. A small hall led to a bath and bedroom.

Nothing inside. No furniture or signs that anyone lived here.

"What the hell? Are you sure you have the right address?" Caroline asked.

Ryker checked his text again. "This is it."

"Then she either moved out and took everything with her—"

"Or this place was just a front," Ryker finished.

"You think the name Gayle is an alias?"

Ryker shrugged. "It's starting to look that way. If she was lying about who she was, perhaps she had reason to kill Eaton."

Agent Manson's brows lifted. "And now she's on the run."

MARILYN GAVE PRESTON TIME to absorb her statement. Face pale, he walked across the room to the window and stared outside. His shoulders shook with emotion.

"You didn't know about the pregnancies?" she asked softly.

He turned back to her. "No. Like I told you, I never spoke to any of those girls after the night of the party."

"Were there any rumors at school about them being pregnant?"

"No, I would have remembered that." Pain wrenched Preston's face. "You said Deborah and Candace were both murdered. What happened with the pregnancies? Was there a baby?"

Marilyn hated to lie to him. If her suspicions were correct, Preston was the father of the infant she'd seen kidnapped the night Deborah had been murdered.

"Was there a baby?" he demanded, his voice rising with anger.

"I don't know."

His jaw tightened. "God." He paced to the bookcase and stared at something on the shelf. A sobriety chip. He traced his finger over the chip, released a deep sigh then turned to her. "I want to know if there was a child. If I had—*have*—a child. Or children."

"I understand." She joined him and glanced at the shelf. He'd obviously worked hard to earn that chip. "I'm sorry I had to tell you this. You showed courage in talking to me today." She squeezed his arm. "If I get information regarding a baby, I'll let you know."

"Thank you." He removed his phone from his pocket and shuffled it from hand to hand. "I think I'd better call my sponsor."

Marilyn laid her card on the shelf, and said a prayer that he would be okay as she let herself out the door.

Ryker glanced at Caroline. "Can you find the manager for this rental property and ask him about Gayle?"

"On it."

"I'll search the house for evidence she was here." He strode through the house again, then went to the kitchen and checked the kitchen drawers. A note, slip of paper with information on it . . . anything that might offer insight into the woman who'd taken care of Daryl Eaton.

He called the analyst at the precinct. "It's Ryker. I need everything you can find on a woman named Gayle Burton. I'll hold."

He opened the pantry door and raked his hand along the shelves. Nothing.

He continued to search beneath the drawers for a false bottom, but the place was cleaned out.

The analyst returned a minute later. "This is strange. Gayle Burton shows up as a home caregiver, but she doesn't work for any company that I've found. There's one reference to her services from an online office supply company that designs and prints business cards for small businesses. I also located a bank account in her name. Funds from Daryl Eaton were automatically deposited in her account for services rendered the last year."

"Can you trace the address associated with that business account?"

"It's the address you were given," the analyst answered.

"Driver's license?"

"The only Gayle Burton in the DMV records is seventy-five years old. Her license expired two years ago, and she lives in New Hampshire."

That couldn't be her.

"Keep looking. Although Gayle Burton could be a phony name so check for similar names and job descriptions. Perhaps she was running a scam to get money from terminally ill patients."

"Good point. I'll let you know what I find."

He hung up as Agent Manson returned. She flipped through her notepad. "Manager said the woman booked the place over the phone. He never met her. She paid cash through their drop box. I asked for the rental application, and he pulled it up, but it was pretty bare."

They were getting nowhere.

"Did he stop by for repairs or see anyone here?"

She shook her head. "She's looking more and more suspicious."

"Like she rented it because she didn't want anyone to find her."

Which meant that she might have had reason to kill Eaton.

MARILYN DROPPED HER HEAD against the steering wheel and dragged in a breath. Preston's brave confession had touched her deep inside.

He had been drugged, taken advantage of, traumatized, and suffered from depression from the attack, which had led to his alcohol and drug dependency.

But he'd received help and was paying it forward.

His mother should be proud of him. But according to

Preston, they were estranged. She'd been ashamed of what had happened to him. Had wanted him to keep silent.

She wiped at the tears she hadn't realized she'd been crying. Immeasurable guilt and shame built up when a person was victimized—Cat Landon, Carrie Ann Jensen, Tinsley Jensen, the victims of the River Street rapist—they had poured out their pain during her interviews.

Her own guilt was born from witnessing a crime and not speaking up.

Her mother should have called the authorities the night of the murder. If they had, Eaton would have been arrested, the Darling case solved, and that baby would have been found.

Preston had broken his silence by talking to her tonight. It was time she broke hers and told the truth. Admitted what she'd seen.

It might be the only way to uncover the truth.

She lifted her head, started the engine and drove toward the motel. She wanted to talk to Ryker. But she needed to tell him this secret in person, not over the phone.

Still, she'd promised to let him know about her interview with Preston, and she was going to keep that promise.

She'd call him as soon as she reached the motel.

CHAPTER TWENTY-FIVE

RYKER PACED HIS APARTMENT, his anxiety mounting. What if the person who'd tried to kill Marilyn had followed her to Delray Beach?

Dammit. She was alone.

He poured himself a scotch, swirled the dark liquid in his tumbler, then tossed it back.

She had done this before. Disappeared when she was investigating a story. But this time, he sensed the stakes were higher. More personal.

Marilyn was in danger. And he could not lose her.

The wind howled outside, beating against the windowpane. A storm was brewing. According to the meteorologist, it could be severe.

Marilyn hated storms.

He wanted her home before it hit. Home with him so he could hold her and ward off her demons.

He called her number and prayed she'd answer.

MARILYN COLLAPSED ON THE motel bed and snatched her phone from her purse. God help her, the storm was really picking up.

She punched Connect, desperate to hear the sound of Ryker's voice.

He was always calming. Understanding without demanding she convey what had happened to send her into panic mode at the sound of thunder and rain and wind thrashing.

"Marilyn, are you all right?" Ryker asked.

She checked the lock on the motel room door, wishing she had her pistol with her. But she'd had to leave it inside her car at the airport. "Yes, I just got to my room, and it's storming."

"I know, baby, I wish I was there with you."

She choked back a sob. "So do I."

Silence stood between them for a moment, then Ryker spoke in a low voice.

"I've got you. Close your eyes and pretend my arms are around you."

She did as he said, emotions welling in her throat. Ryker was her rock. She didn't want to disappoint him.

"I'll always be there for you if you'll let me, Marilyn."

She was too overwhelmed to speak. What had she done to deserve a good man like him?

"I wish I could give you what you want," she said in a low whisper.

"All I want is you, sweetheart, and for you to trust me," Ryker murmured.

"I do trust you," she said. "More than anyone I've ever met."

"But you're still holding back."

A heartbeat passed. Did she have the courage to really confide in him? If she didn't, she might lose him. But if she told him the truth, she might lose him anyway.

"Marilyn?" he said in husky tone.

She inhaled a deep breath. "Not over the phone. In person when I get back."

"I'm going to hold you to that."

And he would. Ryker was a man of his word.

"I saw Preston Richway," she murmured.

A moment of silence, then his deep sigh as if he wished she'd said something more personal.

"What happened?" he finally asked.

She relayed the details of their conversation. "He's using the trauma he experienced as inspiration to help others."

"Good for him," Ryker said. "Do you think he's lying about knowing about the pregnancy pact?"

Marilyn raked hair from her forehead. "I don't think so. He seemed genuinely shocked." The image of that man ripping the baby from Deborah's arms haunted her. "He asked about the baby, said he wanted to know if there was one." She startled as thunder clapped outside. "I think he was sincere, Ryker."

"I suppose it's possible he was in the dark."

"It's sad, isn't it? That he might have stepped up and been a father to that baby." Tears burned her eyes. She had a feeling

Ryker would make a good father.

"Marilyn . . . are you all right, baby?"

"Yes. I just . . . miss you."

The sound of his breath rushing out echoed over the line. She pictured his rugged face smiling, and her heart melted again. "I miss you, too," he said softly. "When will you be back?"

"In the morning," she replied.

"Call me when you land." His voice dropped another decibel. "Until then, remember to imagine my arms around you tonight, my voice drowning out the storm."

She closed her eyes again, and could almost feel his breath against her neck. His lips on hers. His husky voice soothing her until she fell asleep.

"Good-night, sweetheart."

"Night, Ryker."

As the phone clicked silent, she rose, slipped off her clothes and changed into pjs. If Ryker was here, she wouldn't bother. She liked sleeping next to him, skin to skin.

But the chill from the storm had invaded her, and she needed the warmth.

She brushed her teeth and slid beneath the covers, mentally replaying the facts of the investigation in her head, hoping the answer would click into place. Preston was shocked the Darling girls were pregnant. He and his mother were estranged. She'd forced him to keep silent.

She suddenly sat up, her mind ticking.

Hell hath no fury like a woman scorned—or a mother whose child had been harmed.

She'd tried to connect the Darlings to Eaton, but what if Mr. Darling was telling the truth? What if he and his wife hadn't known about the Punisher?

What if Preston's mother had hired the Punisher to make the girls pay for what they'd done to her son?

Chapter Twenty-six

That fucking reporter was in Delray Beach. She'd found Preston Richway.

If he spilled everything, it wouldn't take any time for Marilyn Ellis to put two and two together. If she didn't hate the woman and fear she'd expose her, she might actually like Marilyn.

But she was too smart for her own good.

She should have given up a long time ago. But she'd kept nosing around.

Now Marilyn had to pay for all her questions.

She checked the returning flights from Delray for the morning. An early one then one after lunch. There was no way for her to find out which one the bitch would be on.

Marilyn drove a little red sporty car.

It wouldn't be too difficult to locate the car. She'd stake it out. And when Marilyn landed, she'd kill her.

Then the secrets of Seahawk Island would be safe and the Keepers could continue.

Chapter Twenty-seven

Ryker's phone jarred him awake from a troubled sleep. Panic struck him. Marilyn?

He snatched his phone and checked the number. The ME. He quickly connected. "Detective Brockett."

"I have an ID on the third body from Seaside Cemetery," Dr. Patton said. "You were right. I compared medical and dental records, and the bones belong to Mellie Thacker."

Ryker swung his legs over the side of the bed. "Cause of death?"

"Strangulation. I don't have a definitive time of death, but the best I can say, she died around the same time as the Darling girls."

So somehow the girls had wound up together. And were killed by the same person.

"Can you determine if she was pregnant or delivered a baby?"

A pause. "Dr. Lofton is working on that. I'll keep you posted."

Ryker thanked him, then hung up. If Mellie had been pregnant, then they might be looking for her baby as well as the Darling sisters'.

MARILYN OVERSLEPT AND HAD to rush to the airport to make her morning flight. She checked her messages before she boarded.

Two from Ryker telling her he couldn't wait to see her and to have a safe flight. Then one saying the ME identified Mellie Thacker as the third skeleton.

She texted Ryker. "Can't wait to see you, too. Back soon."

Another message was from her boss wanting her *big* story.

Her promise to Preston echoed in her mind. Some people thought she was cut throat, but she wouldn't expose a story at the detriment of a victim.

Once she boarded the flight and got a cup of coffee, she made notes on the investigation. With the Keepers, she'd focused on the victims' and their families' need for justice. She could continue this theme—that is, if justice was what had driven the killer to take Daryl Eaton's life.

But was there justice in murdering teenage girls?

The four teens who'd drugged and raped Preston and caused Jeremy's accident had committed serious crimes. How could she condone the Keepers killing a serial predator like the River Street rapist or a serial killer like the Skull and not feel these teens had deserved to be punished, too?

Except the lines were blurring. These teenagers had been young and troubled, not serial predators who committed heinous crimes of torture . . .

She accessed the internet and researched Preston Richway's mother. Ironically her name was Joy. But she sensed the woman hadn't experienced much joy since her son was attacked.

Wind thrashed at the plane and lightning streaked the sky, unsettling her nerves. Twice the pilot announced they were going through turbulence sparked by the tropical storm. At one point, they took a nosedive that made her stomach lurch. Finally the treacherous hour passed.

As soon as she deplaned, she rushed to her car. Rain splattered the ground and slashed her windows as she started the engine and pulled from the parking lot. A heavy gray fog shrouded the sky, the palm trees swaying violently with the force of the wind gusts.

Her phone buzzed as she veered onto the main road leading back to Seahawk Island. She didn't recognize the number, but connected.

The pounding rain drowned out the voice. She strained and pressed the handset to her ear. "Hello?"

"I warned you."

Sweat broke out on Marilyn's forehead. "Who is this?"

The phone went dead.

Her pulse hammered. Another threat.

She jerked her gaze toward the rearview mirror and spotted a pair of bright headlights behind her. Water gushed from the tires and collected in deep puddles on the edge of the road, forcing her to slow. She plowed along, blinking hard to see, but the thick sheets of rain and those bright headlights clouded her vision. Her tires churned water, sending it in a wide spray, and she tightened her hands around the steering wheel. The car moved closer, riding her tail.

She braked, hoping the driver would go around her, but instead the car sped up, riding her bumper.

The message on the phone taunted her. *You'll be sorry.*

A woman's voice.

Dear God, was the caller following her?

She took a short cut from the main road, hoping to lose the vehicle. Instead it sped up, its lights coming closer, blinding her as she hit a rut in the road.

Terrified, she punched Ryker's number. If she was going to die, she had to tell him how she felt. That he was the only man she'd ever loved.

That she wanted to spend the rest of her life making up for how distant she'd been.

She pressed his number, desperate to hear his voice.

Static crackled over the line as Ryker answered. "Marilyn, where . . . are you? Are you o . . . kay?"

The wind and rain intensified, and she gripped the steering wheel tighter, fighting to remain on the road.

"Marilyn?"

"Yes, at least for now."

"What the hell does that mean?"

"Just listen. I'm on my way back to see you, but if I don't make it—"

"What do you mean, if you don't *make* it?"

"Someone is following me. But I have information." The connection cut out for a minute and she cursed. It took all her strength to keep the car from blowing off the road. "Ryker?"

"I'm here, baby."

"The source, you asked me who my source was, why I thought Eaton was involved in the Darling case. I . . . should have told you—" The line cut out again, and she sped up slightly and veered onto a side street. The car swerved behind her. "Ryker, I was the source. When I was a little girl, I saw the lighthouse keeper strangle Deborah Darling."

"Jesus, Marilyn," Ryker growled. "Tell me where you are. I'm coming after you."

"I'm near the lighthouse where it all started. There's more. There was a baby with Deborah. Eaton stole the baby. You have to find out what happened to it."

"I will," he said. "*We* will, Marilyn, when you get back here. We'll do it together."

Marilyn choked back a sob. What if she never saw Ryker again? Never got to hold him again?

She wanted that almost as much as she wanted to find that baby. The car inched up though, and she had to swerve to avoid hitting the guardrail. "I've been thinking about Preston Rich-way," she continued.

The car bumped her rear, and Marilyn skidded toward the embankment. She fought to steer her car back on the road.

"Marilyn, you cut out. Are you still there?"

"Yeah, but this car is trying to run me off the road."

"Find a gas station or a parking lot that's lit and pull in. I'll be right there."

"Wait," she said, her pulse hammering. "Listen to me. Those four girls drugged and raped Preston. I think Preston's mother may have hired Eaton to punish --"

Marilyn screamed as the car rammed her rear bumper, and her car flew into a spin. She tried to fight it, but lost control. Her brakes squealed, tires grinding for traction. Her car spun, flipped on its side then rolled. She tried to brace herself as she sailed toward the marsh.

Her head hit the top of the car, and the impact pitched her body forward, then sideways.

Pain ricocheted through her temple just before the world went black.

Chapter Twenty-eight

Ryker clutched the phone in a white-knuckled grip. "Marilyn!" The sound of a crash made his blood run cold. "Marilyn, honey, talk to me. Are you okay?"

He snatched his keys and jogged to the door, but just as he did, a knock sounded. He continued to call Marilyn's name as he opened the door.

Caroline stood on the other side.

He threw up a hand before she could speak, and listened on the phone again. "Marilyn, are you there?" *Please say you are.*

Silence met his question then the phone went dead.

He motioned toward his vehicle. "Let's go. Marilyn's in trouble. I need a trace on her phone."

"I'll call it in while you drive."

Ryker rattled off Marilyn's phone number as they raced to his vehicle. The rain had temporarily ceased, but dark clouds hovered, ready to dump another deluge. The wind howled, trees swaying. God, Marilyn she was out in this mess, alone, and possibly injured.

What would he do if something happened to her?

"Where is she?" Caroline asked.

"Somewhere near the Village."

"I'm on it." Caroline spoke into the phone while he started the engine and raced from the parking lot. "They're trying to trace her," she said a minute later. "Tell me what happened."

"Marilyn talked to Preston Richway," Ryker said. "Apparently the Darling girls, Mellie Thacker and Aretha Franton drugged Preston and Jeremy Linchfield, and had sex with Preston."

"Because of the pregnancy pact," Caroline surmised.

He nodded and pressed the accelerator. "Marilyn claims Deborah had a baby, that Daryl Eaton strangled her and took the infant."

Caroline's eyes widened. "How does she know that?"

"I told you she's good at what she does," he snapped.

"Does she know what happened to the baby?"

"No. Apparently, Preston had no idea he'd fathered a child. When his mother discovered he'd been raped, she went ballistic." He turned onto the road toward the Village. "Marilyn thinks she hired the Punisher to take care of the Darling girls and Mellie Thacker."

"Then she killed Eaton because she was afraid he'd confess on his deathbed?"

"Makes sense." He rubbed his forehead still trying to assimilate everything Marilyn had confided. Although why hadn't the Punisher also killed Aretha? Because she hadn't conceived?

Caroline looked pale again. "Ryker, if the baby survived, maybe Mrs. Richway knows what happened to it."

"That's possible." Perspiration beaded on the back of his neck. " If the baby was Preston's, that means Mrs. Richway is the child's grandmother."

That could have played out two ways. Either Mrs. Richway wanted the child or . . . she'd wanted to get rid of it.

Ryker's mind filled in the blanks. "We've been looking for that caregiver Gayle. What if Gayle is really Preston's mother?"

"That fits." Caroline tapped her fingers on her thigh but averted her gaze as if she was thinking. "She had access to Eaton regularly," she finally said.

"And she could have injected him with heroine," Ryker added.

Agent Manson muttered something beneath her breath. "I'll find out where she lives." Her phone buzzed before she could make the call. She put the call on speakerphone.

"I have the coordinates for Marilyn Ellis's cell phone," the analyst said. "Texting them to you now."

"Thanks," Caroline said. "See what you can find on Preston Richway, specifically his mother's name, contact information and where we can locate her."

"On it."

"I'll hold." She relayed the GPS coordinates, and Ryker swung down a side street toward the marsh. He sped along the narrow road searching all directions for Marilyn's car. Just as he rounded a corner, he spotted skid marks.

Water had flooded the street and collected on the sides of the road. He slowed, scanning the land.

His heart stuttered to a stop.

Marilyn's little red sedan was upside down in the overgrown marsh. Water stood half a foot deep and was seeping through the windows. He swerved to the side of the road, threw the SUV into Park and jumped out running.

Behind him, Caroline called his name. He didn't wait. He had to save Marilyn. If she was trapped in that car and was still alive, she could drown.

He jumped the embankment and slogged through the knee high wet marsh grass, his fear escalating with every step. By the time he reached the car, his lungs ached for air, and sweat poured down his back.

He shoved layers of sea oats aside with his hands and stooped to look in the driver's window. The car was empty.

Dear God, where was she?

He lurched up and began to scan the area. If she was injured, she couldn't have gotten very far. But she'd said someone was following her . . . Panic streaked through him.

"Ryker?"

"She's not in the car!" he shouted. "Help me look for her."

Caroline began combing the area to the left while he searched to the right. Precious seconds ticked by. His boots sank into the wet marsh. Mosquitos buzzed around his face.

If she'd climbed from the vehicle, she'd head toward the road for help. But if someone had forced her off the road, she might be in big trouble.

"Over here!"

Ryker pivoted and jogged toward Caroline. She was bent

over, examining the brush. "Looks like drag marks." She pointed to a flattened section leading across the marsh to a narrow road on the side.

Cold fear seized Ryker. Where the hell was Marilyn?

MARILYN'S HEAD THROBBED, AND her body felt weighted down. What had happened?

She opened her eyes to orient herself. Where was she?

It was cold. Dark. The wall behind her was concrete. She felt along the floor. Concrete as well. Only a sliver of light flickered through the crack in the doorway. No voices outside the door. Only the distant sound of wind and rain and . . . the waves. She was near the ocean, but where?

She rubbed her temple, struggling to recall how she'd gotten here.

A car crash. Someone had hit her from behind. She'd lost control and rolled into the swampland. She'd blacked out and stirred from unconsciousness suffocating. Water was seeping into the car.

Then . . . a voice. A woman's. Calling her name as she dragged her from the car. She'd struggled to see the woman's face. But the pain in her head was so intense it dulled her vision.

It was the female voice from the phone. The one who'd threatened her.

Suddenly the door screeched open. It sounded rusty and old. A shadow stood in the entry. The figure stalked in. A woman.

Tall. An angular body. Hair knotted on top of her head. She wore a dark rain slicker and rain boots that squeaked as she entered and closed the door behind her.

The shiny silver of metal glinted against the darkness. God, she had a gun.

"You couldn't leave it alone, could you?" she said in a crazed voice. "I warned you, but you had to keep nosing around." She began to pace in front of Marilyn, swinging her arms wildly.

Marilyn considered tackling the woman, but doubted she had the strength to overpower her, much less relieve her of the weapon.

"I followed those stories you wrote about the Keepers. I thought you'd be reasonable, that you'd understand. But you're in bed with that cop, and he won't listen."

Marilyn cleared her throat, but her voice was raw. "Mrs. Richway?"

The woman jerked to a halt and glared at Marilyn with rage-filled eyes. "How do you know my name?"

"I . . . pieced together what happened when I talked to your son."

"You should have left him alone!" the woman bellowed. "He was shamed enough twenty-five years ago. He doesn't want this to come out!"

"You mean you don't want it public," Marilyn said. "Your son is a brave man. Keeping silent may have felt like the best choice at the time, but holding all that pain inside eats away at a person's soul."

The woman waved her fist at Marilyn. "How would you know?"

Marilyn inhaled a deep breath, determined to remain calm. "Because I kept quiet about what I witnessed twenty-five years ago, and it's haunted me ever since."

"What are you talking about?" Mrs. Richway demanded.

"When I was a little girl, my mother was a waitress in the Village. One night I snuck away from the diner where she worked and walked over to the pier, then approached the lighthouse."

"You're just stalling," the woman snarled. "Making up a story hoping someone will find you. But no one will."

Marilyn's lungs tightened. Mrs. Richway was right. But if she was going to die, she wanted answers about Deborah's baby first.

"It's the truth," she said, her voice firm. "It was rainy that night, too, and I saw a young girl.

"A . . . girl?"

"Yes, Deborah Darling. She was drenched in rain, barefoot and wearing a thin gown. She was crying and scared as she shoved a canoe onto the shore."

Mrs. Richway's face turned ghost white.

"She was also carrying a baby," Marilyn continued. "She was trying to save her child from the monster who'd been holding her hostage."

The wild-eyed woman shook her head in denial.

"Then I saw the lighthouse keeper. Daryl Eaton. He grabbed the girl and strangled her." Tears choked Marilyn. "I wanted to save her, but I was so little and scared. Then he carried her outside and threw her in the trunk of his car."

Mrs. Richway covered her hands with her ears. "Stop it! Just shut up!"

"No," Marilyn said. "You hired Eaton to punish the Darling girls and Mellie Thacker, didn't you?"

The woman's crazed look said it all.

FEAR THREATENED TO IMMOBILIZE Ryker.

"Ryker, listen to me," Caroline said firmly. "We'll find her. Marilyn Ellis strikes me as a fighter."

Her words splintered the panic paralyzing him. She was right. Marilyn had to survive.

He was in love with the damned woman and he hadn't even told her.

Caroline's phone buzzed, and she checked it. "Let's go. We have an address for Mrs. Richway."

"You think she took Marilyn to her house?" Ryker asked.

She shrugged. "If she doesn't know we're onto her, she might."

They didn't have time to waste.

They ran to his car and jumped in. "It's only a couple of miles from here." Caroline plugged the address into her phone, and Ryker sped onto the road. Dark clouds rumbled ominously, the wind picking up in speed and whistling through the marsh. The road was deserted, the storm warnings forcing people to stay inside, or evacuate if they lived in the flood zones.

Seconds ticked by, each one excruciating and intensifying

his worries. If Mrs. Richway intended to get rid of Marilyn, she could have already killed her . . .

He couldn't think like that. She had to be alive. He needed her, dammit.

His tires churned water as he sped through the flooded sections and veered onto the road leading to Mrs. Richway's. At the end of a narrow street, he found her house. A small older bungalow with a sagging porch. No car in the drive.

Caroline pulled her service revolver, and he did the same as they climbed from the vehicle. His heart hammered as he plowed to the front door. Agent Manson checked the windows and shook her head, indicating she didn't see anyone inside.

He knocked on the door and identified them, but didn't wait for a response. Instead, he jiggled the door. Locked. He kicked it in and stormed inside, gun raised at the ready.

The house was dark, smelled musty and reeked of cigarette smoke.

The possibility that they were mistaken about Mrs. Richway crossed his mind. Then the possibility of finding a body, Mrs. Richway's, or someone else's, sent a chill down his spine.

He flipped a light switch and inched inside through the entry to the living area.

No one was inside.

Agent Manson gestured that she'd search to the right, and he moved to the left toward the kitchen. Empty.

"Ryker, you need to see this!" Caroline shouted.

His breath stalled in his chest. If she'd found Marilyn, he prayed she was alive.

He jogged to the back room and halted beside Caroline. She stood in front of a wall of newspaper clippings, articles and photographs.

Pictures of the Keeper cases. Cat Landon. Carrie Ann and Tinsley Jensen. The River Street rapist victims.

The victims of the Keepers.

More pictures—the Darling girls. Mellie Thacker. Articles about the Darlings' disappearances. A newspaper clipping about Detective William Flagler's accident.

She'd drawn red S's across all the girls' faces. Then double S's.

Another series of article and pictures on the opposite wall. This time, all featuring Marilyn.

Marilyn with double S's slashing her face that resembled blood.

Double S's—the signature of the Keepers.

Chapter Twenty-nine

Ryker and Caroline combed the place for information on the woman. Maybe a second house where she might have taken Marilyn.

The desk was filled with more articles on crimes that had gone unsolved or unpunished, all involving teenage girls. He also found paperwork from the hospital where Preston had been admitted for therapy twenty-five years ago.

"There are old withdrawals slips from her bank," Caroline said. "Large withdrawals."

"Payments for Eaton," Ryker said through gritted teeth.

"And to a Gayle Burton, her alias," Caroline commented.

He dug through the bottom desk drawer and found a journal detailing comments about hiring the Punisher. Making certain the Darlings and Mellie didn't hurt anyone else was the only way she could overcome the shame. Aretha had deserved to be punished as well, but Aretha was contrite and she hadn't conceived.

At one point, Preston had wanted to go public about the rape, because he thought he could help other victims if he did. But his mom had insisted he remain quiet.

He also had no idea she'd hired the Punisher.

Then there were notes about Detective Flagler. He'd gotten too close to the truth and was about to expose her. So Mrs. Richway ran him off the road. Although he survived, he had amnesia and needed intensive physical therapy and had retired from the police department.

Caroline found a photo album in the woman's dresser. "Look at this."

Rage shot through him at the photos of the Darling girls and Mellie Thacker locked inside a room, pregnant.

"Where is that place?" Agent Manson asked.

"I don't know, but we'll find it."

She flipped to another page and gasped. "This is Deborah Darling and her baby." Emotions made her voice warble. "And here is a picture of Deborah, dead."

"And the baby?" Ryker bit out.

"The baby's picture isn't here." A tear slid down Caroline's cheek, showing him a softer side of the agent. The thought of someone harming an infant could shred even the toughest federal agent's composure.

"If we find Mrs. Richway, maybe she can tell us where that child is," he said.

She sniffed and swiped at her face. "But where is she? Where did she take Marilyn?"

Ryker scanned the wall of pictures. Just before she'd crashed,

Marilyn mentioned the lighthouse. The lighthouse where it all started.

Daryl Eaton was the lighthouse keeper. That was where she'd seen him strangle Deborah and kidnap her baby.

He headed toward the door. He couldn't waste time. Every minute Marilyn was abducted meant she might be closer to death. "I'm going to the lighthouse. Stay and wait for a crime team."

"No way. I'm with you." She rushed beside him. "I'll call the ERT on the way."

The rain had started again. A gust of wind was so strong, the windows vibrated as he jumped in the car.

He didn't care if they were in the midst of a full-fledged hurricane. He was going to find Marilyn tonight.

Then he'd bring her home safe and sound, or he'd die trying.

MARILYN HAD TO STALL. Figure out a way to escape. Mrs. Richway's psychosis was escalating. "You don't have to hurt me," she said. "I understand the reason you did what you did. Every mama wants to protect their child, and your son was in pain."

"He was," she cried. "He was so depressed he wouldn't even talk to me. He stopped going to class and dropped out of football, and . . . I didn't know what to do."

"But he finally told you about that night, didn't he? That's because he loves you and trusted you."

"He was drinking and started doing drugs. You don't understand," she shouted. "My son was a football star. He had his entire future ahead of him, and those girls ruined it." She waved the gun as she paced frantically in front of Marilyn. "You have no idea what it's like to walk in and find your son with a needle in his arm, passed out over a toilet. He almost killed himself."

"He told me about that, and I'm so sorry," Marilyn said gently.

The woman's face crumpled. "I forced him to go to counseling, but he was never the same."

"Preston is strong. Although he was wronged, he rose above it and helps others now."

"But those stupid girls robbed him of years." Venom laced her voice. "They were mean and careless. They had no right to have children."

Marilyn sucked in a breath. Arguing with this woman would only intensify her agitation. "You're right. They didn't. They needed to be punished."

Mrs. Richway nodded her head, her eyes wild with rage. "That's right. When I heard about this man who punished sinners, I knew what I had to do."

"Daryl Eaton?"

"Yes, he was a godsend."

"What about the babies?"

Pain flashed in the woman's eyes, mingling with the bitterness. "Those bitches didn't deserve to have children. Children need good mothers, not whores and rapists."

"What did you do?" Marilyn whispered.

"He kept the girls on a little island a couple of miles out to sea until they delivered," she said in a distant tone as if she'd dissociated from reality.

Marilyn struggled to remain calm. "What happened to the babies? You didn't hurt them, did you?"

The woman halted and aimed the gun in Marilyn's face. "Of course I didn't hurt them!" she cried. "I'm not a monster. I was a *good* mother."

"And those babies were your grandchildren," Marilyn said.

She released a sob. "But I couldn't take them and raise them. They would remind me of what those stupid girls did to my son." She wiped at the tears streaming down her face with a shaky hand.

"You couldn't have the Punisher kill them either, could you?" Marilyn said, hoping to calm the woman. "You wanted them to be safe."

"Of course I did! Those babies were innocents. They needed good parents so they wouldn't grow up like the Darlings or those other trashy girls."

An image of Deborah running for her life, trying to protect her infant, roused Marilyn's anger. "What did Mr. Eaton do with the babies?"

Mrs. Richway pushed a strand of hair from her face. "I told him to leave them at a church so someone would find them. That way they'd get adopted into loving homes."

Marilyn released a pained breath. "That was a very caring thing to do," Marilyn said. "You gave them a chance for a future."

Mrs. Richway's look turned crazed again. "But Preston can't know about the babies. It would mess him up again. For Christ's sake, he might even want to find them."

Marilyn sensed that he would, that he was more forgiving

than his mother. "I understand," she said, trying to placate the woman. "You both suffered terribly. But it's time to stop the violence." Hoping to convince the woman to turn over her gun, Marilyn slowly lifted a hand. "You saw my coverage on the Keepers, didn't you?"

"Everyone saw those stories," Mrs. Richway retorted. "I felt for those women. And I admired them. They deserved justice and they got it."

"Just like you did."

The woman cut her eyes sideways as if debating whether Marilyn was trying to trick her.

"Put down the gun and end this now," Marilyn said. "Let me tell your story the way I did the others. Then everyone will understand that you were justified."

She jerked the gun up and aimed it at Marilyn, her hand trembling. "You'll tell them I saved those children from growing up illegitimate."

"That's right, you were thinking of the children."

She lowered the gun slightly. "I was. And I can't be locked away because of it."

"If you allow me to cover your story, the court will go easier on you."

She shook her head vehemently. "No, then Preston will find out and he'll hate me!"

Marilyn gripped the wall. "I've met your son. He won't hate you. You're his mother, Mrs. Richway. He'll forgive you and you can mend your relationship—"

"No! He'll hate me and I couldn't stand that!"

Marilyn pushed to her feet. "Please, let me tell your side. The worst part of being victimized is loss of power. Coming forward helps you regain that power." She gave the woman an imploring look. "You'll be an example for others who're suffering. You can show them how talking can make a difference."

"Talking doesn't help," Mrs. Richway said, her voice cracking. "The only thing that helped was knowing those girls suffered."

Marilyn was losing her. "Only hurting them changed you. You have to let go of the anger and bitterness—"

"Shut up! Just shut up!" Suddenly the woman raised the gun and aimed it at Marilyn again.

But Marilyn didn't intend to die without a fight. She threw herself at the woman and knocked her backward. The gun went off, the bullet pinging against the ceiling.

Marilyn tried to yank the gun from the woman's hand, but she was so full of rage that she shoved her backward. The force knocked the breath from Marilyn as her body hit the concrete wall.

Before she could recover, Mrs. Richway raised the gun again. Marilyn braced herself for the bullet, but instead, the woman slammed the gun against the side of Marilyn's head.

The room spun, stars dancing. Ryker's handsome face flashed behind her eyes just before she passed out.

RYKER PEELED INTO THE parking lot in front of the lighthouse. Marilyn had to be here.

With the storm escalating, the Village was deserted. The pier was empty. Stores and restaurants were closed and dark. Wind battered the windows and awnings, tossing debris across the streets. A newspaper someone had left whirled through the air. Waves crashed violently against the shore.

He threw the car door open, drew his gun and hit the ground running. Caroline did the same, staying close behind him. He scanned the area as they approached the lighthouse, but the area was vacant.

Except for a dark sedan parked on the other side of the lighthouse. The car matched the description of the one that had tried to run Marilyn down in the library parking lot.

He raised his gun at the ready as he pushed the door to the lighthouse open and inched through it. He paused to listen for signs someone was inside, but the only sound he heard was the wind howling.

He gestured toward the staircase. "I'll check upstairs."

Caroline moved toward the second room on the bottom floor, a room holding articles about the history of the lighthouse for tourists.

Ryker raced up the winding stairs, straining for sounds of Marilyn. He had to find her.

Marilyn's head throbbed. She was moving again. But where?

Mrs. Richway's wild rantings jerked her back to reality, and she opened her eyes. "You had to get that other agent Caroline Manson involved, too. That was the end for you. I couldn't let her find out about me and what I did."

Marilyn blinked in confusion. She wasn't making any sense. She kept ranting as she dragged Marilyn across the floor. A dim light flickered in her eyes as a door opened, and rain pelted her. She blinked, desperate to focus. She was outside the lighthouse now. In the rear. There was a back door, but it had been closed off for years.

Wet grass and dirt scraped her legs as Mrs. Richway hauled her across the ground. Rain fell in thick sheets, soaking both of them. The wind was so strong Mrs. Richway staggered against the force of it and the heavy downpour.

The world spun. Marilyn's body ached and she was so weak she could barely move. The storm raged on, launching her back to that horrible night when she'd seen Deborah stagger from the ocean.

They were headed to the water now. Waves thrashed and beat against the rocks, higher than Marilyn had seen in months. The woman dragged her closer, so close she felt the sharp rocks digging into her back. She remained limp, struggling to regain her energy and courage. She couldn't let the woman throw her into the waves. The undertow would sweep her out to sea.

The sound of a voice in the wind jarred her. Ryker's? No . . . a woman yelling, "Stop!"

Mrs. Richway dragged Marilyn nearer the rocky edge. The sound of a gun firing blasted over the wind, and Marilyn rolled to her side. Through the haze of rain, she saw a figure running toward them.

"Stop, FBI!"

Agent Manson. Hope sprouted in Marilyn's chest. Was Ryker here, too?

"Let her go!" Caroline shouted.

"Don't come any closer!" Mrs. Richway fired again, but the agent darted sideways to dodge the bullet.

"Put the gun down," Marilyn said. "It's over, Mrs. Richway."

"No," she cried, her voice warbling in the wind. "My son can never know about her."

Marilyn pushed up and leaned against the rocks while Agent Manson crept closer. "You mean about his babies?"

"Yes." She waved the gun toward the agent. "About *her.* He can't know what I did or about Deborah."

Shock slammed into Marilyn as realization dawned.

Was Agent Manson Preston's daughter? The baby Marilyn had seen Eaton take from Deborah?

CHAPTER THIRTY

CONFUSION MARRED THE AGENT'S face. "What is she talking about?" Agent Manson asked.

"You were never supposed to find out," Mrs. Richway stammered.

"Put down the gun," Marilyn said. "You don't want to kill her, Mrs. Richway. Just think about Preston. And he will find out. There's no way to keep it from him."

A terrified look darkened Mrs. Richway's eyes. "No, he can't know. He'll despise me."

"Find out what?" Agent Manson asked.

"You're adopted, aren't you?" Marilyn asked the agent.

The woman swallowed hard. "Yes, how did you know?"

"I didn't. I just figured it out." Marilyn gestured toward Preston's mother. "Tell her. She has a right to know."

Tears rained down Mrs. Richway's cheeks. "No, I can't say it out loud."

Marilyn licked her dry lips. "Agent Manson, you're Preston's daughter." Marilyn hated to drop a bomb on the young woman, but if it was out in the open, Mrs. Richway might change her mind about shooting the agent.

Marilyn hadn't been able to save her as a baby. She had another chance now.

"When I was a little girl, I saw your mother, Deborah Darling, murdered by the lighthouse keeper Daryl Eaton. She was trying to escape with her baby." Her voice cracked. "I wanted to save that baby, but I was too little, and I was scared. I ran and told my mother, but she was afraid the killer would come after me, and she made me keep quiet."

The agent was frozen still, her eyes wide in shock.

"Daryl Eaton, the Punisher, abducted the Darling girls and Mellie and kept them until they delivered. Then he killed the girls." She gestured toward Preston's mother. "She killed Eaton because she was afraid he was going to tell me the truth."

"I can't believe this," Caroline said in a raw whisper.

"You didn't know you were one of the Darling girl's babies?" Marilyn asked.

Agent Manson shook her head. "My adopted mother died a few months ago. She left me some papers saying she'd gotten me from a preacher who lived on Seahawk Island. I did some research and realized that I was found a few months after the Darling sisters disappeared." She paused and swallowed again. "I thought there might be a connection. That's the reason I requested the assignment here."

"You see, Mrs. Richway," Marilyn said. "If she figured it

out, others will. And if you kill us, the police won't stop looking until they expose the truth. Your only chance to save face with your son is to be the one to introduce him to his daughter."

"No . . . no . . . no . . ."

"The other girls who got pregnant from the pact," Agent Manson said. "Candace and Mellie. What happened to those babies?"

"They were adopted, too, before you were born," Mrs. Richway stammered.

"Where are they?" Agent Manson asked coldly.

"I don't know. The preacher found them homes," Mrs. Richway screeched.

The agent's look hardened. "What was the preacher's name? What church?"

"I don't know his name. The church was that one by Seaside Cemetery," she cried. "But all of you had better lives because of me!"

"My adopted father hit me," Agent Manson said. "Do you call that a better life?"

The woman's face blanched. "I . . . didn't know."

"Caroline deserves to meet her biological father, and he deserves to know about her," Marilyn said.

Tears streamed down Mrs. Richway's cheeks. "No!" She suddenly launched herself at Marilyn.

Agent Manson fired a shot, but the woman hit Marilyn so hard they both sailed over the edge into the water. Waves crashed and rolled over them as Marilyn struggled to fight the woman.

Mrs. Richway seemed to lose her will to live, and flung herself away from Marilyn as if she wanted to be swept out to sea.

Marilyn screamed for her to fight, and swam toward her. But the waves snatched her and pulled them farther and farther apart.

THE SOUND OF GUNSHOTS propelled Ryker down the lighthouse steps. He barreled through the entry and through the side room. Panting, he rushed outside and scanned the area.

The storm made visibly difficult, and the wind tore at his clothes, rain pummeling him. Through the haze, he spotted Caroline by the ocean. He ran down the hill, his heart hammering.

Dammit. Marilyn was in that water.

He raced toward the bank. "Caroline!" He shook her, and she jolted back to reality as if she was in shock.

"She's trying to save Mrs. Richway." Caroline started down the rocks, but Ryker grabbed her arm. "No, the current's too strong. I'll go."

He didn't hesitate. He climbed over the edge and dove into the waves. They careened over his head, the undertow pulling at him. Marilyn was a good swimmer, but this storm made the waves so forceful that he could barely move against it.

He clawed for traction, fighting the current. Marilyn's head disappeared under water. Cold terror seized him, and he fought harder, pumping his legs and arms until he caught her. She was desperately trying to swim toward Mrs. Richway. But the undertow tossed the woman out to sea in the dark.

He caught Marilyn around the waist. Blood oozed from her forehead, and she was strangling. Still, she fought to free herself and save the other woman. "Hang on," he shouted. "Stop fighting me."

She choked, spitting water, and finally gave into him. He dragged her toward the shore. Caroline scrambled toward them and helped him pull Marilyn onto the grass.

"I'll go back for Mrs. Richway," he shouted over the wind. "Call an ambulance."

He dove back in. But the tide was peaking, and the waves were so fierce that he couldn't see the woman. He swam a few feet out, battling the current, dove underneath the surface and searched again, but the darkness swallowed her.

Dammit. He tried again and again, swimming farther out, then diving under again, until his arms ached and he couldn't catch his breath. He'd been out here how long? Several minutes. If he did find her, it would be too late.

Another wave roared over his head and clawed at him, and he went with it, then let it carry him back toward the shore. When he was close enough, he started pedaling with his arms again. He coughed, heaving for a breath, and pumping his arms and legs until he finally felt the ground beneath his feet.

Caroline ran toward him, grabbed his arm and helped him up the bank to where Marilyn lay.

"I alerted the coast guard to search for Mrs. Richway," Caroline said. "And I called it into the station."

"Thanks." He was glad she'd taken over.

All he wanted at the moment was to hold Marilyn and make sure she was alive. She looked pale and weak, and blood streaked her forehead, but she lifted her hand toward him.

He clasped it in his, then collapsed beside her and drew her up against him.

"I thought I was going to lose you," he rasped. "And I *never* want to lose you."

She pressed her hand against his chest and kissed him. "I don't want to lose you either."

He was just about to confess his love, but a siren wailed and the ambulance roared up. He kissed her again, still not ready to release her.

MARILYN STRUGGLED TO REMAIN conscious while the medics lifted her onto the stretcher and carried her to the ambulance. Ryker stayed close beside her, holding her hand, reassuring her.

They'd made it through the storm and survived. And she had the truth now.

Mrs. Richway had known where Deborah's baby was all along. The agent had to be plagued with questions, and the need to find her half siblings.

"Ryker, I need to see Agent Manson," Marilyn said in a raspy voice.

He nodded. "She's right here."

Agent Manson climbed in the back of the ambulance, and Ryker narrowed his eyes. "I'm riding with her," Caroline said.

The paramedic started to argue, but the agent flashed her credentials. "This woman is a witness in a federal investigation."

She and Ryker seated themselves on the gurney facing Marilyn, and the medics closed the door. A second later, the ambulance sped away.

"Someone care to explain what's going on," Ryker said gruffly.

The agent clasped Marilyn's hand. "Is it true?"

"You'll need DNA testing for verification, but yes, I think so."

"Is *what* true?" Ryker asked.

Marilyn smiled at the agent. "Agent Manson is the baby I saw kidnapped twenty-five years ago. Deborah Darling's baby."

Ryker's brows lifted. "Did you know you were connected to the Darlings, Caroline?"

She shook her head. "I considered the possibility. That's what's brought me to Seahawk Island."

Ryker's brows lifted. "That's the reason you were upset when we interrogated Mr. Darling and learned of the pregnancy pact."

She murmured yes. "It made me sick to think that I'd come from that family. That my mother and her sister and their friends raped my father."

"I'm sorry," Marilyn said. "Really sorry, Agent Manson."

"Please call me Caroline."

Marilyn squeezed her hand again. "I wish my mother had let me come forward when I first witnessed Deborah's murder. I was only six though, and she was terrified that the killer would come after us."

"It's not your fault," Caroline said softly. "If it weren't for you, I wouldn't know the truth now." She blinked back tears. "About my father, you talked to him?"

"I did. He never knew about you or the other babies, or what his mother did. He was shocked. Apparently he and his mother have been estranged for years. He said she couldn't let go of the bitterness. He had to find forgiveness in order to move on."

"He sounds like a good guy," Caroline choked out.

"He is. He's helping others with drug and alcohol addiction through counseling."

"So Eaton kidnapped Deborah, Candace and Mellie," Ryker said. "Then he held them hostage until they delivered the babies?"

"He did," Marilyn said. "Mrs. Richway told him to leave the infants at a church where they'd be found and would go to good homes." Marilyn offered Caroline a sympathetic look. "You may have not been conceived in an honorable way, but even though Deborah was only fourteen, she loved you. I saw it in the way she fought to save you from Eaton."

Emotions streaked Caroline's face. "That means Mrs. Richway and Mr. Darling are my grandparents."

Ryker murmured a sympathetic sound. "It's going to be okay, Caroline."

Marilyn's heart ached for the woman. Learning she was the product of a rape, that her grandmother ordered her mother's murder, and that she'd almost killed her, had to be devastating.

A second later, Caroline's look softened. "Odd, isn't it? I thought you were working against me, Marilyn, but all this time you were looking out for me."

The woman leaned over and hugged Marilyn just as the ambulance pulled into the hospital and parked. "Thank you. I'm sorry I was so rude to you."

"Don't worry about it," she said with a chuckle. "I'm a hard person to like."

"No," Caroline said. "You stand up for others and for the truth. I admire you for that."

The door to the ambulance opened, and Caroline stepped out.

Ryker dropped a kiss on Marilyn's cheek. "Even if you are a hard person to like, sweetheart, you're easy to love."

Marilyn stared at him wide eyed as he jumped from the ambulance. For so long she'd hated herself for not coming forward about Deborah and the baby. She hadn't thought she deserved love.

Was it possible Ryker had fallen for her anyway?

Ryker reluctantly released Marilyn's hand as the medics wheeled her into an ER room to treat her injuries. Caroline insisted he be evaluated as well. He hated doctors and barely tolerated the exam, but at least the case was in good hands.

Caroline must be deeply troubled over today's revelations. She was a decent partner, although Marilyn had really cracked the case. Her tenaciousness paid off.

It had almost gotten her killed, too.

A shudder ripped through him, and he hurried to her bedside.

"She's stable," the doctor told him. "We stitched up the abrasion on her head and prescribed pain medication. She swallowed a good bit of water, but her lungs are clear. We'll hold her overnight for observation."

Ryker bit back a chuckle. Marilyn hated doctors and hospitals even more than he did. The only way she'd stay the night was if she was drugged or unconscious. Or if he stayed with her.

Which he would do.

He spotted Caroline in the waiting room on the phone, then his captain stormed through the entrance. Ryker braced himself and walked toward him.

"Brockett, what the hell happened tonight?" Captain Henry bellowed.

He threw up a hand. "We solved the Eaton case and the Darling case, that's what happened."

"You crossed the line and hooked up with that fucking reporter. I warned you."

"Excuse me, Captain," Agent Manson cut in. "But you need to listen. Marilyn Ellis was instrumental in solving both cases. She followed hunches and shared information with us that led to the closing of two cases."

He angled his head toward her. "I want details."

She gestured down the hall. "Let's get some coffee, and Detective Brockett and I will fill you in."

His captain glanced at Ryker with skepticism but gave a brief nod, and the three of them walked to the cafeteria. Once they were seated with coffee, he and Caroline started from the beginning.

By the time they were finished, Captain Henry scrubbed a hand over his face. "Well, I'll be damned." He looked at Caroline. "Are you going to air this on Cold Cases Revisited?"

Worry and indecision flickered in the woman's eyes. "Maybe. First, I'd like some time to deal with it myself. I want to meet my father . . . and now that I know I have siblings, I want to find them."

"That's understandable," Captain Henry said.

The lights flickered off, then on again, the wind continuing to howl outside.

The three of them walked to the ER waiting room, and Caroline slipped inside the room while Ryker stayed to speak to his boss.

"I know you don't like the fact that I'm with Marilyn, sir," Ryker said. "But I know what I'm doing. In fact, if she'll have me, I intend to make our relationship permanent."

His boss shifted as if he didn't know what to say. Then finally he offered his hand to Ryker. "I trust you to do the job and to keep the lines from blurring."

Ryker shook his hand. "Understood." The question now was if Marilyn wanted him.

Marilyn pushed at the covers to get out of bed.

Caroline rushed to her side. "You need to rest, Marilyn. You've almost died tonight."

"But I didn't." Still, she did feel weak and slightly dizzy so she laid her head back against the pillow. "They want me to stay overnight. I hate hospitals."

Caroline laughed softly. "So do I. But if you're going to finish this story, you have to get some sleep."

Hmm, Caroline was good at working people. She knew just how to get to Marilyn.

Caroline clasped Marilyn's hand again. "Thank you for never giving up."

"You don't have to thank me," Marilyn said. "If I'd spoken up sooner, Daryl Eaton might have gone to jail. No telling how many more people he punished with his brand of justice."

"That's not your fault," Caroline said. "You were only a child when you witnessed the murder."

Marilyn turned to Caroline. "I won't divulge any details about you and your father. That's your story to tell."

Caroline released a breath. "Thank you. I hope he wants to talk to me."

"He will," Marilyn said. "He's a good man, Caroline." Marilyn swallowed. "Are you going to look for your siblings?"

Caroline bit her bottom lip. "I want to. But if they're happy and in loving homes, I hate to upset them by divulging the truth about how we were all conceived."

"That's understandable." Although Marilyn knew the woman wouldn't be able to let the situation rest any more than she could. "You could find them and then decide."

"True. I think I'll hire a PI and see what happens." Tears blurred Caroline's eyes. "So what are you going to report?"

"I'll continue the Keepers story, but write about Daryl Eaton and how people—anonymous people—turned to him for help. Maybe it will inspire others to push for justice legally."

"You mean you want to put an end to the Keepers?" Caroline asked.

Marilyn smiled. "I don't think there will ever be an end to victims and their families seeking justice when the system fails. There will always be Keepers."

RYKER SPOKE TO CAROLINE as she exited Marilyn's room. "Are you okay?"

"I will be," she said. "At least now I know the truth."

A harsh truth, but she seemed tough as nails. She just needed time to process the revelations.

"Your turn." She offered him a smile. "She's amazing," Caroline said. "I see why you're in love with her."

"But—"

"Don't deny it," Caroline said. "Just go tell her."

A smile tugged at his mouth even as doubts assailed him. Caroline said good night, and he slipped inside Marilyn's room. She looked groggy, her complexion pale from her ordeal, blood still dotting her hair.

Ryker moved up beside the bed and took her hand. He still felt shaky inside, his adrenaline waning although the fear he'd felt earlier still gripped him.

Marilyn wet her lips with her tongue, and he realized she probably wanted water, so he handed her the cup on the bedside table. She drank deeply, then gestured she'd had enough so he set the cup down.

"Thank you for saving me," Marilyn whispered.

Ryker blinked to clear the images of Marilyn fighting for her life from his mind. "I couldn't let you die, baby."

Marilyn placed her hand against his cheek. "I didn't want to die either," she said with a small smile. "Not without seeing and kissing you again."

His heart raced, and he bent his head over and kissed her. "I'll kiss you ever day from now on if you'll let me."

She slid her arms around his neck, drew him to her and kissed him again. Passion burned through him. Worried about her though, he stretched out on the bed, pulled her into his arms and cradled her against him.

He'd promised he'd take care of her. Tonight that meant letting her rest while he held her.

But he'd nearly lost her and he didn't want to let her go. He leaned his head against hers, and listened to her breathing as it steadied.

Just as she drifted to sleep in his arms, he whispered that he loved her.

CHAPTER THIRTY-ONE

TWO DAYS LATER, THE storm had finally passed. In spite of her protests, the doctors had insisted Marilyn stay at the hospital the first night and had kept her sedated. She'd slept through one of the worst tropical storms Seahawk Island had seen since Hurricane Matthew.

Ryker had stayed beside her all night.

Then he'd driven her home and left to finish the case. She'd showered and rested and finally felt almost human again. But she missed Ryker like crazy.

She could still remember his arms around her, and she longed to feel them again.

She'd watched the news just to get a glimpse of him as he and Caroline gave a recap of the cases. She was surprised—and touched—that Caroline gave her so much credit.

She'd also talked to Piper. Her father, William Flagler, was relieved they'd finally solved the case of the Darling girls' disappearance.

Her phone rang, and she glanced at it, hoping it was Ryker. Instead it was her boss Blakely. "Marilyn, how are you feeling?"

"I'm fine, ready to go back to work."

He chuckled. "Just enjoy a little R & R. You earned it."

"You know I like to be busy."

"Well, you will be. When you return, you'll be the lead anchor."

Marilyn's chest rose and fell with her intake of breath. At one time a promotion was all that mattered to her. But somewhere over the last few days, Ryker had become more important. Ryker and their future together.

"Did you hear me? I thought you'd be jumping for joy."

"I heard you," she said with a smile. "And I appreciate it."

"Don't thank me. You promised a big story and you delivered." He paused. "You did a damn good job, Marilyn. And this was a tough one."

He had no idea.

The doorbell buzzed. "Someone's at the door. I need to go."

"All right, I'll see you soon."

She hung up, tugged her robe around her and hurried to answer it. Maybe Caroline again. The woman had needed a friend, and she and Marilyn had bonded. Caroline was still working up the courage to meet her grandfather and father.

She checked the peephole, her heart fluttering at the sight of Ryker on the other side. In his hand, he held a bouquet of sunflowers. She'd never been a flower kind of girl and Ryker had never been the flower giving kind, but the gesture was so sweet that she threw open the door with a smile.

"I thought sunflowers were the right call after the storm," he said with a sideways grin.

"They're perfect." She wrapped her arms around his neck and laid a lip lock on him. "I've missed you."

He grinned as he pulled back. "Marilyn Ellis missed me?"

"You're damn right she did." She took his arm and led him to the den where she sank onto the sofa. "Where have you been?"

"Tying up loose ends." Ryker's expression turned serious. "We tore apart that secret room in the lighthouse and found notebooks Eaton kept. He recorded all his jobs."

Marilyn's heart stuttered. "You know who he punished?"

Ryker nodded. "There's a list."

"Sounds like another big investigation in the making." And she wanted the scoop.

"Caroline is starting a task force with another agent," Ryker said. "Mrs. Richway caused Detective Flagler's accident because she was afraid he'd find the Punisher and link the man back to her."

Marilyn shook her head sadly. "Anything else?"

"We found evidence connecting her to Eaton and proof that she actually killed Mellie Thacker's mother. Apparently Mrs. Thacker wanted to come clean about what the girls did to Preston. Mrs. Richway ran her down and caused her accident to keep her from talking."

Marilyn grew thoughtful. "Poor Preston. He suffered enough when he was young, and now to learn he has three children and that his mother is a murderer." She rubbed a chill from her arms. "Has he been notified of his mother's death?"

Ryker nodded. "The coast guard recovered her body. He's flying in to make funeral arrangements, but he doesn't know the entire story yet. Caroline wants to be with us when we tell him. It might soften the blow to see his daughter alive and well."

"When we tell him?" Marilyn asked softly.

He smiled and pulled her to him. "Yes, when *we* tell him." But there's something else, Marilyn. Something I have to show you."

She narrowed her eyes as he removed an evidence bag from his pocket. I think you need to see this."

"What is it?"

"One of Eaton's entries. It's about you."

Shock robbed Marilyn of words. Ryker removed the page from the baggie and handed it to her.

"We've already analyzed it for DNA," he said.

She understood and accepted the page. Her heart jumped to her throat as she read.

I didn't ask to be the Punisher. It just happened. My daddy had the job before me. He instilled in me how important it was to help people, especially those who needed help, those who'd been wronged.

This last job wasn't what I expected though. The three girls I was supposed to punish were bad girls. They raped a young boy and drugged another one. He sits in a wheelchair, still struggling with the devastating effects of what they did.

At first, adrenaline drove me. The charge of exacting justice fired my bloodstream like nothing I'd ever felt before. The violence . . . it felt . . . natural. Wrong. But right in a way that bothered me. In a way I couldn't stop.

My father passed the torch onto me. And I couldn't let him down.

But the girls and their babies were different. Part of me craved watching them suffer. Watching them pay for what they'd done.

That was the sick part of me.

I hated it, but it was there.

Then that night . . . the night of the storm. The night Deborah Darling escaped with her baby. I left the board loose for her to find the nail. Made it easy for her to escape. I even left her the canoe.

I watched through binoculars from the lighthouse. Saw her struggle to escape and save her child.

In the end, she'd found redemption. She'd been saved.

But it was too late to save her.

I knew what I had to do.

She had to be terminated. I couldn't continue my role if she identified me.

So I waited until she made it to the lighthouse. They always came there. I knew they would. The light drew them. Led them to safety.

Back to me.

Then I could finish it. End their miserable lives.

Then I saved their children.

But that last night . . . I heard a noise. The tiny squeak of a little girl's cry echoing in the wind and rain.

I peered from the lighthouse and saw her jump behind a tree. She'd seen me.

Knew the monster I was.

I should make it so she couldn't talk.

But something about those innocent eyes trapped me. Reminded me that I had once been human inside. A little boy. A friend. A son who wanted to please.

A man who didn't steal lives or exact cruel punishments.

I tore my eyes from her then ran to save the baby. I had to take the newborn to the church. Give her a chance for a good life.

I couldn't hurt the little girl who'd seen me. She was innocent. She hadn't yet sinned. She didn't deserve to be punished.

That night I passed the torch to someone else. Another Punisher who would exact justice for those the system failed.

I would watch the little girl as she grew up though. Make sure she didn't tell.

I knew her mother. Where she worked. Where they lived. How her mother guarded her and worked hard to keep her safe and raise her right.

The terror in that little girl's eyes haunted me though. She was my hell. My punishment.

She was also my chance at redemption.

For her, I vowed never to hurt another person in my life.

Marilyn shivered, too stunned to speak. She looked up at Ryker with tears swimming in her eyes. "He saw me. He watched me."

"And you stopped him, Marilyn. Don't you see?" He rubbed her arms. "You were afraid he got away with more murders because you didn't come forward, but he didn't."

The guilt that had eaten at her slowly dissipated. Confusion followed. She wanted him to be all bad. Had seen him as a monster.

But he had been torn.

Still, it didn't excuse cold-blooded murder.

But . . . was he so different from the Keepers? And who had taken up the reigns of the Punisher once he gave them up?

"Are you all right?" Ryker asked softly.

She released a weary breath. "I will be."

He feathered a strand of her hair behind one ear. "You are amazing, honey. We make a pretty damn good team. You and me."

"You think so?"

"Yes," he said gruffly. He took the page Eaton had written, put it back in the baggie and in his pocket. Then he took her hand and led her to the bedroom. "I almost lost my mind when you were missing. It only reinforced what I've been thinking."

"And what is that?"

"That I can't live without you," he said in a raw whisper. "That we belong together."

She looped her arms around his neck and kissed him again, her guilt and anguish slipping away as he stripped her robe. "I think so, too."

He wet his lips hungrily. "Maybe we should consider making a permanent arrangement."

Marilyn's throat thickened with emotions. "Ryker?"

"I love you, Marilyn."

She swallowed hard. "I love you, too."

"Then marry me," he murmured.

Marilyn pressed her hand against his cheek. "Yes. But only if you promise to make love to me tonight."

He scooped up and carried her to bed. "Tonight and every night from here on after."

Seconds later, their lips and bodies melded, fiery passion exploding between them. He kissed her bruises and planted sweet tongue lashes along her sensitive skin, suckling her nipples until she begged for more. He slid down her body, teasing her with kisses along her belly then her inner thighs. She clawed at his shoulders, urging him to make love to her.

But he wanted to give her pleasure first, so he raked his tongue along her inner thighs then dipped it inside her heat. She was wet and tasted like passion and desire, stirring his hunger, and he teased her until she cried out his name as her orgasm rocked through her.

His own need escalated, and he rose above her and thrust inside her. This time when he joined his body with hers, it felt different, not just physical. Their love intensified the erotic sensations pummeling him, and made him feel closer to her than he'd ever felt to anyone.

She whispered that she loved him again, her breath bathing his neck. Her soft husky voice triggered his own release, and he thrust deeper. She wrapped her legs around him, clawing his back as he drove them both over the edge.

He held her tight, loving her as their bodies quivered in the aftermath of their lovemaking.

When their breathing finally slowed, he rolled her sideways

and looked into her eyes. "Did you mean it when you said we could make it permanent?"

"I meant it," she whispered.

He snagged his jeans from the floor and removed a velvet ring box from the pocket. Marilyn's breath gushed out as he opened the box to reveal a sapphire and diamond engagement ring.

"I got sapphire because it's your birthstone, and the day you were born was the best day of my life."

Tears filled Marilyn's eyes. "I don't know what I did to deserve you."

"You are just you," he murmured. "The woman I love."

She kissed him, then pulled back and watched as he slipped the ring on her finger. "One more question," he asked softly.

Their gazes locked. "I told you everything," she said. "No more secrets."

He wiggled his brows in a teasing gesture. "You didn't say if you wanted children."

Marilyn cradled his face between her hands and looked into his eyes. "I would love to have a baby with you, Ryker."

His heart swelled with love, and he closed his mouth over hers and kissed her again. Marilyn was going to be his wife, his friend, his lover, and the mother of his children.

"Speaking of mothers," he said. "Mine wants to meet you."

Marilyn laughed. "Do you think she's ready to have me as a daughter-in law?"

Ryker feathered a strand of hair from her forehead. "Of course she'll love you because I do."

Marilyn looked skeptical, but he would keep reassuring her until she believed him, just as he'd reassure her of his love every day for the rest of their lives.

Acknowledgments

I HAVE SEVERAL PEOPLE to thank for helping this project come to fruition:

First, Dayna Linton for her help in doing all the things I can't do—formatting the book, connecting me with a new artist, and for getting the word out on social media! You are a godsend!

Also, thanks to Kim Nadelson, the fabulous copy editor who helped fine tune the manuscript, for forcing me to add more romance, and for always encouraging me to make my book better.

To Lisa Russo Leigh for proofreading, line editing, and her words of praise for the story.

And last but not least, to Jeffrey Olsen for creating a beautiful cover.

Also, thanks to the readers of the KEEPERS series! Happy Reading!

OTHER BOOKS

If you liked *Little White Lies* then please write a review on Amazon! You can also contact Rita at www.ritaherron.com and follow her on Facebook and Twitter @ritaherron!

THE KEEPERS SERIES
Pretty Little Killers (Book 1)
Good Little Girls (Book 2)
Little White Lies (Prequel to Dead Little Darlings – Book 3)
Dead Little Darlings (Book 4)

THE MANHUNT SERIES
Safe In His Arms (Book 1)
Safe by His Side (Book 2)
Safe with Him (Book 3)

THE GRAVEYARD FALLS SERIES
All the Beautiful Brides (Book 1)
All the Pretty Faces (Book 2)
All the Dead Girls (Book 3)

THE SLAUGHTER CREEK SERIES
Before She Dies (Prequel)
Dying to Tell (Book 1)
Her Dying Breath (Book 2)
Worth Dying For (Book 3)
Dying for Love (Book 4)

About the Author

USA Today and award-winning author Rita Herron fell in love with books at the ripe age of eight when she read her first Trixie Belden mystery. But she didn't think real people grew up to be writers, so she became a teacher instead. Now she writes so she doesn't have to get a real job!

With over ninety books to her credit, she's penned romantic suspense, romantic comedy, and YA stories, but she especially loves writing dark romantic suspense tales set in southern small towns.

For more on Rita and her titles, visit her at www.ritaherron.com. You can also follow her on Facebook and Twitter @ritaherron.

59066733R00213

Made in the USA
Middletown, DE
09 August 2019